Christmas at

Suzanne Snow writes contemporary and uplifting fiction with a vibrant sense of setting and community connecting the lives of her characters. A horticulturist who lives with her family in Lancashire, her books are inspired by a love of landscape, romance and rural life.

Her first novel in the Thorndale series, *The Cottage of New Beginnings*, was a contender for the 2021 RNA Joan Hessayon Award and she is currently writing the Love in the Lakes series for Canelo. Suzanne is a member of the Romantic Novelists Association and the Society of Authors.

Also by Suzanne Snow

Welcome to Thorndale

The Cottage of New Beginnings
The Garden of Little Rose
A Summer of Second Chances
A Country Village Christmas

Love in the Lakes

Snowfall Over Halesmere House
Wedding Days at Halesmere House
Starting Over at Halesmere House

Hartfell Village

Finding Home in Hartfell
Christmas at the Home Farm Vets

Christmas at the Home Farm Vets

SUZANNE SNOW

CANELO

First published in the United Kingdom in 2025 by

Canelo, an imprint of
Canelo Digital Publishing Limited,
20 Vauxhall Bridge Road,
London SW1V 2SA
United Kingdom

A Penguin Random House Company

The authorised representative in the EEA is Dorling Kindersley Verlag
GmbH. Arnulfstr. 124, 80636 Munich, Germany

A CIP catalogue record for this book is available from the British Library.

Print ISBN 978 1 80436 911 1
Ebook ISBN 978 1 80436 913 5

Cover design by Diane Meacham
Cover illustration by Hannah George

Printed and bound in Great Britain by Clays Ltd, Elcograf S.p.A.

Look for more great books at
www.canelo.co
www.dk.com

To Jen, with love.

Chapter One

Until this week, the first in December, Erin Hardy had thought she'd forgotten all about her first kiss. Or at least she tried not to think about it because there simply wasn't any point, so it was ridiculous for those memories to be distracting her now. The kiss had been a late one, in her first term at university, and all these years later, Oli Sterling was still her best. It wasn't as though she hankered after a repeat performance either, she'd given up that idea long ago. But now he was about to land back in her life, she couldn't get…

'Ow!' She gave the squirming kitten on the examination table in her consulting room a wry smile and glanced at a thin scratch forming on the back of her hand. Her own fault for allowing her thoughts to drift back to Oli again when she ought to be focusing on her patients. Cuddling baby animals was usually one of the perks of her job as a vet. This tiny tortoiseshell kitten and her brother were especially cute, their fur shades of dark marmalade with splashes of white.

'Nearly done.' She held the kitten with a gentle and experienced hand as she examined eyes, teeth, ears and heart to ensure all was well. A boy was hovering anxiously with his dad, and she offered him a reassuring smile before administering the necessary vaccination and then a microchip into the skin at the back of the kitten's neck. Erin gave her a final stroke and handed her back to her young owner.

'So have you chosen names yet? Your dad says you're keeping them both.' That pleased her, even though she was long used to treating animals still searching for their forever home. After qualifying seven years ago, she'd spent a year in private practice before six months in a temporary role for an animal charity, and she'd found it heartbreaking to treat pets without a loving family of their own. This boy couldn't be more than nine or ten and she had a sharp reminder of herself at the same age; the longing for a pet while understanding it was an impossible dream because they simply couldn't afford another mouth to feed.

She and her mum had moved in with her grandparents when Erin was five, after her father had abandoned them for the dubious prospect of an acting career once he'd tired of family life and an ordinary job. She adored her family, and even though her nan and grandad bickered constantly, they still couldn't bear to be without each other after fifty-five years of marriage.

One day she'd share her home with an animal companion she could cherish, but right now her career and the house she'd bought when she'd moved to Hartfell three months ago were keeping her busy. The thought of sharing her home brought another memory of that startling spring evening in Cambridge twelve years ago; sun glinting above their heads and still unable to heat her skin as much as Oli had; the intent and desire in his unwavering stare as she'd stripped off her ruined white shirt and swapped it for his.

'Nala and Simba.' The young boy spoke shyly. 'We like *The Lion King*, and my mum said they were good names.'

'I think they're brilliant names. So this must be Nala?' Erin hastily dragged her mind back and pointed to the female kitten the boy was cuddling against his chest. 'It really suits her. If you have any concerns just call us, and Elaine in reception will make you an appointment for their booster in three weeks' time.'

'Thank you.' The little boy carefully encouraged Nala back into the carrier and Erin said goodbye as they left the consulting room. She cleaned the examination table and washed her hands before going to a screen on the wall and the keyboard beneath it, adding her notes so Elaine could follow up. A nice, easy consult for a Monday afternoon; two gorgeous and healthy kittens with a loving home and years ahead of them.

She wasn't looking forward to her next consultation and read through the spaniel's notes with a feeling of dread. She didn't really need to be reminded of his recent medical history; she'd been treating Mungo for two months now and his results weren't improving. He was only ten and she knew a difficult conversation about his quality of life was on the way. It was the worst part of the job, and one she'd never quite got used to. She took a deep breath and pasted on a welcoming smile as she opened the door to the waiting room and called her patient's name. The once-lively spaniel lumbered to his feet and her heart plummeted as she caught the anxious gaze of his owners. A jolly and glittering Christmas tree in the corner of reception seemed far too cheery in the face of her clients' despair.

'Come through,' she said quietly, bending down to give Mungo a pat. He wagged his tail, tongue lolling in greeting. 'How's he been?'

Ten minutes later it was all agreed. Erin had taken more bloods, and she'd run the tests. If the results were as expected, then she'd carry out his owners' wishes to put Mungo to sleep in his own home, surrounded by his family. They thanked her as they left, eyes swimming with unshed tears. She took a moment to compose herself as she labelled the bloods and wrote up her notes. The practice didn't often make house calls for companion animals, but she was always willing to make those last moments as comfortable and peaceful as possible. Her new boss, Gil Haworth, was of the same mind, and he was just one of the reasons why she loved working in Hartfell so much.

Yorkshire born and bred, she'd been aware of his brilliant reputation and had leaped at the opportunity to join his expanding practice. When she'd arrived for her interview at the end of August, he'd outlined his ambition to keep the practice at the heart of the local community and adapting to meet new challenges. They'd spent the morning seeing farm clients in the spectacular Dales landscape he'd loved all his life, and he'd laid bare the best and worst aspects of the job. He'd stood aside so she could examine the animals, talk with the farmers, and offer her own diagnoses and treatment plans.

Afterwards he'd taken her to lunch in the village pub, and over plates of outstanding fish and chips he'd offered Erin the job, explaining that her instincts coupled with experience and an ability to work under pressure as part of a team were exactly what he was searching for. She'd found it difficult to hold back a gulp of emotion as she'd thanked him and tried to grasp the swift turn her life was about to take. It would mean a move away from home, her first since returning after university, and it was only the worry about her family that made her hesitate before she'd reached across the table and shaken Gil's hand in acceptance.

The first person she'd called to share the news with was her mum. Hartfell was too far from the town where they lived for Erin to commute or be on call out-of-hours as required, and at thirty-one, it was time she moved out anyway. So the newly re-branded Home Farm Vets would be her opportunity, and her mum had offered congratulations and her usual loving support in whatever ways she could manage.

Erin called her final patient of the day, relieved that this consultation would be less emotional than the previous one. Ten days ago she'd examined a lump on a guinea pig and had been happy to discover it was nothing more sinister than an abscess. It was successfully removed under general anaesthetic and today was a final check-up to make sure all was well. The brown-and-white guinea pig was lively and inquisitive, and she was glad to discharge it and send the patient on her way with two chatty young owners and a thankful mum.

She left the consulting room as spotless as she'd found it, ready for tomorrow. The practice had grown since Gil had taken it over in the summer and the full-time staff now numbered six, with their evening and some weekend out-of-hours work divided between two regular locums. Companion animal patients were increasing as they gained more clients, and he'd discussed with Erin his intention to appoint a third full-time vet in the new year. But until then they were managing with locum support, with a new one joining them tomorrow.

She loved being part of the team and building on the history of the practice. Founded on Home Farm by Gil's grandfather, who'd been a tenant of the estate, eventually the practice had merged with another one in town after both original partners passed away, and Gil joined after qualifying. He'd applied for planning permission to extend into the remaining farm buildings and develop the practice to offer more specialised care and improved facilities, and he was hoping for a decision before Christmas in three weeks' time.

Erin made her way into the waiting room and Elaine, their receptionist, who had put off retiring for another year, paused mopping the floor. A pair of blue glasses suited Elaine's auburn colouring, and her short hair was finally turning grey. 'All set for your house guest?' she asked brightly.

'As I'll ever be,' Erin said, caught unawares by the question. She registered Elaine's surprise at her unusually glum reply and found a smile. 'No, it's all good. I've made the bed and everything.'

She couldn't change her mind about hosting now and let Gil down just because the new locum in question was Oli Sterling and they had history. She hadn't told anyone about Oli, other than her friend Carys from university, who also knew him. Not even her mum, Heather, with whom she shared most things. Heather had once thought the world of him and would probably get straight on the next bus when she did find out, which was the last thing Erin wanted. Her mum still occasionally inquired if she knew what Oli was up to these days. Erin made a point of not finding out, so she was always happy to reply that she had no idea.

She also intended to keep her personal connection to Oli at university private if she possibly could. She dreaded her professionalism ever being called into question, so she fixed her mind instead on the rent she would earn and not the man whose presence at Cambridge had dominated her first year almost as much as the never-ending hours of study had.

Until two days ago she'd been expecting a different locum, someone more experienced and older than her who would slot temporarily into the team. Oli Sterling, as she knew all too well, was neither. But when she'd offered to host, no one could've foreseen that the woman who'd originally accepted the job would be forced to change her plans due to a family emergency.

'I was a bit surprised Gil took him on, to be honest.' Erin used her foot to nudge the mop bucket closer to Elaine. 'Oli doesn't have much farm experience, from what I saw on his CV.'

'Well, Gil was a bit stuck, what with us finally losing Wendy to retirement and Christmas around the corner. Gabi said this new chap comes highly recommended.' Elaine mopped briskly at a muddy patch until it disappeared. Gabi was their practice manager, who'd moved to the Dales from Poland fifteen years ago. She had a fierce eye for detail and was putty around a puppy. 'Apparently she knew someone who'd worked with him, and suggested Gil look him up.'

Erin nodded vaguely. At least January would soon be here, and Oli would be gone, removed from her life a second time. As always she just needed to focus on work; she wouldn't allow him to intrude into her personal life, not this time. But sharing a home with him was a coming reality she hadn't got her head around yet.

As first year undergraduates they'd been allocated rooms in the same building at St Catharine's College, known as Catz, two of the handful of veterinary medicine students the college accepted each year. Since their first meeting she'd always been aware of the pull that existed between them, the exhilarating sense they were always on the brink of something more.

But Oli belonged to a group of students which excluded Erin without even trying – the coolest boys, the effortlessly beautiful girls, all drawn together by an innate confidence she simply didn't share. There existed some invisible thread that bound their backgrounds as clearly as it defined their futures, and even when her social life had overlapped with his, she'd felt separate from him still.

'Look at this!' A ravishing young woman burst into reception. She was brandishing a phone and thrust it urgently at Erin. 'I've just found Oli Sterling's Instagram, have you seen him surfing in Costa Rica? Erin Hardy, I'm thinking we should swap houses for Christmas, like in *The Holiday*.'

'Yeah, but there'll be no Jude Law swigging brandy in mine.' Erin took a step back before her colleague actually rammed the phone into her nose, wondering if they really could swap. Jess, their third-year student nurse, was the most naturally elegant woman Erin had ever met. She made every outfit look stylish, even ordinary green scrubs and black safety trainers, and always added a touch of sparkle. Today it was a jewelled flower clip in her hair, glinting amongst the dark lengths. Her face was a perfect oval, with well-defined cheekbones and evenly spaced brown eyes, ones that Erin always thought of as memorable and striking.

'No, but you've got Oli Sterling instead, and he's way hotter. Look!' Jess tried again with the phone and Erin feigned disinterest, refusing to be distracted. She'd lost nearly a whole evening doing exactly this, and she'd already seen quite a lot more of her new colleague in those shots than she'd planned to. Her mind was tugging her back to the May Ball again; Oli's determination when he'd seized her hand and hurried her away from everyone else, their very last chance beckoning.

'Jess, as of tomorrow he's going to be working with us, and therefore his social media is off limits as far as I'm concerned.' At least it was now. Erin moved to Elaine's desk and pretended to stare at the screen to avoid further scrutiny. Jess had become a good friend since Erin had moved here, and she didn't often take no for an answer when her mind was set on a course of action.

'You could throw a party to welcome him?'

'For a lodger who's only staying three weeks? Are you kidding me?'

'Movie night, then,' Jess said airily, giving Elaine a grin. 'Don't forget we're all coming round to yours to binge Christmas Netflix. Starting with *Holidate*.'

'Oh yeah. I love that film.' Erin had forgotten it was coming up, and quickly tried to recall the details as Elaine chuckled. 'Sorry, remind me again which Saturday we said?'

'You're hopeless, all you think about is work.' Jess exaggerated her eye roll. 'It's two weeks on Saturday, six p.m. You're doing the food and I'm on drinks. Are you going to invite Oli or shall I?'

'Let's just see how it goes. He probably won't want to socialise with us seeing as we'll all be working together.' Erin could but hope. 'I'm sure he'll have his own plans, he's literally just borrowing a bed.'

'Maybe it'll be yours,' Jess said, laughing at the flustered look Erin shot her. Once Erin had wanted that as much as her hard-won Cambridge First. 'Just think, there you'll both be, squeezing past each other in that tiny kitchen and sharing a bathroom. You lucky girl.'

'Not especially.' Erin was imagining it too and her cheeks turned pink; such thoughts were way too close to the surface. She needed to get Jess off the subject of Oli before her friend began to suspect something was amiss. 'Listening to you, anyone would think you're not loved up with Noah now you've bought your first home together.'

'Yeah, but a girl can still appreciate beauty, can't she?' Undaunted, Jess finally pocketed the phone. 'I'm off, you can tell me tomorrow all about your first evening together. Night, Elaine.'

'There won't be anything to tell.' Erin also said goodbye to Elaine and headed outside to her red pickup. She loved her company vehicle, even if it was always full of mud, the multitude of equipment she carried for work, and spare wet weather gear for any eventually. She was making a full and happy life here, and the prospect of Oli Sterling's unwelcome presence was the only cloud on the steady horizon she'd worked hard to establish.

When she'd landed the job, finding somewhere to live was a priority and it was her mum who'd encouraged her to consider buying. For Erin, taking on a home of her own had been a huge leap and she'd worried about leaving her mum too, but they both knew it was time. Gil had let her know about a place that was for sale in Hartfell, and she'd fallen instantly in love with Bramble Cottage's quirky corners and cosy nooks when she'd gone to view it. She already had a mortgage agreed in principle and a decent sum for a deposit after years of saving, and the sale was swiftly agreed. After she'd moved in, the thrill every time she arrived home had still not diminished. Until now, with Oli's arrival imminent.

Frost was glittering on the cobbled lane when she got out of the pickup and crossed the few stone flags which formed her tiny front garden, dotted with pots and plants she hadn't yet got around to replacing. Her neighbour Edmund, a couple of doors down, was a keen gardener and he kept them replenished with winter bedding for her, a favour she reciprocated in cake. Baking, along with the music she didn't play as often as she'd like, were her two main passions outside of her career.

Erin opened the front door and stepped straight into the sitting room, grateful for the heat enveloping her. The previous owners had replaced the windows and central heating a few years ago, and she was very thankful for that and a compact stove on which she burned logs sparingly. Having grown up in town, she'd always imagined herself in some neat new-build, not this two-hundred-year-old cottage with scraps of evidence still speaking its history, like the initials carved into the rough beam for a mantel above the fireplace, level with her chin, or the hand-written recipe books she'd found in a kitchen cupboard and couldn't bear to throw away. It didn't bother her in the least that she could touch the banister at the bottom of the stairs in the kitchen with one hand and the sink with the other – not a selling point the estate agents had thought to include in the details.

A small Formica table and four plastic chairs from a charity shop sat in front of the sitting room window, and her ancient two-seater sofa and matching armchair were chintz. Not exactly the style she was after, but the deposit and legal costs had swallowed her savings, and she couldn't afford to be choosy when she'd been offered them for nothing. They were comfy, which Erin appreciated when she curled on the sofa after a long day of consultations or a difficult call-out. This curious little place was hers now and she adored it, aware of how fortunate she was to be here.

At least Oli's rent would help with the new bathroom she planned to install next year. The current one was wedged beside the kitchen off a squat hallway separating the kitchen from the sitting room. The bathroom dated from the 1980s, the shower a later addition fixed to the tiles above a turquoise bath. Paying the mortgage was her first priority each month and she carefully portioned out the rest of her salary once that was safely taken care of. There was no getting around the fact that repainting, choosing accessories and nicer furniture was on hold for now. But she couldn't wait to celebrate her first Christmas here and decorate the cottage until it sparkled with the joys of the festive season.

She pulled her work boots off and left them on the rack behind the door, her feet in thick socks sinking into a cheerful floral rug over the stone-flagged floor. Three antique hooks hung above the boot rack, and she draped her coat from one, a tremor on her skin reminding her that soon Oli would be doing the same. She was still thinking about making a cup of tea or having a shower before he arrived when she caught sight of a sleek SUV pulling up outside her window.

She'd know his profile anywhere; she'd spent too many hours trying not to be distracted by it when they'd studied together at Catz, sitting up late night after night. So, he was early. Her pulse skittered as she took a hasty step back in case he spotted her staring. His head was bent, presumably checking his phone, and then he got out of the car with that easy, long-limbed elegance she thought she'd forgotten. Her palms were clammy as he went to the open boot, the light illuminating his face. He grabbed a leather bag and, as the boot glided shut, she wondered wildly why she'd ever thought his feet wouldn't reach the end of her spare bed.

She took a long, steadying breath when he rapped on the door, wiping her palms on her legs. Memories of the May Ball were dancing through her mind again, taunting her with the promise they'd held then. She couldn't think any more of that first kiss, his mouth hungry and demanding on hers as he'd slid an arm around her waist to pull her into him, how she'd kissed him back just as urgently.

She blinked hurriedly, trying to force those thoughts away. Oli was facing the lane, and he spun around as she opened the door, the familiar grin she remembered so well already in place. He'd always been able to unbalance her without even trying, and her body was reminding her again about his touch and what it felt like to be in his arms, to have him stare at her with desire and something more. Something she'd never allowed herself to name.

'Hey, you must be Elaine. Great to meet you, I'm...' Oli's mouth fell into a gape as the bag in his hand crashed to the ground and Erin saw his face pale beneath the fading suntan. His smile dissolved as his eyes locked onto hers and a few moments dragged by before he muttered her name. 'Erin? Seriously?'

Chapter Two

Erin had thought the university open day and the inform-
ation she'd received for new undergraduates had given
her a good sense of what to expect, until she'd arrived
in Cambridge on a mild September morning as a nervous
and suddenly uncertain student full of doubts. She was
worried about her mum too, helping to fetch her belongings by train and then bus, before settling Erin into very
pleasant and fully furnished accommodation with meals
catered, a luxury she wasn't used to. Heather was often
plagued by fibromyalgia flare-ups, which brought more
pain and fatigue, and it was one of the reasons why she
and Erin had moved in with Heather's parents all those
years ago.

Erin's life, growing up with her family in an everyday
Yorkshire town, was one of practicalities and without frill
or fuss. Her grandad had retired early from mining with
lungs no longer at full capacity, and they made do with
Heather's part-time hours in a florist shop and her nan's
cleaning job, plus the seamstress work that kept Joyce bent
over her sewing table every day. As soon as she was old
enough Erin had taken over the cooking, trying to ease
the burden on everyone else. Her grandad did what he

14

could, and it still frustrated him that he was no longer the main breadwinner in the family.

Their house was an ex-council one that her grandparents had scraped together enough money to buy, and most of the furniture was older than them. A narrow three-bedroom terrace with a long, thin garden, Erin slept in the box room at the front, which she'd decorated herself after saving up some earnings from her part-time job in a charity shop. Her grandad spent most of his time tinkering in his shed or pottering slowly in the garden, tending the vegetables he loved to grow and which they depended on.

Books and the library had been her escape, and she'd devoured everything, from children's stories and classics like the Brontës and Jane Austen, to James Herriot, non-fiction books on the natural world and every kind of animal. She'd loved animals for as long as she could remember, and volunteered for a local shelter. Later Erin had spent her work experience weeks with a charity providing veterinary care for people who couldn't easily afford it, those for whom life without their adored animals might have been almost unbearable. Occasionally she and her mum took the bus into the Dales for a day out, and Erin would dream of being a qualified vet and living in the place she'd fallen in love with, reading James Herriot's books.

She was a gifted student, aware that hard work and excellent results would give her choices, and might help put her family on a path to a better life. One where they didn't sometimes have to worry about choosing between heat or a hot meal in the winter. She'd left high school with A-starred results across the board and followed up with top marks in three sciences at college. Soon after she'd had offers from both Cambridge and Edinburgh.

She chose St Catharine's, aware that a Cambridge First pinned to her CV could set her apart, and she wasn't leaving home and her family for anything less. Erin dared not even think of the dizzying debt she would incur, despite the increased bursary afforded to those who'd received free school meals. Ahead of her now lay six testing years of hard graft and absolutely nothing was going to stand in the way of her ambition.

Michaelmas term began with Matriculation, students' official registration onto their degree courses. She wore the only suitable outfit she possessed for the formal ceremony, a black dress that sat neatly just below the knee and a gown bought from a previous student. Before leaving home she'd splashed out on her first-ever professional haircut and although she loved the new bangs framing her face, she felt they made her appear even younger than her eighteen years, a milestone she'd passed just three months ago in June. The strange black gown was also unfamiliar, and she wondered anxiously how much she stood out, if the bursary she'd needed to get here and her life in an ordinary Yorkshire town was as obvious to everyone else as it felt to her. She tried not to make herself conspicuous amongst the other students, almost all of whom seemed much glossier and way more confident than her.

She'd waved her mum off outside the Porters' Lodge, trying to hold back her fears for Heather on the return journey and how her mum would cope each day without her help. She had once mentioned not going to university at all and finding a job instead, but her mum had been vehemently against it.

After the ceremony, the freshers made their way to Main Court for the official photographs, surrounded on three sides by magnificent and notable buildings, lining up to take their seats facing an immaculate green lawn and the college's grand entrance between a pair of high stone pillars topped with finials. Erin stared in awe at her new surroundings, still slightly dazed she had joined the historic list of college members and that her name here would live on.

She noticed him immediately; it was impossible not to. Half a head above the boy nearest him, this one already carried the authority of a man, albeit a very young one. Dark auburn hair swept back from a high forehead glinted in the early autumn sunshine and she was near enough to notice a scattering of freckles across his face as he turned to laugh at something his companion was saying. His mouth was outlined by perfect bow-shaped lips above a square jaw, and something strange erupted in her stomach. Thoroughly distracted by both him and the occasion, her left foot caught a chair leg and dislodged it.

'You numpty,' she blurted out. It was her nan's favourite word for nearly everything and the habit had stuck. Erin's arm shot out to catch the chair and she was aware of a few heads turning to stare. Including, she was mortified to see, the tall and good-looking boy on whom her gaze had been clamped.

Horribly conscious of heat staining her cheeks as his amused gaze caught hers, she glared back, silently daring him to suggest she was out of place here because those two words had revealed her to be a plain-speaking Yorkshire lass. Still clutching the chair, her free hand darted to the shorter strawberry blonde curls grazing her shoulders. His eyes followed the gesture and sent her pulse into a spin as his lips widened into a smile. His hand reached out and she felt the unwelcome brush of his fingers as he too took hold of the chair.

'I'm sorry, how clumsy of me.' The only accent evident in his low voice was the one she'd expected, speaking of privilege and private schools. 'Please, let me.'

'It wasn't your fault. It was me who knocked it. Bloody heels.'

'But still.' Between them they righted the chair and there was no reason to linger. She realised eyes she'd thought were grey were actually blue and they were still fixed on hers as other students edged past them. If there had been room in the line Erin would've planted her hands on her hips like her nan did when she was mad about something and asked him what he thought he was staring at.

She was caught, trapped by his attention and an over-whelming feeling of attraction she'd never experienced before. She turned down invitations for dates, and would-be boyfriends drifted away when they realised how much time she devoted to her studies and her dream of securing an independent future, one where she wouldn't be left behind with nothing, like her mum when her father had disappeared.

'What's your name?'

'Why do you want to know?' Her cheeks felt as though they were on fire, and it had nothing to do with the chair she'd almost knocked over.

'Because I just do.' His smile was a lazy one and she couldn't think why he was still lingering, unless it was to drag out her humiliation. Seconds crawled by as she tried to decide how to respond, half hoping her silence would give him her reply instead.

'Okay, so then I guess I'll see you around, stranger.' The amusement in his face faded and she had the inexplicable sense that he'd just seen straight through to her soul, as though every part of her had been laid bare before him. She couldn't even take a step back for fear she'd crash into someone else and embarrass herself all over again. He turned and she took a steadying breath, trying not to follow him with her eyes as he moved away.

–

Erin found out later his name was Oli Sterling and that he was also planning to become a vet. From his voice and the crowd who surrounded him, she didn't imagine that his grandad had played in his old colliery brass band until he hadn't got enough breath left to blow, or his nan worked two jobs to put food on the table in between running the home and helping her grown-up daughter when she was experiencing a bad flare-up.

After the box room back home her accommodation felt huge, and it took Erin a while to settle in. White walls and pale wood furnishings were clean and plain, and she filled the shelves above her desk with items from home, like the cross stich of a Persian cat her nan had made for her, a favourite quote from Christopher Robin about being stronger than she knew, and the photos from her time with the animal sanctuary, reminding her daily why she was here.

Oli was impossible to avoid, especially as they shared a floor in Sherlock Court, and they were often together in small groups, or 'supervisions', to study. She'd sneak glances at him, cross with herself for the curiosity he sparked in her, and blush furiously if he caught her. He'd grin back with that same confidence, and she'd wonder why he bothered with her, certain he saw her as nothing more than a stranger in this hallowed world in which she now lived.

As ever, studying was her salvation, and she threw herself into it. They were soon immersed in an intensive introduction to the practical and scientific world of veterinary medicine, beginning years of learning in animal husbandry and genetics, biochemistry, molecular biology, and physiology. It was a ten-minute cycle to the vet school from her flat and she was thankful every day that she'd saved enough to buy her own bicycle to get her around town.

She loved the ancient Sherlock Library but found her home in the more contemporary Shakeshaft Library instead. Every night after she'd eaten she'd head to her usual spot and study until eleven, unless she and Carys went out first. Erin had bonded with Carys, who came from a hardy Welsh farming family, over pizza one night. She'd recognised a kindred spirit in Carys, another young woman proud of her hardworking background and the sheer effort it had taken to get into Cambridge.

One evening she'd been thrown when Oli had turned up at the library and politely inquired if she'd mind if he joined her. Flustered, she'd told him no, and he'd settled at a desk near hers, and left before Erin did. After that he showed up three or four evenings a week, the only time outside of vet school he wasn't with his friends. They'd work in silence through the long hours and chat quietly in breaks. Usually they'd walk back to Sherlock Court together and she came to treasure those moments, feeling strangely as though they didn't always require words to share a conversation as their bond gradually grew.

Already the end of Michaelmas term was approaching, and Erin was ready for the Christmas break. These first weeks away had been hugely challenging and she missed her family, even though she'd made friends and spent most of her free time with Carys. She'd joined Carys for a couple of weekends in Wales, loving having some real farm animal experience to back up her learning.

She was still in regular contact with home, those messages easing the concern always at the back of her mind for her mum's well-being. One Saturday morning in late November, she was in the library and sneaking glances at her phone, trying not to worry that her mum hadn't replied to yesterday's message. From experience she knew that meant Heather was likely having a fibro flare-up.

She bit her lip and checked her phone again; her nan hadn't picked up the house phone when she'd rung it either. Joyce tended to expect that most callers were scammers or salesmen, and she preferred to avoid both. Erin sighed and placed her phone facedown again; she was probably worrying unnecessarily. She'd made a decision when she arrived at Catz not to go home before the holidays, partly because she missed her family so much and returning would be unsettling, but also for a more practical reason – the train was too expensive.

An hour later there was still nothing from her mum and she swore more loudly than she'd meant to as she snatched up her belongings and fled, trying not to panic. She was going home at the end of term anyway, but she'd already decided this couldn't wait. She was racing across Main Court towards her flat when Oli caught her up, a hand going to her shoulder to slow her, and she halted.

'What's up? I've never heard you say those words in that order before, not even when we had to watch that postmortem of a sheep with liver fluke. What was it you called it? Rank?'

'What?' Erin blinked, staring up at him. 'Give over, Oli, I haven't got time. I've got to get home, like now.'

'Why?' Oli's expression changed to one of concern as the teasing disappeared. 'Take a breath and tell me what's wrong.'

'It's my mum, she hasn't been in touch today and she always replies. Without fail.' She cast a frantic glance around the courtyard, barely noticing the students casually coming and going, the biting winter air making her shiver. 'I need to get to the station. There's a train to Peterborough in a bit and from there I can get to Leeds and then—'

'Can I help at all?'

'You?' Her laugh was a quick one. How did he always do this, hold her with just a look, as though everyone else around them had vanished? Worry made her tone sharp, and her mind was still racing through trains and transport. 'I very much doubt it, unless you can magic up a train right now. I probably won't be there for another twelve hours either way. Mum has fibromyalgia and it can be really bad sometimes.'

'I'll take you.'

'What? To the station?' Somehow Oli was holding her hand, and she stared at their entwined fingers before easing hers free. 'It's fine, I can get a bus. But thanks.'

'Not to the station, to Yorkshire. I'll drive you because you clearly need to go, and I can help.' Drizzle that had been in the air turned to proper rain and Oli tugged his collar up against the freezing drops.

'You're not serious!' Erin laughed again, because there didn't seem to be any other appropriate response. She was searching his face for the tease, but somehow she knew he was serious, and relief was already replacing some of the worry. 'When?'

'As soon as you're ready. You go and get your stuff, I'll sort out a car.'

'Don't you have plans?'

'Yeah, but they'll keep. This is important.'

'Oli, I don't need you to rescue me. I can look after myself.'

'I know you can, but why not let me help,' he said reasonably. 'That's what friends are for.'

It didn't feel like they were friends to Erin, not really. Oli wasn't someone in whom she'd confide, nor would she ever admit that he occasionally featured in her daydreams, which troubled her for multiple reasons, number one being because she wasn't planning to fall in love. 'But where will you get a car?'

'Never mind that. Meet me outside the Porters' Lodge in forty-five minutes. I won't be able to hang around as parking's not allowed so you'll need to be there.'

'Okay.'

He took off and she stared for a moment before racing after him, trying to drag her thoughts into some sort of order. In her flat she dumped her bag and stuffed some essentials into another one, too unnerved by worry over her mum to think through the implications of being driven home by Oli Sterling. It was a four-hour drive, maybe a bit less on a Saturday afternoon instead of a weekday. Why would he even do such a thing, for her?

Forty minutes later she was waiting anxiously on the main road outside the Porters' Lodge, still bemused by the turn of events, when Oli arrived in a small blue Vauxhall. She grabbed the door and leaped inside before he got into trouble; she didn't want to cause him any more problems than she already had. Traffic was worse than she'd expected, the city packed with tourists enjoying the sights of Christmas in Cambridge. To Erin each minute dragged as though it were ten as they crawled along.

'Thank you,' she said eventually, her voice small. 'I really don't know why you're doing this and giving up your weekend. I'll pay you back for the cost of the car.'

It would take her months to do that; she'd have to eke it out of her maintenance loan and make do with less, but that was nothing new. Maybe she could get a job for a few hours each week and send him her salary. She ought to have refused his offer but in those frantic, freezing moments in the courtyard she simply hadn't known how else to get home in a hurry.

'You don't have to do that.' Oli was queueing at traffic lights, and her stomach did the usual flip as their eyes met. 'Seriously, Erin, don't worry about it.'

'How do you know it'll worry me?'

'I dunno. Maybe I know you better than you think.' He pointed to a pair of paper cups sitting in the drinks holder. 'Coffee. I thought you might like one.'

'I don't drink it very often, I prefer tea.' She found a smile. 'I'm a proper Yorkshire lass and we can't get by without a good brew.'

'Is that right? So you don't want it then?'

'I didn't say that.' They both reached for a cup at the same time, and laughed. Erin picked one up, gratefully wrapping her fingers around it.

Now the plan was in motion, her thoughts were racing ahead to home, seeing her family and the old terraced house with its familiar comforts. And what was she supposed to do about Oli then? Invite him into the heart and centre of her life, and expose him to its realities? Or send him away and add the cost of a hotel room to the expense he'd already incurred, because he couldn't drive straight back to Catz after such a long journey. Finally they were on a main road, speeding away from the city, and her shoulders loosened some more now they were heading north and nearing her mum with every mile.

'How long have you been driving? Please don't tell me you've just passed your test and never driven so far in your life.'

'Okay, I won't.' Oli was staring ahead, concentrating as the day darkened. 'I passed a few weeks after my seventeenth birthday, so I've been driving for over a year.'

'Happy to hear it.' That settled her, even though she could tell he was good from his quiet confidence. If they carried on like this, she'd be home and with her mum soon after teatime, a thought which relaxed her some more. Drowsiness overcame her and when she woke again, she was surprised to see they were approaching Leeds.

'Sorry, I didn't mean to fall asleep. I should be navigating for you. At least helping in some way.'

'It's fine, you were obviously tired. And I've got a sat nav for directions.'

Erin glanced at the small screen stuck to the dashboard. They had barely twenty miles to go and one more city to navigate. 'Are you okay? Not too tired?'

'That's a first, you asking if I'm okay.' Oli's laugh was a quick one as he paused at a roundabout to let a van pass, and then pulled out to follow it. The festive streetlights were cheerful, and she couldn't believe these past few months had passed so quickly and that Christmas was around the corner.

'I have got a heart, Sterling, I'll have you know.' She pressed a hand to the top of her chest. 'I just don't always wear it on my sleeve.'

'Except when you're treating animals. I've seen you in action, don't forget.' He threw her a smile. 'Maybe you're someone who needs to look after your heart.'

She was amazed he'd noticed how much she loved being around the animals in the hospital, even though most of their learning was theoretical so far. 'Oli, I just want to say…'

'There's no need to thank me again,' he said. 'If that's what you were about to do.'

'But you didn't have to drive me home. We're miles from Catz, and then there's the cost. And this is one of the nicest things anyone's ever done for me, so thank you.'

'You're welcome.' His voice was low, a layer of gruffness beneath the practicality. 'So when we get out of the city can I turn off the sat nav and trust you to take it from there?'

'It's my hometown, Oli, I could find my way around with my eyes closed. As long as you keep yours open.'

Chapter Three

'Hi, Oli.' Erin was desperate to regain control of the conflicting emotions thudding through her and she stuck out a hand, watching Oli's brows draw together as he took in her arm hovering awkwardly between them. The last time they'd been this close was seared in her soul and it had nothing to do with the formality she was determined to establish now. 'So, er, welcome to Hartfell.'

'You live here?' His startled gaze leaped past her to the sitting room, and she withdrew her arm. Lamplight was gently flickering, a cosy blanket cheerful on the chintz sofa. She'd intended to light the fire before his arrival and now there wasn't time; her plans to prepare herself were in pieces. 'I thought I was staying with someone called Elaine. It was in the email.'

'Nope, it's definitely me.' *Unfortunately* was the word she toyed with adding. She was going to have to step very carefully around their history; it wasn't something she planned to share with her colleagues, and she intended to make sure Oli kept up the pretence. 'Maybe it was a mistake, or you misread it. Elaine is our receptionist, but the email would've come from Gabi, our practice manager.'

'It was definitely from Gabriela, and she said that I was staying with Elaine. The website was pretty basic when I googled the practice.' Oli stuffed his phone into a back pocket and shivered. The evening was already bitter, and Erin reflected if he was just back from Costa Rica, then no wonder he was feeling the cold.

'The new website is still in development. And like I said, it's me. You might want to duck, the door's pretty low.'

His auburn hair was shorter now, still swept back. The beard she'd been expecting from viewing his Instagram had gone, leaving him with shades of a red-and-gold overnight shadow she remembered from their student days, when he'd stumble into vet school at the last minute after a late night. His Levi's were slim fitting with a turn-up and she'd bet her entire life that the black leather biker jacket and lace-up boots hadn't come from a charity shop or even a high street one.

She tucked a stray curl behind her ear and her pulse kicked as his eyes followed that once-familiar gesture. Without the shower she'd planned to have she was still wearing her winter work layers, traces of fur from the pets she'd seen earlier clinging to her clothes. A hoodie over thermals was her go-to, and she'd quickly learned that two pairs of leggings were essential on farm calls.

'Thanks for the warning.' His smile was a taut one too and it was scant consolation to realise he was as uncomfortable as her. He'd only arrived two minutes ago and already she was wondering how she'd ever thought this could work, sharing her home with the man she'd once thought she'd love for the rest of her life.

'You're welcome.' She stood aside as he entered, clutching the leather bag as though it was a shield. Erin slowly shut the door, and it was as though she'd flung open another one right onto their past. Even the walls seemed to be closing in around them, every silent moment crawling into the next.

'So this is it, home. Pretty basic, but it's mine and I love it.' She bit back an apology for the size and state of the cottage. She was proud of it, and of herself for taking this giant leap, even if she'd probably be ready to collect her pension by the time she'd paid off the mortgage.

'Just yours?' The surprise had Oli's eyes seeking hers again and she made herself hold his gaze.

'Yes. I bought it when I got the job here.'

'That's so cool, Erin, congratulations. You always wanted a place of your own, somewhere close to your family.' He lowered the bag to the floor, easing out a breath. 'I suppose I assumed you wouldn't be single.'

'I never said I was single.' There was someone but it was early days, and she was not about to reveal that to Oli; her personal life was very much off limits to him.

'Right.' He nodded quickly and looked around the room again, as though he hadn't properly taken in the details the first time. 'It's really sweet.'

'Is that a euphemism for shabby?' So what if half her stuff had come from a charity shop, and he'd grown up in a country house in Wiltshire when he wasn't away at school. He'd just have to lump it or leave.

'Why do you always do that, misinterpret my meaning? And you do it on purpose, as though you don't want to hear what I'm saying.'

'Maybe I don't want to listen to anything you've got to say, Oli.' She crossed her arms; this wasn't the start she'd envisaged with her new colleague.

'I only meant it's amazing you've already bought your own home, and I think it's charming.' His lips quirked in a wry smile. 'I'm nowhere near that, not sure I'll ever be.'

She ignored that and brought them back to more practical matters. 'So the bathroom is just off the hall, next to the kitchen.' She pointed, to make it clear.

'Downstairs?' Oli's smile faltered.

'Yep. I hope you didn't get the wrong impression in the email about the accommodation as well.' Erin straightened her shoulders, making the most of every single inch of her five feet five.

'My fault,' he said lightly. 'I didn't read it properly, just took in the basics. It was quite long. It definitely said Elaine, though. I would have remembered if your name had come up.'

She wasn't going to be drawn in again by his charm and that easy grin. When they'd first met, she'd imagined him more at home in a city bank like his father, not lambing a sheep in the middle of a freezing February night or performing emergency surgery on a cow in a filthy byre high on a moorland farm. But her perception of him at Catz had changed as she'd come to understand him better. In the veterinary hospital she'd seen for herself his love of animals, and the care and compassion with which she treated them.

'I'll show you to your room.' She half wondered if the sight might have him hotfooting it back into the night in search of the nearest hotel instead. 'You'll need to duck in the kitchen too, and on the stairs.'

She resisted the urge to rush as he followed; there was nowhere far enough to run from how she felt about him. Upstairs, the landing was a small square space with another step into the bedrooms. The two doors were identical, each with a top half glazed and covered with a chintz curtain pinned in place over the glass. She opened the door to his room and squeezed inside so they wouldn't get trapped together on the landing. The mattress on the spare bed was the best she could afford when she'd moved in, so it had cost next to nothing and wouldn't be winning awards for comfort any time soon.

'This is you,' she said, heat racing back into her face as she hit the light switch. Having Oli sleeping a few feet away, just the other side of a thankfully thick wall, was a reality she had so far refused to confront.

'Right,' he replied slowly, his incredulous gaze landing on hers. 'I thought it would be a…'

'Double? Nope, definitely a single. Something had to give to make room for the wardrobe and I chose the extra guest. Hope that's okay.'

Erin made sure it wasn't a question on purpose. Maybe he did have a partner somewhere, but whether he'd read Gabi's email in full or not, she'd been very clear about extra guests. None, not without approval she didn't plan on giving. There was a limit to how much she could take, sharing her home with Oli, and him sleeping with someone else under her roof was it.

'I suppose it'll have to be.' Oli dropped his bag beside the bed and went to the window. She hadn't done a thing with the tiny garden yet and so it was still a swirl of wild borders stuffed with clambering roses and last summer's perennials nudging ever closer to a pocket-sized lawn. Not that he could see it through the dark.

'Do you want a hand with your stuff?'

He turned, leaning against the windowsill and resting both hands on it to regard her, shoulders hunched. 'Thanks, but there's not much more. I travel pretty light.'

'Okay.' She stepped back onto the landing, needing to get out of his space. 'I know the email said that your rent doesn't include meals, but I wasn't sure how late you'd be, and the village shop closes at five. I've made a curry if you'd like to share. Just for tonight.' Her toes were curling at the thought of eating together but she hated the thought of him going hungry. The slow cooker, a moving-in present from her mum, was Erin's salvation. Most days she drove home through the Dales dreaming of the hot meal simmering in her kitchen.

'That's really kind of you, Erin, but I've got plans for tonight.'

'Plans? But you've only just got here!' She snapped her mouth shut before it fell into a gape. He produced that disarming grin she was so familiar with, and now she was glad she'd given him a single bed with its cheap mattress.

How did he already have plans in Hartfell? He'd only been here five minutes, and it had taken her weeks to pluck up the courage to go into the village pub for a meal on her own and begin the tentative effort of making new friends. But then she remembered how much he loathed being alone, a payoff from his days at boarding school and missing home.

'Yeah, sorry. A mate from Catz farms near here and I've arranged to head over. You remember Rob, has that place out in the wilds? Mad about Rough Fell sheep. I haven't seen him since graduation. But thanks for thinking of me.'

'I wasn't thinking of you,' she said quickly, trying to convince herself she meant it. Sometimes she thought there was as much of her nan, who was a feeder, inside her, as there was her mum. 'I'd have done it for anyone and with the hours I work I always batch cook for another day.'

'You're still doing that?' A glimmer of amusement returned. 'You were literally the only one at Catz.'

'Needs must, Oli.' She was stung by his remark, the reminder of the practical skills she'd depended on which weren't exactly a choice. Of all the people she'd known then, he was one of the very few who'd glimpsed the reality of her life at home. They'd moved out of university accommodation in their final two years, and she'd ended up in a house share with a friend of his. He had often been at her place, and sometimes his girlfriend Ingrid would be there too, lounging on his lap and regarding Erin with cool triumph.

Oli moved to the bed and sat down. Erin caught his slight wince, her senses tuning straight back into his. It had always been this way between them; they each seemed able to anticipate the other's mood. She decided she'd better not make him feel too unwelcome, though. She really wanted that new bathroom suite she'd got her eye on. If she was lucky she'd get it in the January sales, and he would be on his way without ever having had the chance to test it.

—

In the morning Erin curled up earlier than usual on the sofa with her breakfast. She'd woken with a churning in her stomach, alerting her to a worry it took her mind a moment to find. And then she remembered: Oli was here, sleeping in her spare room and staying for the next three weeks. Even though his few belongings were mostly confined to his bedroom after he'd fetched them from the car last night, a coffee machine and a box of capsules in the kitchen were making his presence in her home all too obvious. She'd heard him return about midnight, aware of his tread as he'd climbed the narrow staircase from the kitchen and opened the door to his bedroom, then a sharp crack followed by a muttered curse. He must've caught his head on the ceiling where it sloped.

Her phone was in the kitchen, and she hadn't yet replied to the cheery message from her mum, inquiring how her new lodger was settling in. There was a message from Carys too, and it was more direct, making Erin smile when she'd read it: *here if you need me and don't forget you can boot him out if he's an arrogant arse. He's not part of your job description.*

'Morning.'

Erin started, jolted back to the present when she saw Oli at the door from the hallway. A dark blue T-shirt was crumpled above grey shorts, and she drew in a slow breath.

'I hope I didn't wake you last night.' His smile was an uncertain one. 'The thing with Rob turned into a late one and then I got lost on the way back. Sat nav directed me to a track in the middle of nowhere.'

'Probably best not to use it.' She'd also heard him getting into that single bed last night, the frame creaking beneath his weight. 'You might want to apologise to Edmund, though, he's already been round to make sure I'm all right. He found my wheelie bin on its side and was worried.'

'Edmund?' Oli moved to the coffee machine and swapped the plug with the one for the toaster. She'd have to get used to such everyday things for now and tried not to mind. 'Sorry about the bin, it was very dark.'

'It's fine. Edmund's my neighbour, he's lovely.'

'Right. So how did you sleep?'

'Fine.' Good enough, anyway, and she ignored the suggestion of softness in his few words. Erin stood up and collected her breakfast things. She was heading into work early, but first she'd make a flask of tea to see her through the morning out on calls. 'How about you?'

'Yeah.' His smile was more of a grimace. 'All right.'

She quashed a flare of guilt; it wasn't her fault the second bedroom was tiny. 'You should probably know the hot tap takes ages to heat up and the bathroom door...'

'Sticks? Yeah, I noticed. So would you like a coffee, or do you still drink that disgustingly dark tea?'

'A proper brew, you mean.' She'd assumed he would've forgotten that by now. 'No thanks. I have no idea how you even drink that stuff first thing.'

'I need the hit, that's why.'

In the kitchen it was as she'd feared, and Jess had joked yesterday. Erin filled the washing-up bowl and turned for her flask just as Oli reached for the coffee capsules, and if she hadn't leaped back she would have crashed right into him. They both offered a hasty apology, and she felt a surge of electricity pass between them. It was a shock to realise he smelled the same, of vanilla and something spicier that always reminded her of the bourbon he'd sometimes drunk at Catz. She switched the kettle on, waiting for it to boil as he made an espresso and knocked it back in two quick gulps.

'Could you please spare me something for breakfast?' He flashed her that grin and she gritted her teeth. 'I'll go shopping later, I promise. Came straight here from a couple of days with a mate after a flight, so...'

'Help yourself, but as I said...'

'Yeah, I remember. Meals aren't included.'

Suddenly Oli's hand was on her arm, the gentle pressure of his fingers warm and light through her long-sleeved top. 'Don't you think we need a conversation about how this is going to work?' he said quietly. 'Obviously I had no idea about you when I took the job and finding out we're sharing was a...'

'Terrible disappointment? Horrible shock?'

'Neither of those, if I'm being honest.' He withdrew his hand. 'But I'm guessing you knew it was me and still went ahead. Why would you do that?'

'It's very simple. I'd already agreed to host the new locum and I'm saving up for a new bathroom. You've seen the current one so I'm sure you'll understand.'

'So it had nothing to do with us? You and me?'

'Of course it's not about that, there never really was an "us",' she told him hotly. One night with him in the house and already her plans for the morning were falling apart. She grabbed her flask, trying to focus on practical matters. 'All we need to deal with is work, it's the only subject that interests me where you and I are concerned.'

'So that hasn't changed. Studying always did come first for you.'

'What did you expect! You know what my life was like and how hard my family worked to keep our home together. I couldn't fall back on Mummy and Daddy or land some cushy job in the City if I didn't put the hours in, Oli. I have to make every penny of that debt count.'

Erin was not about to let him make her feel guilty for her work ethic. Studying had always been her route to success; she could trust it and she'd never allow herself to be reliant on someone who might break her heart all over again. 'I have to work and I love it. I'm not going to apologise for that.'

'I don't expect you to, nor would I ask it of you. But the past and what happened isn't going to go away.'

'What happened is that you asked me to trust you and then proved that I couldn't,' she said fiercely, hating the wobble in her voice. 'Do you seriously think I want to remember how I felt when I found out about you and Bella that summer, or…'

'There was no me and Bella that summer,' he said sharply. 'But I know I made a mistake and I've been sorry for it since the moment it happened.' Oli raked a hand through his hair and Erin couldn't remember what she was meant to be doing next. 'I tried to explain and apologise, but you…'

'You fooled me once, Oli, I'm not going to let it happen again. My father left my mum and me, and it broke her heart. So you'll have to forgive me for not falling for a dream or trusting in second chances.' The kettle had finished boiling and she went through the motions of filling her flask, the silence and the weight of their history heavy in her mind.

And she couldn't confess all: that part of her had wanted to see him when she'd found out he would be temporarily joining the practice. To test her feelings and her own strength around him now. To prove to herself that she really was over him, could share her home and remain immune to what she'd felt for him at Catz.

'We have to keep this professional. Our personal lives have nothing to do with one another. And no one at work knows and I want to keep it that way. Agreed?'

'I'm not sure it's…'

'Yes or no,' she said bluntly.

'Yes, if that's what you want,' he said quietly. 'And I'm sorry.'

'I don't know if you saw Gil's email this morning?' Erin snatched up her flask and phone; she much preferred talking about work, it kept their relationship on a footing she was comfortable with. 'He's been called away and I'm taking your induction instead.'

'Yes, I saw it.' Oli stuffed two pieces of bread into the toaster and swapped the plugs again. 'That's fine. Reminds me of the old days.'

'Oli, don't, please,' she said helplessly. They hadn't worked together since their sixth and final year at Catz, sharing punishing rotations in the university's animal hospital. That had been forty weeks free of lectures when they'd consulted almost as qualified vets, extending their knowledge across a dizzying range of small animal surgery and medicine, rural farm practice, equine studies, and more. Erin had adored it, her dream and ambition finally within reach despite the constant pressures, preparing case reports, presentations and studying for finals.

Her rotations had coincided with Oli's more than she'd have liked, and her unwritten rule was to behave as though everything they'd shared in their first year and the way it had ended had never occurred. But that hadn't prevented her pulse pounding whenever he walked into a room or the air between them vibrating if they were near, consulting on a case. They'd stood in surgery together time and again, masked, gowned and almost invisible to one another bar the intangible thread which quivered between them.

But her farm clients wouldn't care less about their shared past and what he meant to her now. They'd want to know if he could identify pneumonia in a vulnerable calf or diagnose bloat from a sudden death in a herd of dairy cattle, and prevent any more. Would he understand exactly when to perform a caesarean on a ewe whose labour wasn't progressing before she and her unborn lamb were lost?

Erin really hoped there was a nice, messy cattle de-horning on today's list of calls, or a massive angry bull with a giant stinking abscess to drain. That ought to put a dent in his megawatt smile.

Chapter Four

Yorkshire, thirteen years ago

Erin directed Oli to her street, her discomfort growing with every mile as she wondered how she might be able to avoid inviting him into her home. Outside the house he switched off the ignition and rubbed his temples. The traffic had been heavy around Leeds, and it was fully dark now. She glanced at the house, not needing daylight to read the familiar signs: the stone blackened over the years; the old plastic Santa she'd stuck in the window of her front bedroom every Christmas since she was eight. This year someone else, probably her grandad, had put it up for her and it was a welcome sign of home.

'I honestly don't know what to say,' she told Oli quietly. 'I appreciate this more than you know. If you give me a minute, I'll google a hotel for you.'

Erin turned her phone over to unlock it and shrieked as a hand thumped the window. Her head snapped around to see her nan's cheery face beaming at her beneath a thick woolly hat. She wound down the window, chilly winter air rushing into the car.

'I thought it was you, love. I'm just on me way t'bingo with Margery, then I saw the car an' I said to meself that looks like our Erin inside, but it can't be, cos she's at university.' She bent down awkwardly to stare past Erin to Oli. 'Hiya love, I'm Joyce, Erin's nan. What are you two doin' sittin' outside our 'ouse?'

'I was worried about Mum.' Erin was squirming in her seat, hand on the door handle ready to escape. She couldn't open it yet, not without sending her nan flying. 'She didn't reply to my messages, and you know she always lets me know she's okay.'

'She's takin' it easy, love. She's feelin' rough, but she'll be all right in a day or so. She won't be 'appy if she thinks you've come all this way on 'er account. Anyway, who's your friend?'

'Nan, this is Oli,' Erin said weakly. The relief that her mum was okay was huge, but she was embarrassed too; that she'd dragged him all this way in a panic when there was no need. And now she'd have to explain him to her family and her family to him, and her face was hot. 'He was kind enough to give me a lift.'

'Now then, Oli. You'd best get inside, the pair of you, it's proper cold.'

'It's lovely to meet you too, Joyce.' Oli caught Erin's eye, her hands twisting together in her lap as she fought the indecision over what do to.

'Well, are you comin' in or not?' Joyce made up Erin's mind for her and tugged the door open. 'You'll need a brew to warm you up.'

'Oli's not coming in, Nan,' Erin said desperately, tempted to slam the door and hope he would just take off somewhere else.

'Not comin' in? Don't be daft.' Joyce heaved the door wide. 'The lad'll need summat to eat if you've come all the way from Cambridge, an' I've been bakin'. Get inside, the pair of you, I'll get t'kettle on.'

Erin's shoulders slumped. Her nan might be tiny, but she was mighty, and most people didn't mess with her. 'What about Margery and the bingo?'

'It'll keep for another time, she's goin' with 'er daughter anyway. I'll ring an' let 'er know we've got visitors.'

'Nan, I live here.' Erin got out and went to the boot to fetch her bag, and Oli did the same, locking it after them. 'I'm not a visitor.'

'No, but your friend is. Do you like mince pies, Oli?'

'I love them.' He smiled at Joyce, waiting for Erin to walk up the paved path to the front door ahead of him. 'It's very kind of you to invite me in.'

'Any friend of our Erin's is always welcome 'ere, Oli. Just you remember that.'

Inside, Joyce hollered for her husband and Bill came through to the hall, pumping Oli's hand before wrapping Erin in a hug. She took Oli's jacket and hung it up with hers on the battered old coat stand, its small round mirror reminding her that her face was flushed and her curls wilder than normal. She was trying not to view the house through his eyes as they followed Joyce into the living room, wondering what he'd make of the Anaglypta wallpaper painted a murky shade of magnolia, the 1960s fireplace with its brick surround, green swirly patterned carpet and old beige suite. Joyce pointed to the sofa and Oli took a seat as Bill settled in his armchair beside the fire, his beloved radio nearby and a folded newspaper on the floor.

'I'll just run up and see Mum,' Erin said quickly, still hovering in the door. They'd have a cup of tea, then she'd make their excuses and get Oli out of here as quickly as possible. He had rarely spoken to her of his family,

42

and she knew only that he had a sister. Her grandad was questioning him about Cambridge, so she raced upstairs and knocked quietly on her mum's door in case she was sleeping.

'Mum? It's me.' She carefully opened the door, a lamp illuminating Heather pushing herself up in bed.

'Erin, love, what are you doing here?' Heather smiled and held out her arms. 'Not that it isn't wonderful to see you, because it is. Are you home for the holidays already? Have they let you off early?'

'No, that's next week.' Erin crossed to the bed and held her mum gently, trying to impart some of her own strength and energy in the gesture. 'Just popped in to make sure you're okay. You know what Nan's like with the phone and Grandad's no better.'

'Please tell me you haven't come all this way because of me?' Heather drew a cardigan around her shoulders as Erin settled on the edge of the bed.

'I was worried, Mum, I didn't know what was happening when you didn't reply.' Erin wiped away rare tears before her mum noticed; sitting beside her, the concern this morning and then the hasty decision to accept Oli's offer felt out of proportion now.

'I'm sorry to have worried you, love, but you can't be rushing back every time I forget to charge my phone. There's your studies to think of, and then the cost. I really don't want you spending money on me. How did you get here anyway? The train must've taken hours.'

'A friend brought me, in a car.' Erin jumped in before her mum could list any more reasons why she shouldn't have come. And she still wasn't used to the idea of describing Oli as a friend. He was a stranger in so many ways, and yet.

'Carys? Where is she then, let's go and say hello. I'd love to meet her after all you've told me.' Heather, her own curls already turning grey at forty, pushed the duvet aside. 'Give me ten minutes and I'll be down.'

'It's not Carys.' Erin's face was pink; she was aware her voice wasn't conveying the nonchalance for which she was aiming. 'It's someone else.'

'Well, I still want to meet this guardian angel and thank them for bringing my wonderful daughter all the way home from Cambridge.'

'We're not staying long.' Erin got up and edged towards the door. 'Don't get carried away, okay? He's just a friend.'

'He, is it? Well.'

Downstairs she found herself a bemused spectator as her nan bustled about, popping into the living room to ask Oli how he drank his tea, did he like sugar or not, and how many mince pies could he manage after a long drive like that? Erin perched on the sofa, listening to her grandad sharing the delights of his vegetable garden, offering to show Oli the sprouts he was growing for Christmas and the potatoes he'd safely stored in his shed for winter.

The Christmas decorations were already up, because Joyce liked to be ahead of the curve when it came to chores. A red, green and white paper chain hung across the chimney breast, dangling in front of a round mirror in the centre. The ancient artificial tree they'd had since Erin was small shimmered in a corner and one half of a low sideboard was laden with mini Christmas trees in various seasonal shades. A pair of matching biscuit tins with Santa balanced on top were sat either side of an old wooden advent calendar, and she felt a rush of homesickness as she wondered who'd be opening it in her absence.

She was thinking of Christmas Day, and the us̪.
rhythms and routines of home she found so comforting.
The early morning start so her nan could get the turkey in
the oven, Joyce and Bill grumbling, getting in each other's
way as he peeled potatoes for roasting. The radio blaring
Christmas classics in the kitchen while a brass band played
carols on a record player in the living room. All so soothing
and familiar, and a million miles away from the new life
in Cambridge she was still trying to forge.

'You're stayin' for your tea?' Joyce glanced at Erin as she
set a tray down on Bill's lap. 'It's your grandad's stew an'
I've told 'im that many times about the carrots, but does
he listen? Make yourself useful, Bill, an' 'old this whilst
Erin gives Oli a cup an' a mince pie.'

'Where's mine?' Bill winked at Erin, and she grinned.
At least some things never changed.

'You've already 'ad two, Bill Johnson, an' you don't
want the doctor after you again if your cholesterol goes
back up.'

Erin stood, even more flummoxed to see her nan using
a teapot in honour of their guest. She poured Oli a mug
and handed it to him with a mince pie. She poured her
own tea and took a mince pie too; she was hungry, and
no one made mince pies like her nan. Maybe she could
scrounge a few and take them back to Catz to keep her
going until the end of term.

'These are amazing.' Oli tried to catch the crumbs
falling to his lap and missed, grinning when he caught
Erin's eye. 'By far the best I've ever had.'

'Go on with you, lad, you're just sayin' that.' Joyce,
perched on the arm of Bill's chair, beamed delightedly.
Erin smothered a smile as she heard him muttering
about it breaking under her weight. Their banter was

of her life, and she missed it; she couldn't
...e without the other.'

...eriously, I mean it.' Oli raised a helpless shoulder
...e dropped another on his plate. 'We usually
hav. Christmas cake instead. My parents aren't together
anymore and they both travel for work, so my sister and I
split the holidays between them.'

Heather appeared and in better light Erin saw how pale
she was, and forced away a spike of worry. She'd be home
next week for Christmas and then at least she could help
out in between studying, which was a comfort. Heather
also thanked Oli for his kindness in driving Erin home and
he brushed it off again, assuring them it was a pleasure, and
he'd had no plans he couldn't change.

Once the mince pies were devoured and Oli was asking
Heather about her work in the florists, Joyce suggested
that Erin and Oli eat on their knees in here, seeing as
the three of them had already had their tea. Erin cringed,
imagining that he'd probably never eaten on his knees in
his life, but Oli was quickly agreeing.

'Thank you for including me, it's very kind. The meals
at Catz are great, aren't they, Erin, but I can't remember
the last time I had something homemade.'

'Then get yourself round a plate of Bill's stew.' Joyce
clambered to her feet and Erin was following.

'I'll sort it out, Nan, you sit down. You're not running
around after us.'

Once she and Oli had seen off platefuls of delicious
stew with dumplings and hunks of crusty bread and butter,
plus a generous dollop of Bill's homemade pickled red
cabbage, there was another minor battle when Joyce and
Heather discovered that Oli was planning to stay in a hotel
before the drive back to Cambridge tomorrow.

'I won't hear another word about it.' Heather fixed Erin with a look that said she meant it when Erin tried to protest again. 'You can have Erin's room.'

'Absolutely not.' Oli laughed awkwardly, his gaze catching Erin's, and she flushed at the thought of him sleeping in her bed. 'Sorry, I meant that I'd love to stay if you'll have me but I'm very happy to sleep on the sofa. I really don't want Erin to give up her room for me.'

'Are you sure?' Heather looked doubtfully at the beige couch. 'I don't know if it's long enough for you. Mum, don't we still have that camp bed in the loft?'

'Aye, but it'll be damp. I reckon the couch will do if Oli doesn't mind?' Joyce gave him a beady glance.

'Not in the least.' He flashed Erin that grin she found so perturbing, and even her nan seemed to be having a moment. 'I'm very grateful for your hospitality.'

Erin sat back, letting the conversation carry on around her. When Bill learned that Oli had never seen the Christmas episode of *The Good Life*, one of his favourites, he decided it wasn't too early to watch it again. Erin found it for him and slotted the DVD into the player beneath the television. She found it hard to relax as her family took up their usual positions, squashed up to Oli on one side of the couch with her mum on the other.

Then they got Monopoly out, and Heather excused herself after an hour to return to bed. Bill never missed an opportunity, piling hotels on his Mayfair property and making the rest of them stump up the rent. Joyce was out first, then Bill, and it was left to Erin to maintain family honour and beat Oli, and they shared a high five. Bill was dozing in front of the gas fire and Joyce nudged him awake to go up to bed. Erin's senses were on high alert as she and

Oli were left on their own, nowhere near ready for sleep yet.

'Uno?' She got the little box out of the sideboard where all the games lived. 'Do you know how to play?'

'Of course I do.' Oli shuffled onto the floor, and she joined him, setting the cards out. After beating him in five straight games, she went into the kitchen to make tea and he followed, settling at the small table and chairs for two when she insisted she didn't need any help. She pulled out the chair opposite him and it was easier to talk about Catz, the work they'd done so far, the plans for next term.

'Time for sleep.' She closed her eyes, finally feeling the tiredness pressing in behind them. It had been an unusual and emotional day, and weariness was finally claiming her. 'Grandad will have you out early inspecting his sprouts, and you must be beat after that drive.'

'I'm looking forward to it.' Oli leaned back, covering a yawn. 'I am a bit tired, to be honest. Is this the right moment to tell you I've never driven so far in my life?'

'Oli!' She leaned across the table to bat his arm, and he laughed. 'Why did you do it, then?'

'I hope you know why,' he said quietly. He held her gaze and Erin stood up hastily. This day, that look, none of it made sense in her world.

'I think Nan's left the stuff for your bed in my room, I'll go and get it.'

'Can I help?' Oli was on his feet too.

'I can manage a duvet and a couple of pillows.'

'I know you can. But I'd like to help.'

'Okay,' she said slowly from the foot of the stairs. 'But one word about my bedroom and you'll be sleeping in the car.'

'Got it. So what's wrong with your room?'

48

'Nothing, I love it. I just didn't ever imagine you seeing it, that's all.'

His feet were unfamiliar behind hers, and upstairs Erin opened the door, heart pounding at sharing the memories it contained.

'Am I allowed to say I love it too? It's really cute.' His voice was as low as hers, mindful of her grandparents next door. 'Especially the squirrels.'

'Liar.' She picked up the spare pillow and flung it at him. He caught it easily, tossing it back on the bed. 'I bet your bedroom doesn't look anything like this.'

'No. But I only saw it in the holidays because I was away at school.'

'I'm sorry.' Her reply was an automatic response to the quick pursing of his lips, the glimpse of sorrow in his eyes, before she remembered that boarding school was supposed to represent opportunity in his world.

'Thanks.' He edged into her narrow room, staring at the shelf filled with the cuddly toys she couldn't part with, awards from school, and more photos of animals from the shelter where she'd volunteered.

'Was it a nice school?' She held her breath as he sat on the bed too, the single mattress sinking some more.

'You could say that. But it wasn't home, not like this.'

'How old were you when you first went?'

'Seven when I started prep school.' Oli was staring at his clasped hands. 'I moved to Harrow when I was thirteen.'

'I couldn't think of anything worse,' she blurted out. 'Sorry, that's probably not the right thing to say.' There was so much she still didn't know about him, but she understood that being away from home had hurt, and she wasn't expecting the clench in her own heart.

'No, it's fine. I appreciate your honesty.'

'I think sometimes it's called bluntness. Family trait.' They shared a smile and somehow Erin's hand found its way to his. He slid his fingers between hers and she was staring at this first real connection, their shoulders and thighs pressed together on her blue-and-white galloping horses duvet cover.

'What did you miss most about home?' They'd already crossed a line when she'd agreed to let him drive her here and now he'd seen her world, the room she'd slept in for thirteen years.

'My family, obviously. Although it wasn't the same after my parents divorced.' He swallowed. 'My dad left us for someone else and my sister and I, we'd had no idea that things weren't right between them. We thought they were happy.'

'I'm sorry.' She squeezed his fingers. When they'd first met she would never have imagined expressing her sadness for a situation like his; one of privilege but which had still brought its sorrows and difficulties. 'How old were you?'

'Sixteen. It was right after my GCSEs. Imogen's two years older than me. I know we weren't kids, but it was still a massive shock. Things between me and my dad still aren't great.' Oli paused. 'I don't really know how to forgive him for what he did.'

'I know what it's like.' Erin leaned into him. 'My father left when I was five.'

'It's shit, isn't it?' He turned a troubled blue gaze on hers, and her smile was a brief, understanding one.

'Yeah. Not so much now, it's been years, and he died, so…'

'I'm sorry.'

'It's fine, it doesn't matter anymore. I have my mum and she's wonderful, and you've met my crazy grandparents.'

'They're brilliant, and I love how they love you.' He was staring at a photo of Erin kneeling, her arms around a tall black greyhound. 'Leaving our dog, Honey, was the worst thing. We'd had her since I was four and every time I packed for school, she'd sit on my bed and keep me company. She was always there when I came home, waiting at the door and we'd take off for long walks and swim in the river. I adored her.'

His voice caught as his glance fell to his hand fixed to Erin's between his thighs. 'I wasn't there when she had an accident and had to be put down. I didn't find out until I came home at Christmas, and she was gone. My parents thought it best not to upset me at school as there was nothing I could've done. But there was,' he said fiercely. 'I should've been with her and I hate that she passed away without me holding her and letting her know how much I loved her. She's part of the reason why I want to be a vet, because I want to make a difference. I want to help make animals better if I can. They love us no matter what.'

'Oh, Oli,' Erin whispered. She put her arms around him, holding him tightly. Suddenly his bold and brilliant life at Catz didn't look quite so wonderful now she understood the pain he carried, the separation of his family matching hers even through their vastly different circumstances. 'I'm so sorry. For what it's worth I think you'll make a pretty decent vet.'

'Pretty decent?' He muttered his reply against her neck, and she felt him smile. She'd meant to tease him, to ease him away from the heartbreak, and she was leaning into the unfamiliar touch of his hands on her back. The absolute rightness of it, as though every encounter so far had been leading them to this moment. She was trembling, heat travelling through her body to land a sharp kick of desire in her stomach, a very new sensation.

He eased back and caught one of her curls. 'I love your hair,' he murmured, tugging it gently. 'No one else has hair like you.'

She stilled, her eyes glittering on his. Was she really brave enough to do this? But then where would they be, when they were back at Catz, and he was once again surrounded by his friends and the cluster of beautiful girls all vying for his attention.

'We should get some sleep,' Erin rushed out, letting her arms fall away. She needed to be pragmatic, even though it was the last thing she wanted. But she had to think of her future, to focus on her dream and not her heart. This conversation would be forgotten once they returned to university, and they'd probably feel awkward that they'd let this moment overwhelm them. 'You've got a long drive tomorrow.'

'I suppose.' Oli touched his forehead to hers before nodding slowly and standing up. He gathered the spare duvet and pillows, and at the door he looked back. 'Thanks for listening.'

'You're welcome. And thanks for getting me home.'

'You're also welcome,' he told her softly. 'Sleep tight.'

Chapter Five

Hartfell, present day

Erin didn't ever think she'd take for granted the reality of achieving her dream to live and work in the Dales. Even on this bitter December morning Hartfell was still glorious, despite drizzle threatening to become heavier as she drove Oli to the practice. The fells were shrouded in mist drifting across a grey sky, but even that couldn't spoil the view of snug stone cottages and Christmas lights wound around the topiary in planters outside the pub.

Half a mile from the village she turned into a driveway lined with trees. The farmhouse where Gil lived with his partner Pippa and her teenage daughter Harriet was opposite a paddock on the right. The drive curved around to the courtyard, where the practice was housed in one of three buildings formerly belonging to Home Farm.

Harriet was opening the paddock gate to let Posy, their resident single-minded skewbald Shetland pony, through. Posy loved Harriet and loathed Gil in equal measure. When Pippa and Harriet had moved into the farmhouse last summer, he'd been relieved to let Harriet take over Posy's care. Harriet smiled at Erin, who waved back, as the teenager shot Oli a curious look. Harriet adored animals and was planning her own career as a vet, and Erin enjoyed taking her out on calls to see practice. Harriet was good company, always got stuck in and didn't mind the dirtiest or smelliest jobs, a given in Erin's line of work.

Erin pulled up in the car park. When she and Oli made their way into reception, she was surprised to find the staff had apparently planned a welcome for him. 'Last Christmas' was playing via a speaker, and she smiled; Gil had half-heartedly tried to ban seasonal songs but he'd been firmly overruled by everybody else.

'Oli, welcome to Home Farm Vets!' Jess shot forward, her hair bundled into a loose knot and held in place with an emerald band.

She made the introductions, and he shook hands with everyone as he thanked them. Elaine quickly established that he drank espresso and had a weakness for dark chocolate. She promptly whipped the lid off her tin of homemade brownies and proffered it. Jess was enthusing about how thrilled they were to have him, though Erin really couldn't see why; she wasn't that impressed by his CV as a self-employed locum with a postgrad certificate in small animal medicine.

Already the usual early morning meeting – when the staff gathered with a brew to plan the day ahead – had been sidetracked by his arrival. Oli helped himself to a brownie, and when Elaine returned with his coffee, she persuaded him to take another for later before they all disappeared. Head nurse Steph asked how he was settling in with Erin, and Jess gave Erin a knowing grin when he offered a casual reply. Even Gabi, who ran the practice with a firm hand and did her level best to keep Gil in check, was looking a little less fierce at the sight of their handsome new locum laughing at something else Steph had said.

Erin accepted Elaine's offer of tea and a brownie. Working such a physical job, often outdoors in all weathers, meant she was usually hungry and burned calories nearly as fast as she consumed them. They all took their turn to bake, even Gil, and Elaine was arranging a mince pie tasting closer to Christmas. Oli was charmingly explaining that he'd never baked a cake in his life, and it took Jess, who was expert with eggs, flour, butter and sugar, about five seconds to offer to teach him.

'I'm all packed up at home, though, as my partner and I have just bought a house and we're moving in soon. We'd have to do the lesson at yours, Erin.' She grinned and Erin just managed to avoid rolling her eyes. This was already getting a little too snug for her liking but if she wasn't careful, Jess would smell a rat and want to know why she was so keen to avoid her own lodger.

'That depends on whether Erin minds?' Oli was looking at her too and she shrugged.

'Just don't blow up my oven, and I get first dibs on anything you make as long as it's edible.'

'Deal.' He gave her a grin and she dropped her gaze. After their first year at Catz and how it had ended, she'd had the barrier of studying wedged firmly between them. All she had to protect her now was her professionalism and a determination that they wouldn't get drawn once again into each other's lives.

'Why don't you give Oli a quick tour before we head out,' she suggested to Steph, who was Jess's senior and therefore, Erin hoped, less likely to be susceptible to his charm.

Oli promised Elaine he'd never tasted brownies as good and set off with Steph. Elaine settled at her screen behind the counter with a happy sigh, muttering something about beautiful manners and what a pity he wasn't permanent. Erin, who disagreed with her about the permanence bit at least, ignored Jess as she disappeared into a treatment room with a merry smile, and made for the office with her mug of tea.

It was a squeeze with an expanding staff, and they were all looking forward to the future and a state-of-the-art farm animal building, improved consulting rooms and a new lab. She cast an eye over a large paper diary on Gabi's desk. All companion animal appointments were booked online but this method for recording farm calls had stuck, and Erin loved how it connected the present-day practice to the past one. There was something about names and planned visits on the page in black and white that were solid and real, like the farms and their people. A flicker of satisfaction followed when she scanned her appointments for today: a calf with diarrhoea, a donkey castration and Dorothy Pilkington. Even better.

All perfect for Oli's induction, and it promised to be very different from his usual consultations. She wondered if he might loathe mixed practice in such a rural location and decide it wasn't for him after all. But that wasn't a thought on which she wanted to linger. If Oli left early then her new bathroom fund would be seriously depleted and Gil would have the headache of replacing him. Erin finished her tea and ran over the timings; the calf was first call and most urgent as it could quickly deteriorate without prompt treatment.

Back in her pickup with Oli fifteen minutes later, having collected everything they might need for the day, Erin rolled a shoulder to loosen her tension as they set off. 'So the calf, what do you think?'

She checked for traffic before pulling onto the quiet lane, wipers working furiously now the drizzle had become heavy rain. A thick hawthorn hedge opposite was bare of its leaves on spiky stems and the scarlet berries the birds had already taken.

'How old?' Oli's level tone implied that he too was prepared to keep their conversation professional.

'Ten days.'

'Right. So it's at serious risk then, and I'd be thinking most probably a viral infection rather than a bacterial one. Let's see, shall we?'

Erin crossed a bridge spanning a narrow, gushing river, and drove past the primary school and church with its sturdy square tower. She paused at a T-junction; where the village green was bordered by the river and edged with planting on her right, a crumbling stone cross in the centre beside the remains of wooden stocks. The cobbled main street was empty in this weather, a few white cottages adorned with seasonal lights opposite a pair of larger houses standing behind railings and low evergreen hedging.

She turned left past the Pilkington Arms, built of the same creamy golden stone as Home Farm, smothered in ivy climbing to the rafters. The old youth hostel, which Pippa had bought a few months back and was converting into an art gallery and community space, sat opposite the pub, and the scaffolding hadn't long come down. Tatty rendering on the walls had been stripped back and the pale stone underneath revealed, making the building more welcoming. Pippa was holding a pop-up Christmas craft event on Friday to launch the gallery, and Erin was hoping to find a few gifts and maybe some decorations for her new home.

Oli's gaze was turned to the window as she drove, the radio a background of chat keeping the silence at bay. Low meadows bordered by walls rose to moorland fells, still smothered in mist, and dotted with ancient stone barns standing firm against all the weather flung at them. The river snaked below them, twisting beneath tight hump-backed bridges, and gushing over giant stone boulders to crash into deep rocky pools.

Most cattle were indoors for the winter now the grass offered little sustenance, and Erin noticed some hardy Belted Galloway cows, black with a distinctive white stripe around their middles, roaming loose amongst the Swaledale and Rough Fell sheep, all tough enough to withstand most conditions. The sheep grazed the fells all year round, coloured marks on their fleeces identifying the flock to which they belonged. Most of the ewes would be pregnant and preparing to give birth in the new year, and she felt a thrill of excitement at the busy lambing season ahead.

'It's stunning,' Oli remarked. She nodded, catching his eye when his gaze flickered back to her. 'I can see why those days out with your mum made such an impression and why you wanted to practise here.'

She'd thought he would've forgotten her passion for the Dales and that practising here was the pinnacle of her professional ambition. How many other confidences had they shared that weekend when she'd brought him home to her family and he'd somehow fitted right in?

'Is it always like this, the weather?' He unscrewed a flask of coffee that Elaine had thoughtfully provided. He poured some into a cup and replaced the lid before taking a grateful sip.

'No. Sometimes it's worse.'

'Bit different from growing up in a town,' he remarked. 'It doesn't faze you, but then not much ever did.'

She would never admit that Oli had, tilting her world to a degree she hadn't imagined possible until they'd met. At times she'd resented the feelings she'd had for him then, leading to that unforgettable kiss, the one she still tried not to measure against every other. She offered no reply and ten minutes later was relieved to arrive at their first call and escape any more reminders of their history.

She followed a rough drive alongside paddocks empty but for two grazing horses in navy rugs and a small flock of Swaledale sheep, their horned black faces marked with white around the nose and eyes. She pulled up at a five-barred metal gate fastened to a concrete post with orange baling twine. Usually she had to jump down and open the gate herself, and she looked at Oli meaningfully, hoping he'd get the message.

'Oh yeah. Like being a student again,' he muttered, wincing as he opened the door, and a blast of wind attempted to tug it from his hands. He undid the gate and offered a wry grin as she drove through, and Erin waited for him to close it. He jumped back inside with a shudder of relief.

She parked outside a barn in the yard, the usual jumble of machinery, bales and fencing equipment propped inside, shivering as she pulled on the essential coat, woolly hat, wellies and waterproofs, and Oli did the same. She'd learned never to use the heated seats unless she'd been on the wrong side of a soaking, as leaving the warm vehicle made heading out into freezing wind or blinding rain even worse.

She introduced Oli to the farmer and collected equipment from the boot before following them to a small pen at the back of the barn, separate from the rest of the herd housed in another building. Inside a beautiful red-and-white calf was standing lethargically, head lowered, as its mother looked on.

Erin stood aside so Oli could lead the consultation, and he quickly established the calf had a poor appetite after a difficult birth and the farmer had tube fed the necessary colostrum to provide it with essential viral protection. Its temperature was on the higher side of normal and after further examination he diagnosed pneumonia. He prescribed seven days of medication and advised the farmer to keep a close eye on the calf for any signs of dehydration or worsening of its condition. She was confident the calf would recover as they'd caught the illness in its very early stages.

'Looks like a good outcome.' Back in the yard, Erin glanced at Oli as they disinfected their waterproofs and boots, and changed their footwear. The wind was cutting on her face, and she felt its icy chill the moment she took off her hat and flung it onto the back seat as she leaped into the pickup.

'Yeah, it should be fine,' he said lightly. He hadn't wasted any time getting inside either, and they shared a grin at the calf's hopeful prospects. She raised a hand to thank the farmer as he followed them to the gate and closed it behind them, saving Oli a job.

When they arrived at a smallholding to see their next patient, they learned the donkey was a recent rescue and at three, quite a bit older than was usual for castration. The owner cheerfully explained that it was necessary because his being entire was causing problems for her two females and she wanted all three to live quietly together. She also pointed out that he was a bit of a handful. The donkey was turned out in a paddock, and it didn't take them long to discover he was also a nightmare to catch. It took all three of them a good fifteen minutes to corner him, and Erin couldn't stifle her laughter when Oli slipped in a deep patch of mud near the gate and was sent sprawling to his knees.

Eventually he managed to fling a lead rope around the donkey's neck and hold him steady long enough for her to administer a hasty sedative. Soon the donkey's head began to droop and once she'd followed up with the general anaesthetic, it quickly took effect, and they supported him as he went down on the grass.

Thankfully, the rain had stopped, and she covered him with a waterproof rug as Oli injected local anaesthetic into the appropriate area as well, fingers stiffening from the cold as he worked. She couldn't be certain, kneeling on the wet grass at their patient's head, but it seemed as though the two jennies were watching on with interest, and perhaps even a degree of satisfaction at the sight of their bolshy companion being separated from part of his manhood.

Once Oli had completed the castration and sutured the blood vessels, he administered another drug to reverse the anaesthetic and they waited while the donkey came to, legs unsteady as he climbed groggily to his feet. He tottered meekly alongside the owner into a stable and, satisfied after a short while that he was fine and recovering well, Oli and Erin tidied up and returned to her vehicle to disinfect and strip off outer layers once again.

'Well done.' Wincing – even to her that had sounded patronising – she reached for her flask to gulp a welcome mouthful of hot tea before setting off.

'I know what I'm doing, Erin,' he said flatly, staring at his phone before shoving it back into the glove box. 'I'm not still some student straight out of uni with everything to prove. Gil gets that I'm qualified to do this work, and I spent as much time on farm animal rotations as you did, even if I do have less experience in practice.'

She knew she was falling into the trap of judging him on their history. She couldn't fault his diagnoses or treatments; he'd been warm and friendly with the clients, and he'd handled the animals with a gentleness and sympathy she remembered. She was also uncomfortably aware that it was her own attitude making her unprofessional right now, and she couldn't allow that to cloud her opinion of his experience and skill.

'You're right, and I'm sorry.'

'So who's Dorothy then? Gabi showed me the diary before we left.'

Erin was looking forward to their next visit. 'She's Gil's great aunt, a bit eccentric. You'll see.'

–

Dorothy was Gil's only relative in the village, with his eldest son managing a vineyard in Australia and his youngest at university in Portsmouth. She'd lived in Hartfell all her life and was well known for her preference of animals over humans. The farm she'd inherited from her father had been a sanctuary for animals for over fifty years and she wouldn't refuse anything with four legs or feathers a good home.

At first Erin had found her general disdain for people, booming voice and near six-foot frame alarming, but they got on well, especially since she'd turned out at six a.m. one harsh November morning and surgically reversed a twisted stomach in Dorothy's favourite cow after an unexpectedly early calving. Dorothy had been so grateful to Erin for saving its life that she'd invited her into the farmhouse for breakfast, and they'd happily discussed foot rot in sheep and the merits of Swaledale tups versus Rough Fell ones over doorstep bacon sandwiches and coffee so strong that Erin hadn't been able to face another cup for weeks.

The farm stood half a mile up the dale and was accessed by a rutted track. A driveway swung left in front of the house, and Erin pulled up beside a muddy quad bike connected to a trailer laden with empty feed bags. Weathered barns, roof tiles green with moss matching the shade of the windows, were attached to either end of the large square house built of the same stone, a wide front door standing firmly in the centre.

A wild garden edged with a low wall was compact, given over to grazing sheep. She got out, prepared for the pack of dogs swarming to meet them. She was wary of the small terrier – the reason why post was left at the end of the drive and delivery drivers honked their horns in the yard. The silky red setter loved a cuddle and was more polite than a three-legged lurcher already stuffing his nose into Erin's pockets. The latest addition to the pack, an elderly working collie whose owner had passed away, hung back, still cautious with strangers.

Oli jumped out and she watched as he crouched down to greet the dogs, laughing as the setter tried to clamber onto his lap. She wondered if he still missed his own dog, the one that had been put down when he'd been away at school. Had he ever got another, or was his travelling the reason why not? His arm was around the setter as he tried to persuade the lurcher to abandon its search of his pockets while apologising for his lack of treats. The lurcher licked his chin and even the terrier had ceased yapping as the collie edged a little closer.

'Morning, Erin.' Dorothy's roar was apparent before she emerged from a barn along the track, a low mooing accompanying her. 'I see you've brought your latest. Hope he's up to your standard.' Dorothy wouldn't allow one of their previous locums to set foot on the farm after she discovered he wasn't a fan of goats and had once suggested she might consider rehoming a couple of kids after a billy had run amok amongst the nannies and the birth rate had shot up.

Erin's chin rose a fraction and she registered Oli's surprise at such a welcome. His waterproofs were filthy after the escapade with the donkey, and she hadn't noticed the splash of mud on his left cheek until now.

'Get orf,' Dorothy bellowed as she strode towards them, and he leaped to his feet as though he'd been jabbed with a cattle prod. The dogs slunk away, and Erin was still grinning as she went to the boot to fetch equipment. She knew the patient they were booked in to see but it never hurt to be prepared for anything where Dorothy was concerned.

Gil and Pippa had recently hosted a lunch for Dorothy's eighty-third birthday, and she saw no reason why age should attempt to slow her down. The prehistoric green waxed coat she wore all year round was fastened with orange baling twine above the usual men's suit trousers and a pair of fancy green wellies. The boots had been a gift from Gil and Pippa when he'd discovered that her previous ones were stuffed with carrier bags to keep out the wet. Grey hair was piled on top of her head, spilling from a messy bun, and sharp blue eyes were narrowed on Oli.

'Ruddy dogs,' she muttered in a tone which suggested she meant something else entirely. She stared at him above glasses perched halfway along her nose and held together with tape. He shot Erin a nervous glance and she didn't dare offer a reassuring smile for fear she'd laugh again.

Dorothy sniffed. 'Come on then, let's see what you know about goats. Can't be any worse than the last chap, I s'pose.'

Chapter Six

'You said eccentric,' Oli hissed at Erin, following Dorothy as she set off towards the barn, the dogs falling obediently into line at her heels. 'Not raving mad.'

'You'd better not let Dorothy hear you say that,' Erin replied loudly. 'She let the geese out when she took a dislike to our last locum and informed him it might be her shotgun next time. It was a fortnight before the bruising on his leg disappeared.'

'You're not serious? How does she get away with it?'

'Probably because she hasn't actually shot anyone yet, at least not to my knowledge. I wouldn't like to be in your shoes if you fancy testing that theory. Apparently she did take a pot shot at someone she found trying to steal her quad bike, but Gil said as the bloke was already legging it from the dogs and the geese and was halfway up the track by the time she'd loaded it, he was quite safe. She doesn't leave the keys in the ignition now, just in case.'

'Let me guess.' Oli shot Erin a wry look as he tugged his collar higher, trying to keep driving rain from sliding down his neck. 'She keeps them under her pillow?'

'Nope. Wears them on string around her neck, so I'd say they're pretty secure.'

'Right. Gabi told me to watch out for the bull. Apparently he likes to roam.'

'Oh yeah, I'd forgotten about that. He's fine really, just not that keen on fences. Don't try and stare him down, though. Gil did that once and ripped his trousers when he had to jump over a gate to get out of the way.'

'And just think,' Oli muttered. 'I could be in a nice city surgery somewhere, vaccinating kittens and delivering puppies.'

'Why would you want to do that when you could be here?' Erin gestured to the farm and the fells beyond it. She loved the ancient barns and buildings, built by hands that spoke of the history of this land and its people, their stories crafted in stones laid together and standing firm for centuries. She felt the view settle inside her, grounding her senses, fixing her too to this land. She was at home here and a rush of pleasure brought a smile.

'I really can't think,' he shot back, grimacing at the state of his waterproofs as he took off his hat to run a hand through damp hair.

They caught Dorothy up inside the barn, waiting next to a pen below a loft heavy with last summer's store of precious hay. Erin spotted their patient, a beautiful Golden Guernsey goat, who on first inspection seemed quite comfortable on a thick bed of straw and nibbling from hay in a low wooden rack on the wall.

'Suspect it's mastitis,' Dorothy announced, staring at Oli as though he'd just sicked up something on her carpet. 'What do you make of that?'

'Well, let's have a look, shall we,' he said smoothly, opening the gate and stepping into the pen. In a flash the goat lowered her head and charged, and he shrieked as she butted him very firmly on the thigh. He slammed the gate just before she followed him out to give chase.

'What do you think you're doing?' Dorothy roared. 'Nearly caught her head in the door!'

'What am I doing?' he said incredulously, shooting Erin a plaintive look and clearly hoping for support she didn't plan on giving, not where Dorothy was concerned. 'Didn't you see what happened? If I hadn't got out of the way pretty smartly it would've butted me somewhere a lot more painful than my leg.'

'Too attached to your balls, that's the problem with you lot. Better off without 'em, like m'bull.'

Erin just managed to direct a snort into her hand and caught the wink Dorothy gave her, pressing her lips together so hard they hurt. First the donkey and now Dorothy. This day just got better and better, and she loved her job so much. Right now she very nearly loved Dorothy as well.

'You'll have to be made of sterner stuff if you're going to treat my animals, laddie.' Dorothy glared at him over her glasses as she opened the door to the pen and spoke quietly to the goat, who submitted to her gentle touch. 'I s'pose you want another go.'

'Not especially,' Oli muttered. He entered the pen more warily this time and she consented to hold the goat so he could examine its udders while he asked Dorothy a few routine health questions. Once he'd decided it was mastitis and she'd told him any fool could see that, he outlined a course of treatment and advised her to dispose of any milk the nanny produced. Erin returned to the pickup to fetch the appropriate medication.

'Well, lovely to meet you,' Oli said to Dorothy, checking for any lurking danger as they trooped back into the yard. He held out a hand and she stared at it for a long moment, and eventually he let it fall away.

'Not done yet,' she told him with a glower. 'Got to make use of you whilst you're here.'

'You what?' He shot Erin a worried glance and she shrugged. This was perfectly normal, and as long as there were no other pressing appointments, she was always happy to examine more of Dorothy's menagerie while she was here.

An hour later, they were done, and Oli settled back in the pickup with a weary grunt as Erin pulled out of the yard onto the track, trying to avoid deep ruts full of muddy rainwater.

'Shit, that was brutal,' he said when they'd bounced their way back onto a meandering lane made darker by tall beech hedging on either side. He was sporting a nasty scratch he'd received on his hand after mistaking a feral kitten for a pet one and had undergone a nerve-wracking introduction to Hugo, the allegedly docile and very large Hereford bull, while examining him for a skin condition. Even Erin, after years of practice with cattle on Carys's farm in Wales during the holidays, wasn't certain that Dorothy's method of separating Hugo from his beloved girls in the herd with a short length of blue pipe and a few choice bellows was ideal. He'd ambled into a pen eventually and Oli was able to prescribe a new course of treatment from the right side of stout metal bars.

He'd also dosed a sturdy Rhode Island Red cockerel with a syringe of olive oil to help with an impacted crop, but not before the bird had flown at him with a screech of rage and a vicious-looking beak. Dorothy had grabbed it just in time and wedged it firmly under her arm. She'd informed Oli that the cockerel wasn't especially enamoured of men, but beggars couldn't be choosers if they were going to gorge themselves on too much long grass in the orchard.

'How the hell do you put up with her?'

'Because she adores her animals, and she'd do anything for them. Plus she's Gil's aunt, and they're very fond of each other. As is Harriet, Gil's stepdaughter. She and Dorothy get on like a house on fire and she's often here, helping out after school and at weekends.'

'So it's just other people Dorothy can't stand?'

'Not people, per se. Men, mostly. Elaine said something about her having a partner once but apparently they lived in a caravan in the yard because the two of them couldn't get along in the same house.'

'You don't say,' Oli muttered, closing his eyes. 'Well, at least she's not going to let me back in the yard seeing as I nearly chinned her goat. Small mercies.'

'Don't bet on it. If she'd really taken a dislike to you, you'd never have been allowed near anything else. At least the alpacas didn't spit on you.'

'This time last week I was in Costa Rica,' he mused, staring out of the window again. 'Sunshine and surfing and blue skies. Not like this.'

'Mmm.' Erin had no desire to learn more about his time away or with whom he might have spent it. His Instagram consisted of his travels or animals, and both garnered him plenty of likes. 'Maybe you should go back and volunteer again.' She realised her mistake too late.

'How do you know I was volunteering?'

'It was just a guess. I saw your CV and that you've done it before.'

'Either that or you've been checking out my Instagram.' He shot her a smile and she ignored it, trying to focus on the drive in such heavy rain. 'So you were interested.'

'Not especially.'

Erin was relieved to return to the practice, but she wasn't expecting lunch to be laid on as well. The staff wanted to know how the morning had gone and what Oli made of Dorothy. Gil arrived soon after and the two men shook hands while Erin helped herself to a mug of tea before joining them.

'Erin, hey.' Gil welcomed her with a grin. His dark blond hair was untidy and his blue eyes were bright against a face lined by a life lived outdoors. 'Oli was just telling me about the castration. Sorry about passing it on to you. The meeting at the gallery was brought forward and Pippa needed me there as I'm on the board.'

'It was fine. Nothing I haven't dealt with before.' Erin was smiling at Gil, but her thoughts were lingering on Oli skidding around in the mud as they'd tried to catch the donkey, his determination not to give in, the easy and instinctive way they'd rediscovered their old rhythm of working together and putting the patient first, established during that final year of rotations at Catz. She caught his own gaze on hers, the faint smile as she wondered distractedly if he was thinking the same.

'And Dorothy?' Gil raised a brow. 'I saw she was in the diary.'

'The usual,' she replied quickly, glad to move past that look. 'Oli examined a few extras whilst we were there.'

'And you escaped unscathed?'

'Totally.' Oli's laugh was a wry one and he glanced at the scratch on his hand. 'Well, pretty much.'

'Well done. Not everyone appreciates my aunt, she's certainly one of kind. So what do you think, Oli? Gonna stick with us until Christmas?'

'If you'll have me?'

'Absolutely we will.' Gil clapped his shoulder delightedly. 'Welcome to the team. Let's sit down over a pint sometime and you can tell me about Costa Rica. The surfing must have been incredible.'

'It was.' Oli's gaze flickered over Erin. 'I'd love to go back. Keep travelling.'

'Sorry, Jess is here and I think she wants a word.' She turned away and a silent breath escaped. She needed to fix her thoughts on a new bathroom and not sharing her home with the man who filled her mind with dreams of what might have been if she'd been brave enough to follow her heart and trust him, as he'd asked her to do.

Jess was leaning against a desk, and she thrust a plate into Erin's hands. 'Saved you a piece before it's all gone.' Elaine's pork and cranberry pie was legendary, and Erin had been hoping for a chance to try it. 'So how did it go with Oli this morning?'

'Yeah, fine.' Erin cut off a corner of the pie with a fork, pastry crumbling onto the plate, and her mouth watered greedily. 'I'm pretty sure Dorothy gave him the runaround on purpose, but he coped.'

'So what's the story with you two?'

'Story?' The fork in Erin's hand wobbled. 'What has he told you?'

'So there is one, I knew it. There's always a story when two people can't keep their eyes off one another. And maybe it's just me but you do seem quite familiar. Comfortable, almost, like you really know each other.'

'Don't be daft.' Erin's guilty gaze jumped to Oli laughing at something Gil was saying. She needed to knock that notion on the head before Jess ran away with it. 'We were at the same university, that's all.'

'You what?' Jess dumped her empty plate on the desk and drew Erin away from Steph and Elaine chatting nearby. 'You two were at Cambridge together?'

'Yeah.' This kind of conversation was exactly why Erin was beginning to think she'd made a dreadful mistake in allowing Oli to share her home. Employing him was Gil's choice, but she ought to have seen sense and refused to host him. Three weeks was quite a long time to keep their history hidden from someone as tenacious as Jess. 'We were friends for bit. First year mostly, but not so much after that.' Words that weren't anywhere near adequate enough to describe how she'd really felt about him then.

'Not…?' Jess let the rest of her question tail away and her gaze was sympathetic. 'I'm sorry, it's none of my business.'

'No. Not really, not properly.' Erin knew exactly what Jess had meant. 'We're too different and it would never have worked.' She leaned in and lowered her voice yet more. 'And I don't want that going any further, okay? Cambridge doesn't matter, everyone will probably work it out eventually, but this does. It was a sliding doors moment that didn't amount to anything.'

'Different how?' Jess glanced at Oli, deep in conversation with Gil and Gabi. 'You were at the same university, you both love animals and working with them, understand the pressures of the job. Clearly you share some values.'

'Those are just coincidences, Jess. They're not enough. Once there was a moment when I thought it might work out, but then he went on holiday with another girl.' Erin tried to force away the memory of how she'd felt at the time, not wanting it to overwhelm her now. 'I didn't know until I heard it from someone else. He tried to get in touch to explain but by then I didn't want to hear it. I haven't seen him since we graduated. It's over, we're not even friends anymore.'

'Seriously?' Jess frowned, nodding a 'yes' to Elaine when the older woman held up a mug offering another brew. 'I mean, on the surface that's a really shitty thing to do, but are you sure that's the full story? If you didn't give him a chance to explain...'

'Why should I?' Erin touched the faint thudding in her temples. She hadn't slept well last night, too aware of Oli returning and the unfamiliar noises that came with having someone else in the house. A stranger, and yet not. 'He had his chance, and he blew it. Game over. I've moved on and clearly so has he.'

'So why on earth would you agree to host him after that?' Jess held up a hand as Erin's mouth opened. 'And don't give me some excuse about it being for Gil's benefit, we both know he could've found someone else. Elaine would've probably done it. You did it because you wanted to see him again.'

'Jess...' Erin eased out a harassed breath; telling the story hadn't made it hurt less, but she didn't want to lie to her friend. She'd barely even allowed herself to admit such a thing. 'I didn't want to cause a problem for Gil so late on, and the money will help towards a new bathroom. You've seen the state of mine.'

'Yeah, yeah.' Jess leaned closer. 'You keep telling yourself that if it makes you feel better. But here's the thing. Oli's here, where you are, right now. One of you let that happen, so maybe you both need to move on from your past and think about where you go from here. The way he looks at you, Erin, it's…'

'What are you talking about?' Erin's pulse was clattering and suddenly she wanted to know, have someone else confirm what she already suspected.

'Like it's not over. Far from it.'

'And what about Jason?' Erin whispered. She'd barely given the man she'd met a few weeks ago a second thought in the past twenty-four hours. But Jason was exactly the reality check and distraction from Oli she needed.

'I know you think you should date if you want to settle down with a family one day, but are you sure he's the right place to start?' Jess's smile was sympathetic. 'Noah told me his sister saw Jason's profile on Tinder. He's still on there, he hasn't updated it since you guys met.'

'He doesn't have to,' Erin said calmly. It was way to soon to suggest anything more permanent and she wasn't about to make Jason's online relationship status an issue. 'We're just dating, we're not a couple or anything.' But part of her was hoping it might lead to more, that eventually she would have someone to come home to, someone to share her life with.

'So is Jason still coming to the nativity on Friday?'

'Yes, but he mentioned he might have to see a client first.' Elaine was heading over with a tray of drinks and Erin was relieved to move the conversation from her love life, such as it was. 'Thanks, Elaine, I'd love another.'

'Shall we talk mince pies?' Elaine said briskly. 'What do you think if we do the tasting a week on Friday? Everyone brings in a sample, we each choose our top three and Gil can announce the winner at the party on Saturday. The only rule is that no one enters Violet's from the shop as we all know hers are the best.'

'Sounds good,' Erin said, still thinking distractedly about Oli and what Jess had said. Gil and Pippa were hosting a staff party the weekend after next and the theme was 'ugly sweater'. She was dismayed to realise it would be a social occasion she'd have to share with Oli seeing as he was now a colleague.

'I'm in,' Jess said airily. 'I'm going for the win.'

Erin grinned. 'You haven't tried my nan's recipe yet.'

–

After lunch she settled in the office and put her mind to paperwork. Gil was showing Oli around the companion animal part of the practice and then they'd be consulting for the afternoon. Soon after, idly aware of the buzz from reception as clients and their pets came and went, the email she'd been dreading arrived. It contained the results of Mungo's blood tests, and they were worse than she'd feared. Abnormalities in his white blood cells had increased, and given the worsening symptoms of his chronic form of leukaemia, there was really only one course of action. She read the email again and picked up the phone, taking a moment to compose herself first.

'That was quite a morning. I've decided on balance that you were harder to impress than Dorothy.'

'Sorry?' She turned to see Oli leaning against the door frame, arms folded. The mud on his face had gone and she'd rather be viewing her screen than staring at him. 'You don't need to impress me, Oli. Gil offered you the job on your own merits, not based on what I think.'

'Maybe, but it's clear he trusts you, and if you'd said the word after the induction I might've been out on my ear.'

'Do you mind?' Erin pressed a hand to her temple, trying to smooth away her sadness. How she wished it was different, and she could give Mungo more time. Another Christmas, then a spring and a summer, walks in the woods, splashing in streams. She loathed making these calls and found them upsetting even though they were a necessary part of the job. But she wasn't going to give Oli an opportunity to cast doubt on her professionalism in the face of her feelings.

'I've got to call an owner and confirm results that will likely mean they'll decide to put their dog to sleep.' As soon as the words were out she realised their implication and she didn't miss the flash of pain in his eyes at the reminder of the situation with his own dog. 'Sorry, I didn't mean to…'

'It's okay. I've had to make plenty of those calls too, and act on them.'

'But still, it can't be very nice. Not after what happened with Honey.'

'No, it never is. But I can still do my best by my patient and their family, make it as comfortable as I can.' He paused. 'You remembered her name.'

'Oli, you adored her, of course I haven't forgotten her name.' Snippets of the conversations they'd shared often came back to her at inconvenient moments. Like now, reminded of the dog he'd loved and who'd been denied his comforting presence in those last moments.

'Almost no one else ever talks about her,' he mused. 'But then I don't really tell anyone.'

Erin waited a beat, wondering why she was even allowing herself to go there. 'So why did you tell me?'

'Because I knew you'd understand,' he said softly. 'Because I knew you wouldn't mock me. And I thought you cared.'

'I did, once.' The phone in her hand trembled. 'But now we have to work together, and I need to make this call. Was there a reason you were looking for me?'

'As the newbie, I'm making myself useful and fetching everyone a brew,' he said, some of the lightness returning to his tone, and she sensed he was trying to ease her through the difficult call ahead. 'See, I'm already learning the lingo and calling it a brew. What would you like?'

'Tea, very hot, milk, no sugar. Please.'

'Right. I think I can manage that.'

The door clicked shut behind him and Erin drew in a long breath as she rang Mungo's owners and took them through the results. Amid their tears, the plan was decided. He was comfortable for now and she arranged to see them on Saturday morning. She would be working out of hours anyway and his owners wanted to be together, to say goodbye to their beloved pet in his own home.

Chapter Seven

Yorkshire, thirteen years ago

When Erin woke up it took her a few puzzled moments to remember she was back home in Yorkshire, not in her student flat at Catz, and the familiar sights of her room came into focus. She checked her phone and saw it was almost eight o'clock already. She stumbled out of bed and went to freshen up in the bathroom; she'd meant to be up earlier. She heard her grandparents downstairs, which must mean that Oli was up too.

She dressed quickly and tapped on her mum's door, deciding to leave her to rest when there was no reply. In the living room Oli's temporary bed had been tidied away, the duvet folded neatly at one end of the couch. She went through to the kitchen and saw him sitting at the small table with her grandad, her nan at the hob frying bacon.

'Morning.' Her pulse pattered as Oli smiled at her and she was thinking of last night, of them holding each other. The decision she'd made to pull back when he'd touched her hair and how she'd been afraid to explore what might have happened next, the exhilaration when she'd known he'd wanted to kiss her.

Her gaze skidded over to her grandad; she couldn't count how many mornings she'd seen her grandparents doing exactly this, and Oli looked almost as much at home as they did. 'Smells good, Nan.'

'Sit down, our Erin, your grandad's already 'ad 'is. I'm just making some for Oli before 'e goes outside.'

'Outside?'

'Aye, to see t'shed.' Bill clambered stiffly to his feet and Erin felt a rush of love for the familiarity of home and her family. 'What time are you two 'eadin' off?'

'We haven't talked about it but soon, I suppose.' She didn't imagine Oli would want to stay any longer than they had to.

'I'm in no rush.' Oli was holding a mug of tea the colour of creosote and she wondered if her nan thought that might compensate for the lack of coffee in the house. 'I don't have to return the car until tomorrow.'

'I'm puttin' a chicken in t'oven, Erin, so you can 'ave your dinner before you set off.' Joyce wiped her brow with a tissue from the pocket of her housecoat, bacon hissing in the pan as it browned. 'You can take Oli into town an' show 'im round.'

'Nan, really, you don't have to make our dinner as well,' Erin replied helplessly. She'd never brought a boy home before and even if this one was only a friend, it wasn't a huge surprise her family were laying out the red carpet. 'And Oli won't want to see the town.'

'Actually, I'd love to, if you'll take me?' He finished the last of his tea and carried his mug to the sink.

'Right then, you're on,' she muttered. 'What do you know about brass bands, rugby league and the Brontës?' That'll teach him to go along with her nan.

'Almost nothing.' Oli grinned at her as he stuck his hands in the washing-up bowl and began clearing away the few dishes inside it, making Joyce beam with approval. 'But I'm willing to learn.'

Erin's heart did that annoying flip again and she thought crossly that if her mum had just charged her bloody phone, then none of them would be in this ridiculous situation. She and Oli would still be at Catz, and he'd never have driven her home and met her family, let alone spent the night on their old couch.

'Come on, lad, I'll show you me shed while Erin 'as 'er breakfast.' Bill winked at Erin, and she smiled; she always knew where to find him if he wasn't in his armchair beside the fire. He had a camping stove in the shed, and he'd potter all day long, making brews, tinkering, fixing things and potting up his plants. He'd even rigged up a doorbell so Joyce could fetch him without having to march down the garden. Erin knew he disconnected it when he didn't want to be disturbed, but she wasn't sure her nan did.

After Oli had been taken on a tour of the shed and the garden while Erin ate a bacon buttie and stuffed her few things back into her bag, they set off to walk the short distance into town. After the intimacy of those moments on her bed and all they had talked of, it took her a few minutes to find more ordinary conversation as they wandered past grand Victorian buildings and the usual range of shops alongside some independents.

They walked to a museum, once the home of a Victorian textile millionaire, and on to the rugby league ground where Erin watched matches with her grandad. She learned that Oli had played rugby union at school and teased him for it, airily informing him it wasn't even rugby unless it was played under league rules. He made her promise to take him to a game sometime so he could decide for himself, ribbing her too when he discovered she'd followed her grandad into his old colliery brass band and played the cornet.

Being with him was more natural and easier than she'd ever imagined, and she felt a rush of love for her grand-parents when she saw the extra place laid for lunch at the bigger table in the dining room they rarely used, her nan's sewing temporarily cleared away. They'd welcomed him as they did every other visitor, with kindness, humour, and food, and she had to remind herself sternly that he'd very likely never see them again. Her mum's fibromyalgia flare-up was easing, and she joined them to eat. Such time with her family was precious and Erin wouldn't allow herself to think of the days when she'd be without them.

When they were ready to leave, Heather and Joyce hugged Oli and thanked him for bringing Erin home. Bill shook his hand again, eliciting a promise to return in the summer and see his vegetable garden in full bloom, and Joyce pressed a packet of chicken sandwiches wrapped in greaseproof paper on them, along with half a dozen mince pies. Oli thanked her and Erin hugged her family too, trying to hold back tears at having to leave them again.

Traffic was heavy for a Sunday, and they pushed on. Erin didn't want to stop at the services and have Oli incur extra expense on her behalf, and owe him any more than she already did. Now that the adrenaline panic of yesterday had fled, she was beginning to dread the reality of having to face him every day at Catz now they'd spent a weekend together and understood more of each other's lives. Conversation was stilted on the drive back and eventually they slipped into silence.

When they reached Cambridge, they agreed he would drop her off at the Porters' Lodge and she'd grab their things so he could park the car ready to return it tomorrow. At some traffic lights, a quick pause in their final moments together, she found the words that had been in her mind all weekend.

'Oli, I really don't know how to thank you.' She willed the lights to stay on red long enough to explain. 'What you did for me, it was incredibly kind and generous.'

'You don't have to keep on saying it. Your family were very welcoming, and I thought they were great. It felt like a real home, and that's been a while for me.'

'I'm glad,' she said quietly. 'They really liked you; my grandad doesn't show off his shed to just anyone.'

'That's nice.' The lights were changing, and Oli rushed to speak. 'But if you do want to thank me, then say yes to a ticket for the ball. They go on sale at the end of January, and we get the first release.'

'A ticket to the ball?' Her mind was too full of the work that lay ahead to think about the end of their first year. But she did know that the Catz May Ball, held in June just before the end of term, was legendary. The college went all out on the entertainment and a theme, with live bands and DJs all through the night and on to daybreak. It was the highlight of the student year and the hottest ticket in town. Already she'd heard it being talked about with excitement and anticipation as details were gradually posted on social media. Erin had barely given it a second thought; she had exams to deal with first.

'For me?' She wasn't expecting the sharp rise in her tone and the words felt thickened as she wondered why Oli Sterling would buy her a ticket to the ball on top of everything she already owed him.

'Yes, for you.'

She wanted to ask why and didn't dare. Was it because he had wanted to kiss her in those moments in her room and was inviting her to be his date? Or because he felt sorry for her now he'd seen the reality of home and assumed she couldn't afford a ticket of her own?

'That's very nice of you, but I don't think I'll be going.' Her mouth was dry, and not actually showing up for the ball had never occurred to her until this moment.

'Not going?' He shot forward on the green light, almost stalling the car. 'But why? It's going to be amazing, and everyone will be there.'

They would, and if she was there with him they'd be staring at her too, and wondering why he'd picked an ordinary Yorkshire lass like Erin Hardy to be his date when he could have anyone he wanted. Then he'd realise it could never work between them and she would be the one with a broken heart, pretending she was oblivious to him and the feelings he stirred up in her. It was a new sensation, to realise that for once her emotions were threatening to run out of control. The gates at the entrance to Catz were just up ahead and they were out of time.

'I want you to be there, Erin,' he said quickly, braking sharply outside the Porters' Lodge, and a horn honked angrily somewhere behind them.

'Thanks Oli, but you've done so much for me already. I couldn't possibly expect you to pay for my ticket as well.' She jumped out to grab their stuff, slamming the boot shut. She raced through the gates into Main Court, bags bumping against her legs. She left Oli's bag outside his door so she wouldn't have to see him again and explain how she'd love to go to the ball but simply wasn't brave enough to say yes in case he felt sorry for her.

May Week and the end-of-year celebrations were already upon them, and Erin hadn't expected to feel such regret when she arrived early for the ball. She'd barely been able to eat all day and she'd be exhausted once it was over, but for very different reasons than most of her contemporaries. Even Carys hadn't been able to talk her out of the decision she'd made weeks ago. She'd spared herself the search to find the perfect dress, the accessories and heels to accompany it, time spent on flawless hair and make-up to complete the effect.

Her first year at Catz was almost over and there were aspects of university life she'd miss over the summer: the friends she'd made, the camaraderie and fun, the success of her new life here. And Oli. She would miss him too and she planned to see out these last days without letting him suspect how she felt about him, as she had done for the past few months. She'd never expected their worlds to collide in quite the way they had back in November. Instead of that weekend bringing them closer, she'd retreated even further into her studies, determined that independence and hard work would see her through. She could rely on those; it was her heart she didn't trust.

She stood through the briefing with the rest of the staff working the ball, tugging awkwardly at her uniform. Students were already arriving, transformed into glittering versions of their usual selves and intent on partying hard into tomorrow, a wild excitement thudding through the air adding yet more buzz to the atmosphere. Erin couldn't help it, she was half listening to the briefing and searching for Oli through the crowd. Her stomach dropped when she spotted him, dazzling in black tie, surrounded by the usual group of riotous friends. And Bella Browning, the cool, blue-eyed blonde who'd been circling him for months. They were all stunning, they all seemed to belong here in a way that she never would. Erin raised her chin defiantly; so what if he saw her looking like this.

Their burgeoning friendship had altered since the weekend he'd driven her home, and tonight she was even more aware of the distance she'd placed between them. There was a coolness evident now and when he came to the library to study, they no longer walked home together. Those precious moments she'd cherished, when they'd drifted together outside of vet school, had vanished too, and she missed them. Sometimes Erin wondered if he regretted sharing about his family and the loss of his beloved dog with her. If he felt he'd gone too far with someone who didn't understand his world, that glimpse he'd given her into a life just as imperfect as her own. Occasionally it felt as though they actually had been a couple who'd broken up and had no idea how to proceed, studying together day by day.

She knew the moment Oli saw her, the thrill darting across her skin as ever alerting her to his gaze. Balancing a tray of empty glasses, her pulse spiked as incredulous eyes locked onto hers, pinning her in place with an appalled stare as he took in her uniform. The plain black skirt and white shirt, the comfortable flats that would keep her on her feet until the morning was light and her work done. She glared back; happy in some strange way that he'd seen her like this and would realise she could never stand at his side wearing the perfect gown. But she wasn't expecting him to leave his friends and storm towards her.

'What the hell, Erin,' he yelled above the music, elbowing his way into a thin gap between students to tower over her. 'Why are you doing this? You should be celebrating too, and this is our night, the end of our first year. Maybe the end of everything for you and me.'

'There is no you and me, Oli, there never was,' she shouted back. 'Why are you so angry with me? Why do you care if I'm in a dress or not?'

'Because I do. Sometimes I wish I didn't.' He leaned down to drop the words into her ear. 'Why didn't you tell me you were going to work tonight? I would've done it with you if I'd known.'

'No, you wouldn't. Your friends would have laughed and talked you out of it.'

'Well, I guess you'll never know, because you never gave me a chance. You never gave us a chance, Erin.'

There was a danger glittering in his eyes that she'd never seen before, the formality of his suit perfect against the dark auburn colouring. Years of rugby had brought a maturity to his frame that other boys simply didn't possess, and she'd never noticed them anyway. Oli was the one who filled her heart and mind, and she clung to her studying and the drive to succeed to hide from these crazy feelings that made no sense. She wasn't going to think of what this evening might have been like if she'd been brave enough to step out of her life for a few magical hours, and wear a dress instead of a uniform.

'Why do you always have to be different?' he said roughly, catching her hand when she put the tray down and went to stalk past him.

'Because I am! Because you and me, we're from different worlds and we just don't fit.' After the view he'd had of her life back home, she needed him to understand that she had to send him away. They couldn't ever be a couple at Catz, and surely that weekend had made him see it. 'I have no idea who your date is tonight, but I know she'll be someone who suits you more than I ever could.'

'I didn't bring a date. She turned me down.'

'I bet that was a first.' She wanted to laugh but something in his eyes stopped her, and her breath stuttered as everything else around them fell away.

'Yeah,' he said bitterly. 'It was you, Erin. It's always been you. I didn't offer to buy you a ticket because I thought you couldn't afford it or because I felt sorry for you. I wanted you to be my date, to find out what you and I really are before we go home for the summer. To see if we have something to come back to.' He let go of her hand and shoved it through his hair. 'But you know what? You're wrong about you and me being too different. You know you are, because underneath we want the same things, the ones that really matter.'

The hand holding his bottle flicked towards her and she gasped as an icy wet puddle landed on her stomach, trying to unravel the shock at the sight of his beer splattered across her white shirt. He dumped the bottle on the bar and grabbed her hand, towing her through the crowd. Erin was caught in his wake, too stunned to free herself as he stormed past dancers and the band on stage; barely aware of fairground rides and casino tables, the dozens of students intent on having the best night of their lives. Her feet were following Oli's, their hands clamped together, and he didn't pause until they reached the Porters' Lodge and ducked out of sight behind a hedge.

'Do you really hate me that much?' Erin cried, snatching her hand free and yanking her ruined shirt from the short black skirt. 'So now you've finally managed to humiliate me, is your work here done? You utter bastard.'

'It would be easier if I did hate you,' he said simply. 'Then I could move on and forget that I haven't spent the last nine months thinking about you.'

'You don't mean it,' she whispered. Her chest felt tight as dizziness made her stumble, desperate to evade the truth finally laid bare in his eyes. It wasn't even dark yet and those blue depths were flashing with dangerous intent.

'Do you seriously think I'd throw my drink over you just to humiliate you? You obviously don't know me as well as I thought, Erin.'

'Oli,' she muttered. 'Don't do this, please. I have a job to do. I have to get back.'

'Don't do what?' He reached out and gently cupped her face. 'Admit it's always been you, even when I tried so hard not to let it because I thought you didn't want me?' He huffed out a laugh and she was trapped by his hurt, the reality of his feelings she'd brushed aside in order to protect her own. It was as though she'd been dragging herself back from a precipice time and again, and now she was about to topple over, powerless to save herself.

'You and I have never danced together, gone on a date, or even kissed. And now it's almost too late. You look straight through me, as though I don't even exist for you.'

'Because you terrify me,' she cried. Dare she believe this might actually be happening, that she could admit how she felt, and they would find a way to be together? Was she truly brave enough to follow her heart and allow him to hold it? 'How can I trust you, when I'm so afraid of loving you?'

'Do you mean it?' he said roughly, and suddenly his hands were tugging her against him.

She nodded frantically and her last thought, as his mouth landed on hers, was that waiting so long for her first kiss, the only one she'd ever dreamed of, would be worth every second. There was haste and hunger in their urgency to discover one another, and she wound her arms around his neck to hold him close. It was a furious and fiery kiss of longing and possession, and she gave herself up to it, pressing against him in any way she could. Erin was the one who eventually ended it, and only his arms were holding her up as she trembled against him.

'I've got to go back. I can't just disappear, it wouldn't be fair on everyone else.'

Oli nodded reluctantly, resting his hands on her waist. He kissed her forehead and then her cheek, and she found his mouth again, impatient for more. He lifted her up, and she was drunk on this new and dizzying exhilaration. Dusk was approaching, stars beginning to glitter above them, and she'd never felt more alive in her life.

'I'm sorry about your shirt.' His smile was a rueful one as he put her down. 'I just wanted to get you out of there and my drink was the first thing that came to mind. Maybe it won't show if you tuck it in?'

'Swap with me.' She laughed at his surprise as she rapidly undid the buttons on her shirt. He watched as she pulled it off and stood before him in her black skirt and a white lace bra.

'Erin, you have no idea what you do to me,' he said hoarsely. 'Do you really have to go?'

'Yes. I won't let them down. I'm not staying here, not even for you, Oli Sterling.' She tossed her shirt into the air, and he caught it. 'Give me yours.'

He slipped his dinner jacket off and undid the bow tie, stuffing it into a pocket. The jacket fell to the ground, joining her shirt now he'd dropped it. Oli unfastened his own shirt, and her breath caught as he took it off and held it out with a lazy grin. 'I think it's too big for you.'

'I don't care. It's yours and I'm going to wear it.' She slid it on and fastened the buttons, tucking it into her skirt. It smelled of him, a heady vanilla and bourbon scent that filled her senses whenever he was near. She turned to leave, assailed by a panic that very soon they'd be going their separate ways for the summer.

'When will I see you again? When will we find the time?'

'Soon,' he said quickly, tugging her against his bare chest for one last, lingering kiss. 'I don't know how, but we will. Trust me, Erin.'

Chapter Eight

Hartfell, present day

By Friday and the end of their first week, Erin was gradually settling into a new routine at home with Oli. She avoided him in the mornings by eating breakfast early and arriving at the practice before everyone else, and he would follow about thirty minutes later. They sat through the staff briefings and wherever possible she confined conversation to work and little else. He'd eaten out every evening so far and she had no idea where he went; she was generally in bed by the time he returned.

She and Gil usually split the farm calls in the mornings and picked up whatever else needed doing in the afternoons, from consultations and routine tasks like dentals, to other surgeries and emergencies. This evening there was a live nativity procession through the village, followed by carols with the local brass band outside the church. She would be on call from Saturday and was hoping for a relatively quiet weekend. For now out-of-hours calls on weekday evenings were covered by two alternating agency locums.

She had intended to go home and shower before Oli arrived but an emergency call to a cow with a nasty gash on its face put paid to her plans. The farm was almost twenty miles away and the day was already edging towards dusk when she set out. A cold, frosty evening was on the way, and she always carried extra layers, snacks and a shovel in the pickup in case of snow.

When she reached the farm the cow was already secured in a metal crush, a narrow pen holding her firmly in place, and the worried farmer explained that he thought she'd caught herself on a post she'd worn loose scratching herself. Erin examined the beautiful red-and-white Dales Shorthorn cow and set about neatly stitching the wound back together, arranging with the farmer to remove the stitches another day.

Oli wasn't in when she arrived home, and she was glad to warm up beneath a shower. She darted into the hall afterwards, thinking about whether she could one day extend the kitchen and put a sofa bed in the sitting room so her mum could…

'Oh!' She skidded to a halt at the sight of Oli at the kettle, a mug in his hand. Clutching the towel tightly with trembling fingers, her face flamed. 'I thought you weren't coming back!'

'What, ever?' he quipped, busy with the box of teabags.

'No, before tonight,' she muttered, trying not to shiver. She told herself it was because of the cold.

'I was making you a brew. Thought it would be a chilly one, treating that cow.' He turned around and the mug in his hand clattered onto the worktop. 'Sorry. I didn't realise you weren't, er…'

'It's fine.' It wasn't at all. Her pulse was racing, and she hadn't missed the low note in his hurried apology and the way his eyes had skimmed over her. The last time she'd faced him similarly dressed she'd whipped off her shirt to stand before him in her bra and a short skirt right after they'd kissed. She was thinking of it now, his mouth demanding and skilful on hers, and how she'd instinctively known how to respond even though she'd never been kissed before.

'Would you mind some company at the nativity?' Oli hastily turned away and switched the kettle on. 'I thought maybe we could walk down together. Jess mentioned everyone's going to the pub afterwards.'

'Isn't it a bit… rural, for someone like you?'

'And what do you mean by that?' He sounded more amused than annoyed, and Erin tried to clarify.

'I didn't have you down as someone who enjoyed village life, that's all. I always imagine you more at home in the city.'

'I can do rural with the best of them. So what else do you imagine about me?'

'Nothing.' She swallowed, clutching the towel a bit tighter. She could do without that playful tone. 'Will you be ready in time? I'm leaving soon.' They could arrive together, she supposed, it wasn't like she'd have to spend the entire evening with him.

'Right now I'm more ready than you.' Oli's eyes flickered to her face, and she saw the smile he was trying to hold back. 'What about your brew?'

'Sorry, I don't think I've got time. It was a nice thought, though. Thanks.'

'Another time,' he said lightly. 'Meet you down here then?'

'Okay.' Erin edged past him and ran up to her bedroom. Fifteen minutes later she was layered up in a Fair Isle sweater over a thermal vest, with jeans and knee-length boots beneath her winter coat and a woolly hat, the curls she'd grown longer since graduating loose. Oli was ready too, a green beanie in place. The evening air was bracing when they stepped outside, stars sparkling in a clear sky.

The shop window had been transformed into an old-fashioned sweet shop for the festive season, with candy canes, a gingerbread house and jars of sweets nestled amongst a snowy background. Erin greeted people she knew, some of them clients whose animals she'd treated. She'd already asked Edmund if he'd like to join her, and he'd thanked her but refused, as he was eating with a friend first and planned to arrive later. Children were skipping along, presumably hoping for a glimpse of Father Christmas. A few little ones were in shepherd costumes, ready to take their place in the procession.

The brass band was gathered on the village green opposite the pub, head torches in place to light up sheet music pinned to their instruments. Erin felt a sharp pang for the days when she'd played in her grandad's old colliery band, her cornet gifted by an elderly member who had no more use for it. A few stalls offering refreshments had been set up and she waved to Kenny from the pub, serving mulled cider and wine from one with his partner Vince.

'Can I tempt you, Erin?' Kenny called, waving a paper cup. 'Although you don't look as though you need warming up.'

'Yes please.' Erin hadn't eaten in the pub often, but Kenny was always lovely and welcoming whenever she did. His cropped hair was gunmetal grey, matching a short, sharp beard. The food, cooked by Vince, who'd trained in Paris, was amazing and she was planning to take her mum for lunch one Sunday. She wasn't on call until tomorrow so she could treat herself to one drink, and she accepted the delicious-smelling wine Kenny offered.

'Thanks Kenny.' She was aware of Oli halting at her side. 'This is Oli, who's working as a locum with us until Christmas.'

'We've already met, my darling.' Kenny winked at Erin and Oli laughed as he accepted a cup of mulled wine. 'He's eaten with us every night this week, I adore finding new regulars. I keep asking when he's planning to bring you along as well, but he won't say. I do love a man who won't kiss and tell.'

'Oh!' Erin's gaze jumped to Oli, and he raised a shoulder. She'd wondered where he went each night but hadn't imagined he was so close. Did he hate her company so much that he'd rather eat an admittedly very nice but not cheap dinner in the pub to avoid her every evening? Perhaps it was her fault; she hadn't exactly thrown him much of a welcome and had made clear he was on his own when it came to meals and cooking.

'So will I see you both later, for drinks after the carols?' Vince was busy serving another customer, and Erin nodded at Kenny. 'Perfect. I've reserved a table for the practice, got to make sure there's room for you all.'

'Thanks, Kenny. See you later.' She looked at Oli, wanting to make amends. 'So can I buy you a turkey roll, as a belated welcome?'

'I'd like that. Thanks.' They joined a queue and once they'd got their rolls, filled with turkey, stuffing, cranberry sauce and sausages, laughing as they tried not to let anything fall out, they made their way over the bridge towards the church to wait for the procession. Elaine was there with a friend and Erin waved at Jess queueing for drinks further down with her partner Noah.

'So you were right, this is all very quaint.' Oli rolled his empty wrapper into a ball and tossed it into a bin. He held out a hand for Erin's too, and she thanked him as he disposed of it. He stamped his feet as the procession on the green began to assemble into some sort of order.

'You would say that.' She caught the gleam of his smile through the dark. 'Didn't they have the story of Jesus's birth in Marlborough, then?'

'I think they probably did but I can't say I've ever seen it performed live. Anyway, I was referring to the brass band. I've never forgotten you signing me up for rehearsals when we were freshers and conning me into thinking it was the real ale society. It sounded like a load of cats trying to fight their way out of tin cans when I turned up.'

'That's bloody rude,' Erin retorted, shoving him in the ribs with an elbow, and he laughed. 'I was trying to educate you. You obviously have no appreciation of proper music.' She was remembering her surprise when he'd actually showed up and found a roomful of students rehearsing. He'd been nonplussed for a few moments before his charm had kicked in and he'd excused himself, but not before flashing her a grin that promised some form of retribution. She'd received an email not long after, welcoming her to the university's improvised comedy club. She'd gone along to a workshop just to prove a point and Oli wrong about her willingness to at least check it out. 'I can see now my efforts were in vain.'

'I have all the education I need, thank you very much. No plans to study anything ever again. Except maybe brass bands, let's see if you can convert me this time.' The nativity procession was beginning, circling the green as marshals in hi-vis jackets cleared a path through the crowd. 'Is that Dorothy, leading an alpaca? I can't see her face, but I reckon that's her coat. She might not even be inside it, it could well be walking on its own.'

'Yep, and Alfie's leading the other one. He's Harriet's boyfriend, another young farmer. Maybe it's the alpacas slowing everyone down, they're such plodders.'

'And spitters. Please tell me they're not really wearing antler headbands?'

'I can't, because they are.' Erin laughed as Oli shot her a sardonic look. 'I suppose available reindeer are in short supply at this time of year and they're having to make do with Rufus and Rupert.'

Dorothy had rescued the alpacas a few years ago and they lived a very comfortable existence on her farm, being indulged by her and Harriet. Pippa wasn't keen, having been spat on at first introduction. Erin saw her outside the gallery with Gil, arms wrapped around one another as Harriet walked slowly past with Posy the Shetland pony. Posy was on a very tight lead rope in case she attempted to take off in search of food or trouble. She was also sporting a reindeer headband, and when she shook her head, it flew off to land on the cobbles.

'Erin, babe!'

An arm was thrust around Erin's shoulders as someone shoved their way into a space beside her, and she staggered into Oli. His hands went to her waist to steady her, then fell away just as quickly when she was tugged backwards, landing against a solid chest. The man who'd just arrived sported a body honed by hours in the gym and a face she was startled to realise she was beginning to find more attractive than his personality. Tonight his long brown hair was tucked inside a grey beanie instead of fastened in the usual man bun.

'Jason, hi,' Erin replied, trying to disguise her surprise. She'd forgotten she'd invited him tonight and didn't want either man to notice her discomfort now their paths were about to cross.

'Hey, you.' Jason took her hand. 'So my guy was running late and he wanted to talk through his event. He suggested we do it over a quick beer. You know how it is, I couldn't turn him down.'

'Well, at least you made it.' He always had an excuse for his lack of timekeeping, she'd noticed. Never an apology.

'And miss all this?' Jason smirked at the nativity procession walking slowly past, the band marching to the tune of 'O Come, All Ye Faithful'. 'I was going to let you know I was on my way but I'm here now. You look, er, nice. Is that a new hat?'

'No, I wore it last time I saw you.' When he'd taken her to a run instead of brunch because a client was racing, and he'd wanted to watch. They'd all ended up at the pub afterwards, and he'd barely even tried to include her in the conversation.

'Anyway, it suits you.'

Erin wasn't quick enough to dodge Jason's mouth heading for hers, and she tried to quash her irritation. He'd never once attempted to greet her with a kiss before. He leaned past her to look at Oli.

'I'm Jason, Erin's, er…' He stuck out an arm, reaching across her, the explanation already abandoned. 'So you are…?'

'Oli Sterling.' Oli shook Jason's hand firmly. 'How do you do?'

'Oli's our new locum, Jason, he's working with us until Christmas.' She jumped into the silence before it became an awkward one. 'Jason's a joiner, Oli, a really brilliant one. He's from Darlington originally but lives in…'

'And a personal trainer,' Jason said quickly. 'I run two businesses and I'll be giving up the joinery soon. Got plenty of demand for the training and that's where the money is when you find the right clients.'

'Good for you,' Oli murmured, and Erin sent him a warning glance.

Jason was still holding her hand, and she wasn't sure she liked the possessive weight of it around hers, but decided to go along with it for now given they were dating.

'So what happened to that other locum, Erin, the one who was staying with you? Never showed up?'

'Her family circumstances changed, and she had to alter her plans.' Erin's even tone belied the sudden swirl in her stomach at what was coming next and how Jason might take it. She hadn't been expecting him to remember the change in personnel at the practice. 'So Oli stepped in instead.'

'Right.' Jason's fingers around Erin's tightened. 'So where are you staying then, mate?'

'With Erin,' Oli replied smoothly, and she cringed at the amusement in those two words. He'd enjoyed that and she'd be having words later, but he hadn't finished. 'She's made me very welcome, and the cottage is so snug. I have to keep remembering to duck but that's all part of the experience, right?'

'You never said, Erin.' Jason huffed out another laugh and she didn't think she was imagining the edge in those few words.

'You never asked,' she told him flatly. She wasn't about to apologise for whom she invited into her own home, and certainly not to a man with whom she'd had six dates.

'Erin, look, I think Alfie's having trouble with his alpaca.' Oli pointed and she spotted Alfie trying to persuade it to stay in line instead of hauling him into the nearest garden. 'Do you remember that time at Catz when we had to examine one with an abscess on its jaw? You were the first who dared go near it, then got slathered in pus when the needle went in, and the abscess exploded.'

'Thanks for reminding me,' she said. 'It was a perfect introduction to the stink that comes with being a vet. The pus leaked through to my T-shirt as well, took me about three washes to get it out.'

'Catz?' Jason inquired. Erin freed her hand; she'd had enough of hers being held as though she were a toddler about to run away.

'Sorry, yeah.' Oli flashed him a grin. 'Erin and I were at Cambridge together. Catz is the nickname for our college, St Catharine's.'

'Nice. Never went to university, didn't see the point in wasting all that money. Better off earning it instead. So you two are old mates then?'

'Not really,' Erin said, fixing her gaze on the band heading out of sight towards the church, torches bobbing in the dark. 'We didn't see that much of each other outside vet school, it was seriously full on.' She'd done her best to avoid Oli socially after the end of their first year, guarding her heart for all she was worth.

'So how did you and Erin meet, Jason? Which one of you swiped right first?'

'Oh, Erin would've swiped for me but she's not on Tinder.' Jason laughed, fumbling for her hand again to squeeze it. 'No, we actually met IRL, and it's quite a funny story, isn't it, babe?'

'Not especially,' she replied, taking a swift dislike to his use of the abbreviation. Her toes were curling at the thought of Jason explaining and what Oli would make of it. 'I was with Jess at…' But Jason was already speaking over her a second time.

'It was at a beer festival, Oli, and I'd just been giving CPR to some guy who'd keeled over. He was fine, by the way. Ambulance came and they said I'd done everything right and probably saved his life. Anyway, I picked up my beer, a mate whacked me on the back to say well done, and I threw my drink all over poor Erin.'

She didn't dare look at Oli. Already she was right back there with him, the evening of the first May Ball. The cold shock of his drink against her skin, the warmth of his fingers clutching hers, his urgency as he'd hurried her away from the crowd. Her very first kiss, the feel of his mouth finally claiming hers after all those weeks of waiting, the completeness she'd felt in holding him and being in his arms. His surprise and then his desire when she'd undone her shirt and taken it off, and watched him do the same.

'You're right, Jason, it is quite funny. Apart from the nearly dead guy, of course.'

She couldn't let Oli see that she was wondering if he was thinking the same. How much she'd wanted him then and how devastated she'd been when she'd seen those images of him on holiday with Bella Browning just a couple of weeks later. He'd smashed her trust out of the park and taken her love with it. And she especially didn't want him to know that now he was here, all those old feelings she'd long thought she'd put aside were rising once more to the surface.

'Yeah, apart from him,' she said lightly, tilting her head to smile at Jason and remind herself of the man she was dating. 'I know you can't make the pub afterwards, Jason.

You said you were busy so don't worry if you have to head off soon.'

'No, actually I think I can make it,' he said quickly, sliding an arm around her waist. 'The boys won't mind if I jump online a bit late, it'd be great to meet your friends and see this country pub you've been going on about.'

'Right.' Erin tried to feel pleased; a casual drink in the local pub was one thing, his actually meeting Jess and the rest of her colleagues was quite another. And she'd literally mentioned the pub once, suggesting they eat there one night, and he'd cancelled at the last minute to fit in a client instead.

As they joined the crowd following the procession to the church for carols, it felt to Erin that the two halves of her life had collided in spectacular fashion. Oli represented her past and her first love, those long, hard years of studying, and the very young woman she'd been whose experience of a harsh world was balanced out by the care and support of her family. Jason was a reflection of now, the home she was making in Hartfell alongside a flourishing career and the independence she'd established.

She dodged Jason's attempt to hold her hand again, self-conscious about such gestures with Oli here and cross with herself for minding what he might think. When they reached the church, a rough stable complete with bales and a manger was ready, and as the birth of Jesus was proclaimed, shepherds and wise men arrived to deliver their gifts. The brass band played carols between each reading, finishing with 'O Holy Night' and the exquisite tone of a small choir, voices rising and falling to the music. For Erin it was a bittersweet reminder of home; Christmas with her family and the concerts she'd played in, the years of festive routines the same until she'd left for university. Jason nipped off to take a call, and she heard him muttering behind her about the lack of signal.

Most people with children took them to meet Santa, who'd also arrived at the church, and Erin, Oli and Jason strolled back down over the river to the pub. A crowd was gathered outside on the cobbles, holding drinks and braving the chill. Inside they were welcomed by merry festive music, and Erin caught Kenny's eye at the bar and returned his wave. She spotted Elaine, Jess and Noah alongside Gabi and her wife Michelle, seated at a large table in the corner. A fire was blazing, and the Christmas decorations were subtle and stylish, evergreen with occasional splashes of scarlet and silver. Jess waved them over and everyone shuffled up.

Erin introduced Jason and they took their seats as Oli headed to the bar to make good on his promise to buy a round for his new colleagues. Jason removed the beanie and his coat, fixing his man bun in place and outlining a pair of impressive biceps in a snug T-shirt. Noah was lovely and although Erin had only met him a couple of times, she'd always felt he was the perfect foil for Jess's exuberance.

Oli returned with a tray and Elaine moved along to make room for him. He took a seat opposite Erin, who was aware of his every little gesture, trying hard not to notice and focus instead on Jason to her left. She attempted to draw him into conversation, but he'd connected to the Wi-Fi and was busy on his phone, swiping the screen. Oli was chatting with Gabi, Elaine and Michelle, and Erin caught bits of their conversation as he leaned in to listen, a hand resting around a pint of craft beer. When Jason finally put the phone down, she was relieved to have someone other than Oli to occupy her thoughts. By ten p.m. most people were drifting away, and she decided to join them, surprised Jason had stayed so long.

'Sorry, I'm going to make a move.' She leaned across to speak to him, staring at his phone again. 'I'm on call from six a.m.'

'Want me to walk you home?' He spoke without looking up, but she was already gathering her things.

'No thanks, it's fine, barely five minutes.' Erin wound the scarf around her neck and pulled her hat on. She hadn't meant to sound dismissive, but if Jason came home with her now she'd feel obliged to invite him in and that was the last thing she wanted with Oli there and an early start in the morning.

'I'll walk Erin home, Jason.' Oli had stood too, and he shrugged into his coat. 'I'm heading in the same direction, and you mentioned you're meant to be online with your friends by now. I'm guessing you're a gamer?'

'Right, yeah. Cheers.' Jason followed them outside and she submitted to a goodnight kiss, wondering if he was dragging it out for Oli's benefit. She'd been clear about just dating so far but Jason was getting impatient about taking things further and she knew she wouldn't be able to delay it much longer. Hopefully long enough to get Oli out of the house though; she cringed at the thought of Jason spending the night with Oli just the other side of her bedroom wall. She and Oli set off for home, a full moon lighting a path along the cobbles.

'Oli, don't do that when I'm with Jason.'

'Do what?'

'Play the "when we were at Catz" game. You did it again in the pub as well, just to annoy him. And mentioning that you have to duck in the cottage, it's perfectly obvious he's not as tall as you.'

'Just a bit of fun. Sorry.' He didn't sound it, and Erin heard, rather than saw, the smile in his reply.

'It's not that funny for me. And did you have to be so insistent about walking me home? He was only trying to be nice.' She bit her lip; even she wasn't convinced that Jason would've wanted to see her safely to her own door if there was no chance of him coming in.

'You think?' Oli pushed his hands into his coat pockets. '"Nice" where Jason is concerned is maybe a pejorative term. Tosser is more like it.'

'My relationship with him is my own and your opinion of both is irrelevant. I hope you remember that and treat him with more respect next time.'

'I'll start treating him with respect when he shows you some, Erin.'

Her lips tightened as she drew out her keys and opened her front door. She hurried inside and straight up to bed, forgoing her usual late-night tea to avoid Oli and any more uncomfortable truths he might be tempted to reveal.

Chapter Nine

Erin crept downstairs in the morning, still keen to avoid Oli. She was on call for the rest of the weekend, and he was working too, taking routine Saturday morning appointments. She made tea and sat on the sofa to appreciate it. After her call to Mungo's owners earlier in the week to confirm his results, she'd arranged to meet them today. Over the years she'd got more used to the emotional ups and downs that came with her career, but she'd never lose the sadness and empathy for tasks like the one she had to carry out this morning.

But it wasn't only thoughts of her patient and his family unsettling her. Oli's presence in the cottage was something she couldn't ignore; his coat hanging beside hers, boots propped neatly in front of the sofa, every small detail making it appear he was at home here too. She heard him upstairs and went to the kitchen for her flask; if she was called out to an emergency she could be gone for hours.

'Morning.' Oli's tread was slow, deliberate, as he made his way downstairs, and Erin wished she'd left five minutes earlier. His auburn hair was still tousled from sleep, and he ran a hand through it, covering a yawn with the other one. 'Are you off to see that dog?'

'Yes.' Work made perfect sense when what she felt about Oli really didn't, and she was glad he'd kept the conversation to practical matters. 'I'm due there in thirty minutes.'

'Coffee before you go?' He stepped past her to the machine, opening the cupboard to find a capsule and swapping plugs with the toaster. 'Just this once? The caffeine might help.'

'No thanks. I'm still a tea morning, noon and night person.'

'I've no idea how you even begin to function without coffee.' He removed the water tank and filled it. 'I can barely blink before I've had my first.'

She remembered that about him and she was doing it again, falling into his smile and the memories they shared. 'Sorry I don't have any espresso cups.' She eyed the too-large mug he'd been using all week. 'I should get you some.'

'Don't apologise, the coffee still tastes the same.' He paused, the mug in his hand. 'Would you like me to come with you, to see the dog? I don't have to be at the practice until nine.'

About to rush out a refusal along with a retort about why he thought she might need company for a task she'd performed so many times already, she paused. She remembered Honey and how distraught Oli had been over her passing, that he hadn't been able to be with her. 'No thanks,' she ended up whispering, before clearing the catch in her throat. 'I'll be fine.'

Erin checked she'd got everything she needed then offered a hurried goodbye as she left the cottage. Ten minutes later Mungo's owners welcomed her with tremulous smiles and showed her into the sitting room, where he was lying on his comfortable bed in front of the fire. She bent to greet him and gently rubbed his head, blinking back her sadness when his tail thumped a welcome.

She turned to his family and talked them through the procedure, satisfied they were certain about continuing. Moments later it was done. She checked for a heartbeat and confirmed he had gone, offering her sincere condolences. His family cried as they held him, and Erin stepped aside, not wanting to intrude. They thanked her for coming and helping Mungo to slip away in peace at home, sharing a distracted goodbye. Outside she sat for a few moments behind the wheel, waiting for her sorrow to subside.

Shortly after she took a call about a cat who was vomiting and arranged with the owner to bring it into the surgery that afternoon if there was no improvement. She drove back to the village, thinking about going home instead of into the practice, and pulled over to check her phone when a notification arrived. Oli had been added to the staff group chat and she wasn't expecting a new message to be from him now he was in her contacts again.

> Meet me at the shop if you've got time? My shout.

She was nearby, so she left the pickup; it would only take her a minute to run back if she was called out. She adored the village shop, once the front room of a cottage, and popping in to chat with Daphne and Violet, the two sisters who ran it. Violet had worked there all her life and Daphne had joined her a few years ago after the end of her marriage. Violet's baking was legendary, and every weekend Erin picked up something delicious to enjoy at home.

Oli was waiting outside, propped against the wall and causing her stomach to flutter annoyingly. He was wrapped up against the chill too, the beanie and a scarf back on, his smile one of understanding edged with sympathy.

'Okay?' He straightened up and she nodded. There was a softness in his question and she had a sudden, unwelcome image of coming home to Jason, trying to picture him wanting to know if she was all right, and simply couldn't. But perhaps that wasn't fair; he didn't understand the emotional highs and lows of being a vet in the same way Oli did.

'Yes. Thank you for asking.'

'So I haven't got long but I thought you might appreciate something to warm you up. You always did love a bacon buttie and I've put in an order with Daphne, so you don't have to hang around. Gil told me they're the best in the dale.'

'You didn't have to do that.' But the idea had already taken hold, and Erin couldn't decide if it was his thoughtfulness or the anticipation of tucking in that was pleasing her the most. Maybe both.

The bell above the door tinkled as they entered and made their way past shelves laden with almost every kind of necessity. One wall was groceries and another was books, greeting cards and maps, a large American fridge between them. The wooden shelves behind the counter still held old-fashioned jars of sweets with a set of scales for weighing, and there was even a haberdashery section at the far end, with cooking utensils alongside basic tools, batteries, and bicycle pumps. The shop had recently become a hub for Amazon, and it was a lifeline for all who lived in the village.

'Morning, Daphne.' Oli paused at the counter with Erin, and she also greeted the woman, whose warm hazel eyes were emphasised by a pair of green glasses. Daphne had been very kind since Erin had moved to Hartfell, and Erin bought all her milk, bread and vegetables here. Daphne had recently added homemade frozen ready meals to their range, which kept Erin going when sometimes she was too busy and tired to cook for herself.

'You're right on time, Oli, they're ready.' Daphne's smile encompassed both of them and Erin's mouth watered when she placed two hot sandwiches wrapped in greaseproof paper on the counter. 'One well done with brown sauce, no butter, and one with egg and ketchup, both on sourdough. Have I got that right?'

'Perfect, thanks Daphne.'

Erin was surprised he'd also remembered exactly how she liked her bacon butties. 'How's Violet?' she asked instead, glancing along the corridor to the kitchen to see if Daphne's older sister was in sight. Violet lived with dementia and found some everyday tasks beyond her now, but her gift for baking had never altered.

'She's all right, Erin, thank you for asking.' Daphne's smile was a resigned one as she completed Oli's payment. 'Her mince pies are flying out of the shop almost faster than she can make them. Pippa's ordered some for the gallery opening and I keep asking Violet if it's too much for her now, but she insists that it's not and she's happiest when she's busy. I suppose it's what she's always known, and I keep a close eye on her. I am going to advertise for some help though, in the new year.'

'I'll let you know if I hear of anyone,' Erin promised. Another thing she loved about rural farm work was that it kept her in touch with the people who didn't live in the centre of the village and news was passed along the dale from farm to farm as it always had been. One retired farmer had let out his land and moved into a cottage in the village. He loved to sit at the bus stop and chat with the people passing by, either locals going about their business or visitors passing through, and she appreciated his stories when she had time to pause.

They thanked Daphne and returned outside. Erin loved these sharp, clear days, the high fells glistening with a scattering of snow, frost clinging to bare branches like icy fingers.

'My car or yours?'

'Mine,' she told him, setting off. 'Then I can chuck you out if I get a call and have to go.'

Back inside the pickup, which wasn't much warmer without the engine running, Erin bit into her buttie. 'Thank you,' she muttered after the first mouthful. 'This is amazing and exactly what I needed.'

'You're welcome. I thought it might set you up for the day.'

It would help, but it was his kindness that was forefront in her mind. That he'd remembered how she liked her bacon, had ordered for her so she wouldn't have to wait long if she needed to go.

'Are you going to the gallery opening later?' She'd heard him chatting about it with Elaine yesterday; all the staff were popping in at some point, excited to see the changes to the youth hostel that Pippa and a team of builders had been working on these past months.

'That's the plan after I finish at the practice. My dad's difficult to buy for and I thought I might see something there. He likes art.'

'Will you be at home for Christmas?' Erin wasn't even sure where home was for Oli; she'd already heard that he kept a virtual business office address in London and rented a studio flat in Hertfordshire.

'At my sister's. She and her partner have bought their first house together and they want to do the big family Christmas.' Oli sighed, scrunching up the paper now he'd finished eating.

'And you don't?'

'I usually go away, I'm not that into it. Still can't quite get past those memories of coming home for Christmas and finding out Honey had died. And it's never been the same since my parents split up, so…'

'I'm sorry.' Erin adored Christmas and couldn't imagine not spending the day as she usually did, enveloped with her family in their routines and celebrations. When she and her grandad had played in the brass band, December was always a busy month with concerts and carol services every week. It had set up the season for her and she still couldn't hear brass instruments without being tugged straight back to those days.

She needed to get a move on with her Christmas shopping too; her mum and her nan were easy enough, while her grandad said there was nothing he needed and not to spend her money on him. But she always found him something he'd love, whether it was heritage seeds for his vegetable garden or an old recording of a brass band he'd treasure.

Her phone rang and she picked up the call, immediately switching into work mode as she listened to the farmer on the other end. Oli understood what was coming and he raised a hand as he got out of her car. She started the engine and set off once she'd got the details. When she reached the farm she layered up to examine a pig with a suspected infection in a rear claw, pulling on her wellies and waterproofs.

Inside a barn divided into pens by sturdy concrete walls she saw a large British Saddleback sow with its distinctive black body, white front legs and a white band around its middle. She seemed quite content lying on her side, but Erin had spotted the outer rear claw and couldn't blame the sow for wanting to take the weight off it. She was happy to have a first look from outside the pen and not disturb or upset her more than absolutely necessary.

'The coronary band looks inflamed but there are no obvious signs of an abscess or swollen joints,' she informed the farmer. 'Let's have a closer look, if she'll let us.'

The farmer entered the pen first, bending to scratch the sow between her dark ears. She grunted satisfyingly and Erin followed, running a gentle hand down her leg to examine the hoof. 'Some slight cracking but it's not too bad. She's probably nicked it on something. I'll give her anti-inflammatories and a course of antibiotics that will penetrate the tissue. Seven days to be on the safe side and it should help prevent the infection heading into a joint, but obviously keep a close eye on her.'

Erin returned with the medication and efficiently injected the sow, thankful she didn't react adversely and try to corner her, or worse. She advised the farmer to call the practice if there was no improvement after three days, when a change of medication might be required. Back at Hartfell there were no more calls for now, so she decided to visit Pippa's gallery while she could.

The old youth hostel and former coaching inn – since renamed the Ivy Walker Gallery in honour of Pippa's great-grandmother, who'd been a local farmer and an artist – stood at the head of a T-junction with the pub opposite and the village green across the lane. Alongside setting up the gallery, Pippa had been supply teaching art at college and was leaving at the end of term. The official gallery opening was in January, when a launch was planned to display a local landscape artist who'd never shown before.

Erin joined the throng of people milling inside, feeling a little self-conscious in her winter work layers. The main gallery was on her left, chalky white walls fresh beneath a beamed ceiling, a traditional fireplace renovated to its original black. The smaller room on her right was also finished and she spotted Harriet and another young girl helping serve guests queueing for mulled wine, hot chocolate and mince pies. Erin waved and Harriet grinned back.

Strolling along the tables while a harpist played traditional carols in the background, Erin picked up a pair of navy-and-white handwarmers her mum would love, plus two glass baubles for her Christmas tree. Heather was coming over tomorrow and bringing a box of their old decorations so Erin would have something from home on her own tree. She also bought some floral bath bombs for her nan, who didn't hold with showers. One stall was selling striped Christmas candles in jars, and she chose a pair of cinnamon ones for her fireplace before falling quickly in love with a set of Christmas stockings made from old woollen sweaters, which was when Gil found her.

'Hey, Erin, thanks for coming. Isn't it brilliant? I'm so pleased for Pippa at how many people have turned out.' He raised a hand to someone else he recognised in the crowd. 'Kenny's been very generous in letting us use the pub car park too, this one's full.'

'It's fantastic, and the gallery looks gorgeous,' Erin agreed. The phone in her pocket pinged and she checked it quickly; it was just her mum's usual daily message. She had a different notification for work calls, but she liked to keep an eye so as not to miss anything important when she was on call. 'Harriet mentioned how busy Pippa's been, getting everything set up.'

'It has been a rush, the scaffolding only came down a few days ago but she was keen to open today and support local craftspeople as it's the first Saturday in December. I'm so proud of her vision and determination to remember Ivy this way and find new artists to show. So how's the day looking?'

'Fine, I might have to see a cat later but so far quiet.' Erin was planning to have a hot chocolate if she had time; they looked mouth-wateringly delicious laden with thick cream and dusted with powdered chocolate.

'Erin, how wonderful to see you. Thank you for coming.' Pippa joined them, looking especially lovely in an orange-red floral print tea dress paired with slouchy dark green suede boots, her blonde hair falling to her shoulders. A gifted artist in her own right, Erin knew she'd recently sold some of her paintings to collectors.

'My pleasure, my shopping bag is getting heavier by the minute. Congratulations on the gallery, it's beautiful.'

'Thank you, that's very kind.' Pippa smiled up at Gil, and Erin wondered if she'd ever look at someone in quite the same way. 'It's been a real labour of love, hasn't it?

The building had been empty for over a year so it was a bit grim when we bought it. My friend Cassie is here somewhere too, she's been brilliant on social media and getting the word out. Isla, her daughter, is helping Harriet on refreshments.' Pippa pulled a face. 'Raf said he would try and make it, but he cried off at the last minute.'

Erin had been secretly hoping to meet Pippa's glamorous brother, who until recently had played drums in their dad's Eighties rock band Blue at Midnight. The band had recently completed the final dates of a world retirement tour ending in Australia. Jonny was still out there, settling into the house he'd bought with his partner, Vanessa, and their two youngest children, Phoebe and Freddie, Pippa's half sister and brother.

'And I just wanted to thank you for taking Harriet out to see practice, Erin.' Pippa leaned closer to speak over the chat. 'I love my daughter dearly but there's no denying she's very determined when she's set her mind on something.'

'Oh, she's very welcome,' Erin replied. 'I'm always happy to take her.'

As the only grandchild of a world-famous rock star who'd lived in London for most of her life, Harriet had the kind of confidence, even at fourteen, that Erin could only dream of. She was also kind underneath her sharp wit, and blessed with an innate ability to read people. Erin had never been surprised that she got on so well with Dorothy.

'She's very keen, and Gil told her that she couldn't do better for a role model than to learn from you.'

'Oh!' Erin allowed herself a moment to indulge the pleasure Gil's compliment brought her. 'That's very generous, but I've still got a lot to learn.'

'Only the truth,' Gil replied. 'Harriet's dead set on Cambridge too, so she's bound to quiz you and Oli. She helped me with a PM on a sheep the other day and didn't even flinch when I opened it up. The pus literally erupted, and we were…'

'No pus, please. Not here.' Pippa placed a finger against his lips, and he laughed, bending to kiss her cheek quickly.

'Maybe Harriet would like to come round and eat with us one evening, and chat about Cambridge.' Erin flushed as she realised how naturally she'd referred to her and Oli as 'us'. 'I'm sure Oli would share his experience too.'

'Oh, Harriet would love that, thank you.' Pippa beamed at her. 'I'll let her know and she'll be wanting to plan a date as soon as you're both free. Did you know she's persuaded Dorothy to join Instagram?' Pippa shook her head as Gil rolled his eyes, and Erin laughed. 'She told Dorothy photos of the animals would do wonders for their fundraising efforts, but really? They posted some pictures of the alpacas in reindeer headbands from the nativity and apparently they've gone down a storm since Raf put it on his stories.'

'I was just glad Posy behaved herself and didn't fell half the village on her way to the nearest feed bucket,' Gil said wryly. 'I did warn Harriet not to take her, but she wasn't having any of it. And Dorothy's just as bad, egging her on. Gave me one of her looks when I asked how many alpacas did she think were present at the birth of Jesus. Told me they might well have followed a star across the Andes to Bethlehem and she counted the evening a success seeing as only one person complained about being spat on. So that's all good, I suppose.'

Pippa leaned in. 'Apparently she's been getting strange messages too, and someone asked for a photo, so Dorothy sent one of a placenta after a calving. I'd like to bet that wasn't what the chap had in mind. Harriet had to intervene and update Dorothy's app settings. Oh hi, Oli, so lovely of you to call in.'

Erin was still laughing about Dorothy when Oli halted beside her. She glanced up and caught the flicker of his gaze on her, the quick smile warming her from the inside.

'Thank you for the invitation, Pippa. What a gorgeous space.'

'Thank you. We've still got a way to go before the lift's installed and the community room is ready upstairs, but I'm delighted with it so far.' Pippa waved at someone, and Gil excused himself to take a call. 'Erin's very kindly offered to invite Harriet over for a meal sometime so she can talk to you two about Cambridge.'

'Sounds great,' Oli replied, and Erin was aware of his eyes on her again. 'There's loads we can share, isn't there, Erin?'

'Absolutely.' She wasn't going to be caught out by the suggestion of amusement in his reply, given there was also plenty she wouldn't share. 'Maybe you should cook, Oli.'

'Sorry, would you excuse me? I can see the *Yorkshire Life* photographer beckoning.' Pippa edged away into the crowd and Erin checked her phone again, thinking about a date for Harriet and dinner.

'So are you buying Christmas gifts?' Erin hadn't meant that to sound quite so nosey. 'I'm guessing you don't need decorations if you go away for Christmas.'

'Not usually, no.' His eyes narrowed as she took something from her bag of shopping and handed it to him.

'Got you something I thought you might like.'

'For me?' Oli's voice rose as he accepted the package, and he grinned once he'd unwrapped the tissue paper. 'I love it, thank you.' He was holding an enamel espresso cup, decorated with woodland animals sitting around a Christmas tree. 'Now I feel as though I should recip-rocate.'

'Please don't, you can leave it behind when you go.'

'What if I want to keep it as a reminder of Hartfell?' he asked softly, and she was relieved to escape that look when her phone rang. She answered it quickly and turned to make her way outside.

Chapter Ten

Erin's weekend continued with two more call-outs, one to a cow that had gone down with mastitis and a very tricky breech calving on Saturday evening. On Sunday morning, arms still aching after pulling the calf out with the aid of a calving jack and a very fit female farmer, she returned home from the practice after seeing the vomiting cat from yesterday in time to start preparing lunch.

Thoughts of hosting Christmas and having her mum over to celebrate kept her cheerful. Much as she'd love her nan and grandad to be here too, they'd decided to stay at home as they found outings tiring now. She and Gil were planning the Christmas rota this week and she was certain to be on call for some of the bank holidays.

She'd put a joint of beef in the oven earlier and the smell was very welcome once she'd let herself into the cottage. She started on the vegetables, peeling potatoes to par boil ready for roasting, followed by carrots and swede for the steamer. She had wondered about telling her mum she was busy this first Sunday after Oli's arrival, but Heather was bound to find out about him eventually, and Erin had decided she might as well get it over with.

'Morning.' His voice was low when he came down the stairs and a tremor travelled through her, skin tingling as if he'd touched her.

'Hi.' Erin slid the carrots into the steamer with the swede, still thinking what her mum might have to say about Oli. She turned around and her mouth fell into a gape.

Barefoot and holding a towel, a pair of dark grey boxers hugged his hips, and her gaze hurriedly took in shoulders honed from years of rugby tapering to a narrow waist. His skin still held the trace of a Costa Rican suntan and dark hair covered his chest, running down to a firm stomach. She spun around to the sink, trying to pretend she hadn't observed every detail, and her elbow caught the chopping board. It crashed to the floor, sending peelings flying. She dropped down at the same moment as Oli, fumbling wildly at the mess to scoop it up, and their heads almost smacked together.

'Shit, sorry. I wasn't trying to splatter you in peelings on purpose,' she muttered, trying to focus on bits of carrot and swede, and not Oli's bare chest almost brushing her face. Her senses were full of him and the warmth emanating from skin that smelled of vanilla. They lunged for the same pile of peelings, and she yanked her arm back as though she'd been stung when her fingers brushed the back of his hand.

'Let me. Thanks for helping, but there's not enough room for both of us.' Not in the kitchen certainly, probably not even in the cottage now she'd seen him like this. She wished her hair was loose and not held back in a ponytail so it might disguise her burning face and the desire glittering in her eyes. She eased out a breath as he stood and picked up the towel he'd dropped.

'Erin, I've been thinking, and I'm sorry what I said about Jason on Friday. You're absolutely right, it is none of my business and as long as you're happy, then…'

'Thanks. I am.' But neither of them could take back what had passed between them when they'd walked home in the dark and Oli had laid bare his unease. He couldn't hide the emotion in his gaze then and she'd recognised it, because she was battling not to feel the same way. Part of her longed to return to those early days at Catz and maybe this time write a different ending for their story.

She busied herself with the meal as he disappeared into the bathroom and closed the door. When Oli passed her a second time, the towel around his waist, there were no more words, only the scent of vanilla lingering as he ran upstairs.

Heather arrived at midday, and they shared a hug once she'd left the Christmas decorations in the sitting room and a marmalade bread and butter pudding in the kitchen. She was slight, and the strawberry blonde hair Erin had inherited was now grey, though her mum still wore it in the curly bob she always had. Erin had been ten before she'd realised that her mum cut it herself to save money. Heather batted away Erin's concern about the journey over on two buses, always insistent that Erin was too busy to drive over and fetch her. And when Erin was on call, she couldn't.

'Mum, I'm fine,' she replied to Heather's own enquiry. She still found it disconcerting that a glance seemed to be enough for her mum to understand how she was, as Heather's eyes ran over her with motherly care. 'I'm more interested in how you are. Have you had any more flare-ups since we spoke? Nan said…'

'I'm all right.' Heather brushed that off as well; dealing with her fibromyalgia was ongoing and something she had learned to cope with. 'Your nan's right, we manage and there's nothing for you to worry about.'

'What about the pain, did the...'

'I'm managing, and that's all you need to know,' Heather said firmly, hanging her coat and scarf behind the front door. Oli's coat was half hidden by Erin's, and she wondered how her mum had missed it.

'I hope you're not working too many hours, love.' Heather patted Erin's arm as she joined her in the kitchen. 'Make sure you find time to rest and relax next weekend.'

'I will, don't worry about me. I'm on call and you know what it's like.'

'I can't help it, it's what mums do.' Heather smoothed the tinfoil covering the pudding. 'This needs a good forty minutes, don't let me forget to stick it in the oven when we sit down.' She glanced upstairs, as though wondering where Erin might have hidden her house guest. 'So how are you getting on with your new lodger? You were very vague in your messages.'

'Fine. It's been a busy week.' Already the first one of Oli's stay had passed and Erin was glad to land on the truth as the reason for keeping messages to her mum brief. He hadn't reappeared since his shower so her hopes that he'd be out before her mum arrived had fled. She was dreading the awkward encounter on the way, but she couldn't expect him to hide out in his small bedroom like a student whenever she had guests.

'What's she like?'

'Nice.' Erin cringed as she adjusted the timer on the steamer and put the lid over a layer of kale, a gift from Edmund's garden.

'Nice? That's it?'

'Yes, I expect you'll meet them eventually. Please would you do the table, lunch isn't far off being ready.'

'Right.' Heather opened a drawer, gathering place mats and cutlery. 'How many are we, love? Three or four? I take it Edmund's coming?'

'Just two. Edmund's nephew is taking him out and I said I'd save him a meal for tomorrow.'

It wasn't unusual for her neighbour to join them for Sunday lunch. When Erin was on call, Edmund accepted parcels for her and she often came home to find a note through her door and a meal in the little outhouse in the garden, so sharing Sunday lunch was one way she could thank him for his kindness. As a local historian of considerable expertise and long retired from the security services in London, Edmund was brilliant company, and she loved listening to the stories he was able to share.

'Has your lodger gone out, then?' Heather called from the sitting room. 'Remind me again, what's her name? Melissa, wasn't it?'

'Melanie.' Erin lifted a scalding tray of golden-brown roast potatoes from the oven and set it on the hob. The Yorkshire puddings were perfect, gravy was simmering in a pan, and she went to the fridge, about to remove a jar of horseradish sauce. 'About Melanie, Mum, there's something I've been meaning to tell you.'

'Go on then, spit it out.' Heather was back and she removed two glasses from a cupboard. 'You're being very cagey all of a sudden, our Erin.'

'There was a change of plan and I have a different lodger,' Erin said hurriedly. 'It was all very last minute, and I didn't really have time to think it through. I just decided to go along with it and...'

'You don't need my permission to have someone staying in your own home, love.'

'Mum, shush!' Erin took a deep breath, the memories of that weekend when Oli had driven her back to Yorkshire still so fresh in her mind, as though it had been just a few months ago and not thirteen years. But her mum was bound to have forgotten anyway, so worrying what Heather might have to say about him being here was pointless. 'His name is Oli.'

'Oli? How funny your lodger should have the same name as that lovely boy who drove you home when I was poorly that time. He had the nicest manners of anyone I've ever met, and he was so good with your nan and grandad too, they thought he was marvellous. Do you remember him rushing off to Asda because we'd run out of... Erin, love, you've gone pale. What's the matter?'

'There aren't two Olis,' Erin muttered. 'Just the one.'

'You mean it's him?' Heather's brows rose with her voice. 'Your Oli, the one you were so keen on at university? The one that drove you home?'

'I wasn't that keen on him, Mum,' Erin replied hastily, glancing at the ceiling lest he might overhear. Her face was scarlet, and she'd forgotten why she was at the fridge. 'We were on the same course, that's all. And he's very definitely not *my* Oli.'

She turned her attention to the beef and began to carve, slowing down when she saw the thick slice she'd hacked off in her haste. 'Melanie couldn't come and Gil found Oli instead. I had nothing to do with his decision, and it would be great if you would remember that we're just colleagues staying in the same house and treat him accordingly.'

'Treat him accordingly,' Heather said incredulously. 'So you've forgotten, then, what he did for you?'

'He drove me home, Mum. Once. That's it.' Erin always tried to diminish it because it still didn't make any sense, that'd he put himself out for her. Back then the answer was too incredible to believe and now it was too late to do anything about.

'You're right, he did drive you home just the once, even though I always expected he'd turn up again. But he didn't hire a car and drive you all the way from Cambridge to see if I was all right, love. Oh, I'm sure he wanted me to be fine, but every mile, every pound he spent, every minute on that old couch with his feet sticking over the end, he did for you, Erin. You might not think so but it's true. So where is he, why isn't he having lunch with us?'

'Because I didn't ask him and he'll be going out!' The plates she'd picked up hit the worktop more forcefully than Erin intended. 'Cooking for him is not part of our arrangement and we don't eat together.'

'But don't you think it would make sense, seeing as you're both working long hours in all weathers?' Heather said quietly, filling the glasses with water from a jug in the fridge. She'd never been someone who shouted and a calm word laden with disappointment had always been more effective than yelling where Erin was concerned.

Heather made it seem very simple, and Erin's teeth were clenched together as she slid a knife into the carrot and swede to test them. This was all her own fault; she ought to have anticipated that her mum was like a dog with a bone once she got started on something, and having her over for lunch with Oli here was clearly a very bad idea.

'Pooling your resources would probably save you money in the long term. It's not going to cost much more to make a shepherd's pie or a chilli for two than it is for just one. Your energy costs will go up if you cook separately.'

'I'm not daft, I've factored that into his rent,' Erin said impatiently, tilting her head to the sitting room. 'Why don't you go and sit down? I'll bring it through.'

'Erin, this isn't you,' Heather said quietly, resting a gentle hand on her arm. 'We've always shared, even when we had next to nothing.'

Both their heads swivelled to the stairs as a door opened above them. Erin was cringing again, wondering if Oli had heard every word. The breath seemed to have left her body as he made his way downstairs, and a glance was enough to take in his casual lounging clothes. Their eyes met and then the familiar grin was back as he held out a hand to her mum.

'Heather, how wonderful to see you again. It's been years.'

'It has, Oli, far too long.' Heather grasped his hand and tugged him close. 'Oh, give over with shaking hands, I can't stand all that formality with friends. Come here and let me give you a proper hug, I've never forgotten what you did for me and our Erin that time.'

Oli's laugh was a startled one as Heather wrapped both arms around him, and he bent down to hug her back. Erin just wanted the pair of them out of her kitchen; lunch was ready, and she didn't want anything going cold. Right now she was very tempted to leave the house and let them have lunch on their own. She'd been counting on Heather's practical common sense seeing straight through Oli's dazzling smile and perfect manners, not staring up at him like he'd just rescued a kitten from certain peril.

'Mum, why don't you take the gravy and horseradish to the table?' Erin had had enough of all this reminiscing.

It made her uncomfortable, especially when she saw Oli glance into the sitting room and take in the cosy table set for two. Another wave of shame followed, and she opened her mouth. But Heather was ahead of her.

'Oli, won't you join us? Erin wasn't very clear on your plans for lunch, but you don't look as though you're going out. Sit down, we'll bring you a plate.'

'That's very kind, but I'm quite happy to sort myself out once you're finished.' He shrugged at the chaos in the small kitchen, trays and pans waiting to be washed up littering every surface. 'I don't want to be in the way.'

'Of course you're not in the way,' Heather said briskly. 'We have plenty, and there's enough pudding to feed six.'

'If Erin doesn't mind?' Oli's gaze landed on her and she was relieved to hide from it as she retrieved another plate from the cupboard.

'Of course not,' she told him. It was absolutely the right thing to do, and she was glad her mum had stepped in after all. 'You go on through with Mum.'

'Can I help at all?'

'You can help by doing the clearing up later,' Heather said firmly. 'I'm not stopping long, I'm off to the cinema with a friend and I don't want to get caught in that rain they've forecast. It was the only afternoon she could do.'

She handed Oli an extra place setting as Erin loaded the plates, saving enough for Edmund. The rest went onto Oli's plate; it was one way she could make up for her meanness for not inviting him in the first place.

'Stick another potato on Oli's plate.' Heather pinched one from her own and waved away Erin's protest. 'I've got plenty and I should think it takes quite a bit to fill him up.'

'Another reason why I'm not cooking for him,' Erin muttered. 'He'd cost me a fortune.'

'Give him a chance, Erin,' Heather said quietly as she was about to carry two plates through to the sitting room. 'You've both got a bit of making up to do, wouldn't you say? And I'd hate to see you go through life mistrusting everyone because of your dad and what he did to us. It's different these days, I don't see why you can't have your independence and still love someone.'

'There's nothing going on, Mum,' Erin told her exasperatedly. 'We're colleagues and that's it.'

At the table conversation was easier than she expected, largely thanks to Oli asking Heather about becoming a freelance copywriter since leaving her floristry job. Heather was interested in his travels and life as a self-employed locum, and he had plenty of funny tales to share. When they'd eaten he thanked Erin for the meal, and she was happy to escape and clear the plates away. He also promised to reciprocate, adding a rueful caveat that it was unlikely to be anything quite so good given his lack of cooking experience.

'Erin can teach you. She's very good.'

Erin shot her mum a glare from the kitchen. The bread-and-butter pudding was perfect, golden brown with caramelised sugar crisp on top. She fetched a tub of custard and one of cream from the fridge, and returned to the table.

'And how are your mum and dad, Oli? Are they still in Marlborough?'

'My dad's in London now.' He glanced at Erin before continuing with something that wasn't quite a smile hovering on his lips. 'I'm afraid my mum passed away seven years ago. It was very sudden, and we weren't expecting it.'

Seven years ago. The year they had graduated. His mum had died seven years ago, and Erin hadn't known. Her stomach was in knots, sorrow clouding her mind with regret. She removed the lid from the custard and passed it to him with a trembling hand.

'I'm so sorry,' she whispered, her thoughts caught on what he and his family must have gone through, scorched with shame and sadness that she had blocked him from her life and hadn't been there for him.

'I'm very sorry for your loss.' Heather reached across the table and patted his hand.

'Thank you. It's fine now, sort of.' He found a smile, a cheerier note back in his voice. 'You're spoiling me with this meal, it's very kind of you both.'

Oli refused another helping of pudding when Heather tried to press it on him, insisting she take it home or save it for Edmund instead. After tea for Erin and Heather, and coffee for Oli, which they had around the table as well, Heather got up and found her coat and scarf.

'I'm off before that rain comes,' she said. Erin and Oli had stood too, and Erin watched as she hugged him again and told him how wonderful it was to see him and that he'd better not leave it so long next time. At the door she hugged Erin too, who did her best to avoid Heather's meaningful look and early exit. 'Bye, love, mind how you go. Love you.'

'I will, love you too. Text me when you're home and I'm here if you need me.'

'Will do.' Heather was watching Oli in the kitchen, emptying the sink of its clutter. 'You know, Erin, sometimes a person just strolls into your life, and even if it doesn't make any sense, it's still meant to be. You and him need to talk about what happened that summer.'

131

'Mum, it was years ago, and we've moved on,' Erin muttered. 'We're both busy with our own careers and he's leaving at Christmas in two weeks. I don't need that sort of complication in my life.'

'And what about this chap you're supposed to be seeing? Where does he fit into all this?'

'He doesn't,' Erin told her frustratedly, trying to recall Jason's features. Good body, man bun, that was it. Not dark auburn hair swept back from a face she knew almost as well as her own. 'We're just dating, we're not together or anything.'

'I'm glad to hear it.' Heather was already walking down the lane to the bus stop. 'Because your nan was at the bingo the other night and Margery showed her his Tinder profile. Her granddaughter's on there and your nan said that he looked like a right…'

The rest of her words were blown away by the wind and Erin was glad she'd missed whatever criticism about Jason her mum had to offer. And how had her nan and her elderly friend even heard of Tinder? She shuddered, that wasn't a thought on which she wanted to linger.

Chapter Eleven

'Explain to me how this works.' In the kitchen Oli had put the plates in the roasting tin and Erin winced. Now they would be greasy on the bottom as well, and she half wished he'd leave her to it.

'I see your cooking ability extends to clearing up as well.' Other than breakfast, he hadn't eaten any meals in the cottage since he'd arrived. Last night he'd brought in takeaway pizza, and she'd been very grateful for it after a busy day.

'So teach me,' he said airily. 'You fill the bowl with hot water, add soap and scrape with the scrubby green thing? Then what? Do the kitchen fairies show up and sprinkle everything with magic dust to dry them?'

'Something like that. I'll wash up, I don't trust you.' Erin opened a drawer and chucked a clean tea towel at him. He caught it and came to stand alongside her. There was the scent of vanilla again, his body close to hers. 'But when the fairies are busy gathering lost teeth to decorate the fairy queen's castle, we have to use one of those. And I'm not leaving you in charge of putting my kitchen right after a Sunday roast, I'm not that daft.'

'Ouch. So do you believe in the Easter bunny as well? And Father Christmas?'

'You mean you don't?' She pressed a hand over her heart, leaving a soapy patch behind. 'You're killing me, Oli, really.'

'Never saw the point,' he said quietly. 'I'm not big on fairy tales.'

'Me neither.' She wouldn't be trying to decipher any meaning in that remark. His life was none of her concern, just like hers wasn't his. 'But Father Christmas doesn't count, everyone knows he's real. Looking at you now, it's not difficult to imagine you've never washed a dish in your life.'

'I have,' he said indignantly. He seemed about to flick her with the tea towel and thought better of it. 'There was that time at Catz when the dishwasher broke and I'd run out of everything, even the pizza boxes were green. I did it all in the shower, though, because the kitchen sink was rammed.'

'Gross. Don't even think of trying that here.'

'I won't, don't worry. Your shower's barely up to washing me, never mind mouldy mugs,' he said, carefully inspecting a plate to make sure it was dry. 'So you don't think naked washing up will catch on?'

Erin's traitorous mind immediately leaped back to that morning and Oli on his way to the shower. Letting him lodge in her home was one thing, thoughts of him half naked were quite another. 'It had better not,' she warned. 'I've led a very sheltered life.'

'I believe you,' he mused, adding another dry plate to the pile of clean ones. 'You never played pub golf at Catz and woke up with your head in the toilet.'

'You got me there,' she told him casually, tipping dirty water out of the bowl and running the hot tap to replace it with clean. 'My middle name's boring.'

'No it's not, it's Iris. Because it means rainbow and your mum loves colour.'

The plate she'd just picked up plopped into the sink, sending hot water flying, and she grabbed a cloth to wipe it away. 'How do you know that?'

'Because you told me, that weekend. When we were in the car.'

She was trapped into stillness by his words and the sense that he could see into her deepest self, the part where all her fears, hopes and desires, and most especially her feelings about him, were kept hidden. They'd spent hours together then, and shared all kinds of insignificant details that were still fixed in her memory.

'So what's my middle name?' Suddenly his casual question sounded anything but and she was relieved to be spared a reply when her phone rang. She hurriedly dried her hands and answered it, her thoughts turning instantly to work as she listened to rushed details a worried owner was trying to impart.

'I've got to go.' Clearing up abandoned, she stuffed the phone into a pocket and was already on her way to the front door, snatching up keys. 'Someone's bringing a Vizsla down now, she's been in labour all day and isn't progressing.'

'I'll come with you.' The intimacy of those last few moments had deserted them, and Oli raised a shoulder when she looked at him. 'I know you can manage, but it sounds like it could be a caesarean and if so you'll need more hands. I can help.'

'Thanks.' It made sense as only one nurse was on call and the puppies would require support the moment they were born. She shrugged on her coat and boots as Oli did the same, and they emerged into a wet and darkening afternoon, running to her pickup.

The practice always felt strangely quiet out of hours, as though it was missing a piece of its heart without the rest of the staff and clients coming and going. Erin welcomed the owner and their beautiful, rust-coloured Hungarian Vizsla into a consulting room. She introduced Oli and the woman informed them that the soon-to-be first-time mum, Cleo, had been in stage one labour of whelping for around twelve hours. After the examination and once Erin had checked her general health, she concluded that they ought to carry out an emergency caesarean.

She promised to ring the owner with news as soon as possible, and she and Oli carried Cleo through to the prep room to ready her for surgery as Steph, the nurse on call, arrived. Steph held a paw as Oli clipped away hair and attached a catheter to administer medication as Erin scrubbed up. How swiftly their Sunday afternoon had switched into something different, she thought, as she felt the usual adrenaline rush ahead of the procedure she was about to perform. Once Cleo was asleep with Steph monitoring, Erin began with a neat incision.

'Got one.' A few minutes later she lifted out a tiny, russet-gold puppy and handed it straight to Oli, waiting with a towel draped over outstretched hands. He turned away to begin clearing membranes and mucous from the puppy's mouth and nose, stimulating respiration and circulation as he dried it. Soon it began to squeak, a welcome, high-pitched sound, and they shared an exultant grin. He placed the puppy in a crate lined with snug bedding, smiling at the adorable face with its scrunched-up eyes.

'And another.' Erin was working with quick efficiency, years of experience guiding her, and she laid the second puppy in Oli's waiting hands. Soon there were six puppies in the crate, four girls and two boys, all breathing, squeaking and squirming. Once Erin had completed the surgery and Cleo was awake, resting in a recovery room and slowly coming to, he brought the crate of puppies through. Steph left to return to her niece's birthday party and the end of the celebrations.

Erin eased the puppies towards Cleo, guiding the newborns to a first feed full of the essential colostrum and antibodies they needed to give them a flying start. She settled on the floor with Oli on Cleo's other side as the puppies wriggled close and tried to latch on. She called the owners, who were ecstatic with relief and excitement, and would return soon to collect the new family.

'Thanks for your help, Oli. It did make a difference.' Erin closed her eyes; it had been a busy weekend and tomorrow she would be back at work as usual.

'You're welcome. A perfect outcome for a Sunday afternoon surgery. How do you feel?'

'Yeah, elated, relieved. And tired. You know what it's like. I hope I never lose the wonder and miracle of birth. The puppies are adorable and I'm very glad they and mum are okay.'

'Totally. There's nothing quite like that moment of fear and adrenaline when you begin a surgical procedure. After I qualified I think I lived on both of those things for about two years. I had all the theory but putting it into practice on my own was terrifying at first.'

'Same.' Erin had relished the challenges too, and it had allowed her to channel all that energy and training into her career. Having Oli here now, working together for the first time since they'd been nervous students finding their way in rotations, was thrilling. And concerning, lest she get too used to his presence in her home as well.

'Are you tempted by one?' He eased out a long leg to stretch it, his hand gentle as he stroked one of the puppies. It managed to latch onto Cleo and plopped onto its tummy to feed.

'Maybe one day.' When she was certain she could afford the extra cost, the long-term financial and time commitment required. She allowed herself a happy little dream of bringing her own dog to work, taking it for long walks in the sunshine. 'Do you think you'll ever have another?'

His smile was a wistful one and she glimpsed the sadness flare again in his eyes. 'Hopefully. If I ever stop living like a student and settle down. What you've achieved is amazing, Erin. A career you love in the place you've always wanted to live, a home of your own.' He fixed a long look on her. 'What else is out there for you, apart from a puppy?'

'To keep going and help my family, I suppose,' she replied quietly, shifting positions to get comfortable; the floor was hard and cold. The only risks she took were work-related ones, when she had to balance every carefully thought-out decision against a potential life or death outcome. 'Don't we all want the same things in the end? Security and work, home, a place to call our own where we feel loved and valued?' She realised he'd made exactly this point during their time at Catz, and she'd dismissed it then.

'Yeah, but home doesn't have to be the same roof over my head every night. I make my home wherever I am.' Oli's gaze was unflinching, and Erin felt as though they were suddenly having a very different conversation as his tone lowered. 'Why did you let me come and stay, knowing it was me? Why not ask Gil to make other arrangements, given our history?'

'Hello? Have you met my shower?' She'd wondered this herself, lying awake before he'd arrived. Worrying about seeing him again and yet afraid of passing up the opportunity.

'So it's all about the bathroom? You weren't curious about me at all?'

'Maybe a bit.' She paused, the words that had been stuck in her mind since lunch finally bursting free. 'I'm so terribly sorry about your mum, Oli, I had no idea.'

'Thanks. Eventually you find a way to get used to it. I'm not sure the grief ever goes away though, I think you just learn to live with it. There's still stuff I want to tell her, things I'd like to share.'

'I'm sorry I let you down and wasn't there for you when she died.' Erin had failed him, and the realisation caught her breath. 'Especially after what you did for me.'

'It's not a debt you have to keep on repaying, Erin.' Oli was staring at the tiny puppies, content and dozing after a first feed. 'I did it because I cared about you, even though I wasn't brave enough to let you know how much. I think I was hoping somehow you'd realise.'

'I sort of did. I was just scared of allowing myself to believe it.'

'I sent you a message, the night Mum passed away.' He eased out a sigh. 'Or rather, I wrote you one, because I couldn't send it. I assumed you'd blocked me for good after graduation because of the way things ended that summer.'

She had, and had gone so far as to evade university reunions and even the wedding of his best friend Rory in the Highlands. Rory's girlfriend had been part of Erin's house share at Catz in those final two years. When the wedding invitation had dropped into her inbox, she'd pleaded pressure of work, unwilling to spend the day avoiding Oli and whoever he was with at the time.

Her hand reached across Cleo to find his, and he let her hold it. She stared at their hands resting lightly on his thigh; hers pale and small, freckled, her skin not as soft as she'd like with the constant washing and scrubbing. His felt similar, rougher still, and his fingers twined between hers, stroking them absently. All the years they'd known each other and yet they had barely touched. He was the man against whom she measured every other one and she couldn't help it; he'd been her first kiss and the best, her first love. Even a friendly gesture like this, trying somehow to extend her sympathy for his loss, felt like so much more.

'What did it say, your message?'

'I wanted to tell you what Mum meant to me and how it felt in those first few hours to be without her. How shocking and sudden it was, and how lost I felt. I wanted to borrow a bit of your strength because my own felt so diminished. For you to tell me I'd find a way to be okay without her.'

'Oh, Oli,' Erin whispered, her fingers tightening around his. 'I would've come if I'd known.' The thought had never occurred to her and yet it was true. She would've dropped everything if she'd understood what he was going through, just as he had for her. She couldn't imagine a life without her mum, and it was crushing to think that Oli had wanted her at his side when he'd lost his own.

'It's okay, I'm not saying it to make you feel bad. I understand why you didn't trust me, I knew we were fragile and needed nurturing. I should've fought harder for you, for us, and then you wouldn't have had a reason not to trust me.' Oli hesitated. 'I know I let you down, Erin. I'm really sorry about what happened that summer. The house was already booked when you and I got together, and I had no idea that Bella was going to be there.'

Erin was still gazing at their hands fixed together, wanting to free herself and yet afraid to break the bond. If they separated now then she might never know what happened. The end of their first year at Catz at the ball was clear in her memory; the giddy excitement of all they'd achieved and the promise of more beckoning, a new love growing, thriving into the future.

Until it was obliterated by the photos she'd seen of him and Bella on holiday in France; Bella on his lap, her arms round his neck, splashing in the pool, heads together as they talked. Their intimacy and the harsh reality of life with someone like Oli had floored Erin then, and the shattering of her heart had felt almost physical. Blonde and beautiful Bella Browning, who understood his world perfectly because she'd grown up in it.

'She'd just broken up with someone and she was fooling around, there was nothing in it.'

'Nothing?' The word was hollowed out with scorn. 'And it never occurred to you how it would look to me, waiting for you to come home?'

'Maybe this sounds naive, but no, because you were the one I was thinking about, Erin,' he said simply. 'You were the one I was missing, messaging every day. Bella came to my room one night and suggested we should get together, that we'd be the perfect couple.' Oli paused. 'I told her no.

I also told her about you and that's why I wasn't going to be with her. I don't know how you came to see those photos, but I can guess.'

Erin's stomach dropped and her hand in his trembled as he offered the explanation she'd never given him the chance to share before. He'd messaged his apology right after she'd seen the photos and, numb with shock, she'd blocked him immediately. Somewhere deep in her heart she'd been half expecting some reason why they couldn't ever work, and she'd spent most of the summer pulling long hours on Carys's farm in Wales. When they'd returned to Catz for the second Michaelmas term, Erin had done everything she could to avoid him whenever possible.

He'd tried to talk to her and each time she'd refused to listen, aware the only way she could protect herself was to keep him at a distance. Eventually he'd backed off and their friendship had faltered. The following year he and Ingrid were together, and until now Erin had never doubted her decision.

'I thought you'd kissed me at the ball and said those things for a laugh because you knew how I felt about you,' she whispered sadly. 'And that I was never the one you really wanted.'

'How did you feel about me?' Oli's voice was low, uneven, and she caught the hurried plea in those few words.

'I'm not going to spell it out, Oli.' She owed herself that much dignity at least. 'My father left us with nothing and I saw how hard my family had to battle to survive, so I wasn't going to put my heart in the hands of someone I didn't trust to hold it.'

'Want me to say it first?'

'Say what?' She swallowed down her sadness, the desire to understand what had been in his heart then. 'It's pointless, it doesn't mean anything now.'

'If you think I kissed you and said those things at the ball to mock you then you don't know me as well as I thought,' he said roughly. 'I did it for one reason only, and that was because I was in love with you. And I know you felt the same, you don't even have to say it. It was there every time we were together, and we only had to look at each other to know it was true.'

She didn't want to let his words settle inside her but couldn't prevent it; they were warming her and hurting her all at once. How much had they missed, how might their lives have been different if she'd allowed her mind to believe what her heart already knew? She freed her hand from Oli's and checked Cleo, focusing on her responsibilities and not their past. Their silence was broken by the puppies snuffling and squeaking, while Erin stroked Cleo as she battled to contain the feelings their conversation had stirred up.

'Whatever happened then, we've both moved on, and we lead different lives now. If you hadn't taken this job then we probably wouldn't have seen each other again. It's too late to go back.'

'I don't want to go back. Maybe I want to look forward for once,' he said quietly. 'And I know you're not going to like this, and I'm supposed to back off where Jason is concerned, but I'd still be saying this if it was my sister or any other person I cared about.' He drew in a long breath. 'You should end it with him. You deserve so much better, and he's not for you.'

Erin stood up awkwardly, her legs stiff after sitting on the hard floor, and fumbled for her phone. Cleo was more alert, and it was time to call her owners again and let them know they could collect her.

'Whatever your intentions are for saying that Oli, our history doesn't give you the right to comment on who I'm with. Jason and I are fine as we are and I don't need any more, I can look after my own future. And your middle name is Cameron. Because it was your mum's family name and she wanted you to have it.'

Chapter Twelve

'I might be imagining things, but I'm pretty sure we didn't have two ponies on the premises when I left this morning.' Gil appeared in the office on Tuesday after his farm visits with the family dogs, Lola and Maud, at his heels. Erin looked up from where she'd broken for lunch before an afternoon of testing cattle for tuberculosis. 'I've just seen a piebald cob in the paddock and Posy's got it cornered. Either Harriet or Dorothy is responsible, and my money's on Harriet. She took off first thing before breakfast and I haven't seen her since.'

'I haven't seen her either.' Erin thought even Harriet might make herself scarce if she'd fetched an animal home without Pippa or Gil's permission. With a grin, she got up and pulled on her coat, hanging on the back of her chair. 'Let's have a look, then.'

Word quickly spread and by the time Erin had caught Posy and persuaded her not to make her displeasure with the new arrival more apparent, the entire staff had trooped out to take a look at an underweight and very sorry-looking black-and-white pony. Despite her condition she was a sturdy build and Erin guessed around thirteen hands high.

'It's a mare,' Gil said grimly. He'd found a spare head-collar in the stables and led the pony inside out of the rain. Erin had brought Posy in too, and left her secure in her own stable, where she went to the back to sulk. 'She must be a rescue, judging by the state of her.'

The pony's thick winter coat was filthy, more black than white, and matted in places. It was clear her feet hadn't been trimmed for some time and were overgrown to a degree that had made her hobble uncomfortably across the yard. Her feathers – thick hair growing beneath her knees to her hooves – were dirty too, coated in mud. In the stable her head hung down, hip bones protruding and eyes dulled, and Erin felt desperately sorry for her. Gil ran a hand from her neck along her body and sighed when he felt her stomach, more distended than the rest of her. 'Anyone else think she might be in foal?'

'Looks that way. What do you want to do?' Oli had hung back now the rest of the staff had returned to the surgery.

He and Erin had been polite and careful with one another since they'd talked on Sunday afternoon. They had agreed to share the shopping and cooking, and this morning he'd filled the slow cooker with ingredients for a chicken casserole tonight. She'd never really put into words what she'd felt for him at Catz, and hearing him say that he'd been in love with her then was proving impossible to forget. Bits of their conversation kept popping up at inconvenient moments – like now, while assessing the welfare of this bedraggled little mare apparently in need of a loving home. His eyes caught hers and she looked away.

'First, let's get her dry and warm. Water and feed too, then when she's feeling a bit brighter we'll clean her up and take some bloods. She'll need worming and we'd better scan her to make sure she actually is in foal. There's probably a rug around here somewhere that'll fit her.'

'So she's staying?' Erin was relieved, dreading the thought of turfing the starving pony back out into the depths of winter. Not that Harriet or Dorothy would let that happen.

'For now.' Gil slowly shook his head. 'No doubt Harriet has other ideas. I bet Dorothy put her up to this; I'll be having a word with my aunt when I see her. And Harriet, when she gets home from school.'

'She'll need a name, if she hasn't already got one.' Erin was stroking the pony's neck, trying to let her know that she'd be okay now and they wouldn't let anything worse happen to her. 'I bet she doesn't have a passport.'

'What about Flo?' Oli suggested. 'She looks like she might be a Flo.'

'She does.' Erin threw him a grin. 'I like it.'

'Right, Flo it is, unless Harriet's got a better suggestion.' Gil slipped the headcollar off and gave Flo a gentle pat. 'Poor little girl, let's get you sorted out.'

'I'll do it, if you want to get some lunch?' Erin checked her phone. 'I've got another hour before I need to be at Roland's for the testing.'

'Thanks, Erin.' Gil closed the stable door and made sure to kick the bottom bolt in place too, the dogs ready to follow him back indoors. 'Make sure Posy's shut in too. I wouldn't put it past her to escape and let Flo out as well, probably see her off whilst she's at it.'

Oli was on his lunch break too, and he and Erin quickly made a clean bed from the blocks of shavings Harriet stored for Posy. They banked up the bedding high and deep so Flo could lie down in comfort if she chose. Oli filled a clean water bucket and Elaine appeared with a kettle so they could add some warm water to entice Flo to drink. Erin slid a few handfuls of haylage into a net; the pony would need to be fed little and often so her weakened digestive system wouldn't be overwhelmed. Posy was on a permanent low-calorie diet to keep her laminitis condition at bay, so Erin offered Flo a little of Posy's feed in a bucket, gratified to see that she ate it. Flo would need something different to build her back up, but Posy's food would do for now. Erin and Oli left Flo standing on the thick bedding, out of the rain and freezing air, and they planned to check on her later with Gil.

–

When Erin returned from TB testing the herd of dairy cattle, she was cold and ready for a hot drink. The cattle had been unsettled by the change in routine and a few had escaped into the yard, leading her and the farmers a merry dance before they were rounded up. She heard Jess chatting with Oli in the office in a quick break between consultations and from the sound of it, Jess was helping him choose an ugly sweater for the staff Christmas party on Saturday. Gil had drafted in extra cover and planned to be on call if required so everyone else could have a night off. They'd agreed on Secret Santa for their first Christmas as a team and Elaine had suggested they draw names at the party and exchange gifts on the twenty-third, which would be Oli's last day.

Erin was already half regretting inviting Jason to the party. Pippa and Gil had been kind enough to include partners and in defiance of Oli's words on Sunday about her relationship, she'd messaged Jason yesterday and blurted out the suggestion. She'd already agreed to be Jason's plus-one at his cousin's wedding in the new year. Surprisingly, he'd said yes straightaway to her invitation, and she was wondering if it was because he didn't have a better plan lined up. In reality it felt too early in their relationship to have him join her for a more formal work event than a gathering at the pub, but she'd asked him now and at least it meant she wouldn't be arriving alone.

'Erin, hi. What do you think of this?' Jess appeared in the kitchen as Erin was filling the kettle, still musing on the party, and thrust a phone she recognised as Oli's towards her. 'Oli's not that keen but I think it's perfect and he suggested you should have the casting vote.'

'Me?' Erin laughed, automatically reaching for mugs to make her colleagues a brew. Elaine had gone home, and it was Steph's half day. Gabi was on a training course and would be back on Thursday. Word had got around now about Erin and Oli being at Cambridge together, and everyone had accepted they'd been friends. Erin was hopeful that only Jess knew things had been different. The man in question propped himself against the door as she woke the coffee machine up, his eyes on hers full of amusement. 'I'm not sure my experience of ugly sweater parties, which is none, is up to choosing outfits for other people.'

'So you don't like it?' Jess waved the phone again and Erin had a proper look this time.

'Actually, I sort of do. There's something about a scowling green sprout that would really suit you, Oli. Goes with your hair.'

'Decision made.' Oli accepted his phone back from Jess and ran his fingers over the screen. 'Done. I can pick it up from the shop tomorrow.'

'Can't wait,' Jess said airily. 'So when are you putting your decs up, Erin? I'd offer to help, seeing as we won't be having any this year, given the state of our house, but I don't want to be in the way if Oli's helping you instead.'

Erin gave her friend and colleague a pointed look, and Jess laughed, undaunted. 'Soon, I hope. My mum's brought over some old decorations from home, and I've got a few new ones to add.'

Exploring all those old childhood memories the decorations held made her feel nostalgic and a little sad. It was another shift away from her usual routine of decorating her grandparents' house together. Celebrating a first Christmas in her own home was another step into a fully independent life.

'Don't I get any say in all this Christmas planning?' Oli folded his arms, and Erin was thinking of his mum, and the reminder that he'd be spending another Christmas without her.

'Is that an offer to help?' She was pretty sure she wouldn't get Jason round for such a mundane task if she asked him. 'But it's totally fine if not, I understand.'

'I think even I can manage to help you string a few lights around a tree.'

'Well, it's not just lights.' Erin handed Jess herbal tea and Oli an espresso, and they thanked her. 'Decorating the house for Christmas is one of my favourite days of the year, it's so much fun.'

'How bad are we talking here?' A smile was hovering on Oli's lips, and she read one in his eyes, too. 'On a scale of *The Grinch* right through to *Elf*?'

'Oh, full on *Elf*, definitely. Imagine *Elf* crossed with *National Lampoon's Christmas Vacation* meets the shop in *Last Christmas*, then you're getting close.' She hoped he wouldn't find her plans upsetting, given the situation with his own family.

'Seriously?' Oli huffed out a sigh she felt was exaggerated, the amusement in his gaze still lingering. 'Gabi didn't put that in the welcome email.'

'We didn't want to scare you off,' Erin said lightly. 'While we're talking about movie night, Jess, I was thinking of sticky cranberry sausages and halloumi in blankets, with s'mores to finish.'

'That sounds amazing. I can't wait and Steph's really looking forward to it.'

'What do you think of *Holidate*, then *Elf* and *The Holiday*? If we start early enough we should be able to make three.'

'Perfect. Maybe we could squeeze in *Last Christmas* too, I love Henry Golding in that movie.' Jess was nursing the mug between her fingers. 'So will Jason be there?'

'I haven't invited him as it's a work thing, not couples.' Erin was keen to get Jess off the subject of Jason in front of Oli. 'Not that we're a couple, we're just dating.'

'Yeah, so you keep saying.' Oli's narrowed eyes made it clear what he thought of that, and Erin glared back. Whatever had passed between them on Sunday night, sitting in the empty practice after carrying out emergency surgery, he still had no right to make his feelings about Jason quite so plain, especially in front of Jess.

'So you'll be there, Oli,' Jess said quickly, and Erin could've kicked herself. She'd walked right into that one. 'What's your favourite festive movie?'

'I don't really have one.'

'Oh come on, everyone does!'

'Not me, but I suppose if you pushed me I'd say *The Muppet Christmas Carol*,' he said wistfully. 'There's just something about those characters that's so comforting, and the story is timeless. I used to watch it when I was a kid.'

'Then we should watch that too,' Jess said immediately, looking at Erin for confirmation. 'We could swap out one of the others, I don't mind which.'

'We can talk about it later. I'd better get on. I've got stuff to do online before I finish.' Erin was thankful to have a reason to end this conversation. This was exactly why she preferred to avoid all discussions at work where her private life was concerned; it was getting a little too public for her liking. It was different with Jess as she'd become a friend and, for all her frivolity, Erin trusted her.

Forty minutes later she was going over some test results from the lab. They'd taken bloods from the vomiting cat Erin had seen out of hours last weekend and its kidney results were concerning. She needed to see it again to discuss those and other symptoms, and plan for possible treatment. She was about to pick up the phone when Oli stuck his head around the door.

'Sorry, Erin, have you got a minute? Dorothy's brought in a kitten, and I could do with a word as Gil's not here.'

'Sure.' She followed Oli into his consulting room. There was a cardboard box on the table and, when she took a look inside, her heart clenched at the sight of a tiny and beautifully marked ginger tabby kitten. Marmalade shades on its legs and tail were darker than those on its back, and the lower part of a very sweet little face and its chest were dusted with white fur, making it appear as though the kitten was wearing a bib. Its coat was damp and dirty, a tiny tummy shrunken and empty, and she wanted to weep.

'Desperately underweight and the eyes look sore.' She glanced at Oli and saw his own troubled expression. 'Any discharge or raised temperature?'

'Nasal discharge and she's sneezing. Temperature's elevated to thirty-nine point eight, not overly concerning.'

'Female?' Erin felt that made the kitten seem even more vulnerable, and he nodded. 'Any signs of bloody diarrhoea?' Even though she longed to stroke the kitten, she wouldn't until she was satisfied it wasn't feline parvovirus. Oli shook his head.

'Dorothy noticed it around the farm with a young adult and she'd been leaving food out for them but hadn't been able to get any closer. She thought the mother looked well enough but was also underweight.'

'Was?'

'She found its body on the road an hour ago, and the kitten was under the hedge nearby. She thought it was dead too but realised it wasn't quite and brought it straight here.'

'Oh, the poor little love, and her mum too.' Even as sorrow settled over her, Erin's mind was racing to the next step, what they could do in a situation like this. 'That's awful.'

'Yes, absolutely. We can run bloods to make sure it's not parvo so Dorothy can be clear about the risk of infection on the farm. I suspect it's probably FCV.'

'That wouldn't be the worst thing she could have. I'd prefer cat flu to something more sinister,' Erin murmured. 'She's what, about eight weeks?'

'I should think so, her eyes are green, not blue. I haven't weighed her yet. There are no signs of ulcers or swellings to indicate a more virulent strain of the virus.'

'That's good.' The kitten sneezed and the sound was a tug on Erin's heartstrings.

'So here's the thing.' Oli cleared his throat as Erin straightened to face him. 'There's no microchip, she's almost certainly feral, without a home or vaccinations, and she's very sick. Dorothy has no idea when she last fed, and she may well have been surviving by suckling from her mother. She's clearly very underweight and dehydrated, and lacking antibodies if her mother wasn't vaccinated either.'

'What did Dorothy say?' Erin knew exactly where Oli was going with this. Dorothy adored her animals, but many years of caring for them had taught her she couldn't save everything.

'That she'd love to have her back but she's pragmatic enough to know that the kitten probably won't survive, even with careful nursing, and that takes time. If Dorothy hadn't found her when she did, it would've been dead overnight anyway without shelter or food in this weather. And then there's the cost of treatment and care, without insurance or owners to pay for it.'

All practical considerations Erin had heard so many times before and she'd be saying the same to her client if one was stood on the other side of the table with the box and its critically ill ginger bundle between them. The kitten sneezed again, and she caught a glimpse of green eyes amongst the dampness surrounding them. Was she imagining the exhaustion in that weary gaze, the fight to survive fading along with her life? The kitten's tummy was hunched, and Erin couldn't bear to think of her homeless and hungry.

'It might be kinder, Erin, given she's had a terrible start and probably won't make it anyway, to let her…'

'I'll take her. And I'll cover the cost.' Erin was already reaching for a pair of surgical gloves, her work in the lab temporarily forgotten. She very rarely spent anything without first considering the implications, but this was literally a life-and-death situation, and it wasn't a decision she needed time to make. 'Let's weigh her and get a catheter in, then we'll take bloods and start a line to get fluids going. We can try her on some food when she's more comfortable, but it might need to be syringed.'

'You're sure?' Oli's hand went to her arm and his voice was gentle. 'I didn't want to sway you, but I'd hate to give up without giving her a chance either.' He hesitated. 'I'd have taken her myself, but I won't be…'

'I know. You won't be here much longer.' She looked up. How was it only two more weeks until Christmas? 'And of course I'm sure. We can always rehome her when she's well again.'

They shared a grin and Erin's adrenaline was racing as they swung into action. The tiny ginger girl offered no resistance bar a squeak when they clipped away dirty and damp fur on a thin front paw and carefully inserted the catheter. By the time Oli had carried her through to a kennel kept in isolation for such cases, the entire practice had heard and popped in to take a peek.

'She needs a name,' Jess declared. 'We can't be calling her the kitten or the ginger the whole time.' She had two cats at home and was keeping a safe distance. Erin had already offered to nurse the kitten so the other staff didn't have to make contact, and Oli said he would do his share. They couldn't catch or transmit the virus to other patients themselves, but it could be passed on if other cats came into contact with bowls and litter trays. It was vital they wore protective clothing around the kitten and disposed of it before leaving the isolation kennel, alongside every other virus control in place in the practice.

'Ginger?' Oli suggested.

'No, something sweeter, she has such a gorgeous little face.'

'Marmalade,' Erin offered. 'It seems to suit her somehow.' She'd placed a bowl of hot water nearby so the steam could help the kitten's breathing. They'd taken blood samples, and a litter tray was set up on one side of the kennel, the space so large its tiny occupant was barely visible in her cosy nest.

'It does.' Oli dropped down to his haunches to join Erin beside the kennel. 'Maybe Marnie for short, Marmalade's a very big name for such a little girl.'

'Marnie. I love it.'

'Just don't get too attached,' he warned. 'She's got a long way to go.'

'I know,' Erin said fiercely. 'But we're going to do everything we can to get her there.'

'I'll leave you two to it, then,' Jess said drily. 'Brew on the way.'

Erin had already cleaned Marnie's eyes, applied drops and given her an anti-inflammatory injection to help bring down her temperature and ease her symptoms. It was a relief to have fluids steadily flowing into Marnie's body, but Erin would be happier once she'd taken a drink on her own and had swallowed a tiny bit of something, even if they had to syringe it into her. It promised to be a long night, and she was thankful not to be on call, so she didn't have to leave Marnie just yet.

Chapter Thirteen

The following morning Erin was back at the practice at six a.m. to check on Marnie. The kitten had spent the night in isolation, and Erin and Oli had taken turns to nip back and make sure she was okay. Relieved to see that Marnie had made it through the night and was looking brighter since leaving her at midnight, Erin topped up her meds and curled into the only comfy chair in the office to close her eyes, jerking awake again after what felt like five minutes.

'Morning.' Oli was leaning against a desk nearby. 'Sorry, I didn't mean to startle you but it's seven thirty and everyone will be in soon. Here. Made you this.'

'Thanks. There's never a time I don't need tea.' She felt sluggish, slow after a nap she wouldn't usually take, and accepted the mug he offered, tea brewed just the way she liked it. Oli's hair was damp after a shower, and she liked the stubble he was letting grow back into a beard after telling her he needed every layer he could get to stay warm here.

'I've just had a look at Marnie. She's still subdued but I think she's a bit better than yesterday.'

'Yeah, I thought that too. The meds and fluids will be helping.' Erin drank some tea and put the mug down, about to get up. 'She's due a feed and…'

'You stay there and finish your brew, I'll do it. You've had a disturbed night.'

'So did you.'

'Yeah, but I wasn't here at midnight and then back at six.'

Oli disappeared and Erin sat back to enjoy her tea. Her neck felt stiff and she yawned, thinking of the calls she was making later. A lame horse, a heifer in calf who was off her food and pregnancy scanning a small flock of rare breed sheep. A recent storm had given way to a cold, sharp day, and snow closer to Christmas was a possibility. Much as she loved to see the landscape swathed in white, it would bring problems for everyone and especially the farmers as they battled to keep their livestock fed and safe.

She washed up her mug and went through to the isolation kennel, pausing at the sight of Oli stroking Marnie inside the crate. Yesterday the kitten had been too weak and poorly to offer any resistance, and even though she still had a long way to go, her feral instincts to defend herself could flare at any moment. A quick look revealed the litter tray had been used and she watched as he carefully opened Marnie's mouth to check for ulcers before syringing the prescription food they'd started her on last night. All good signs, and Erin hoped if she continued to improve then Marnie might be able to come home with her in a couple of days.

'She was ready for that.' She was heartened by the sight of Marnie lifting her head and sniffing for more when the syringe was empty.

'Yeah, we could let her try the next feed on her own.' Oli settled Marnie back on her bed again, mindful of the catheter still attached to a line providing fluids. If she began to drink on her own, they could remove it later.

'How's she doing?' Gil stuck his head around the door, Lola at his heels. He kept a hand on her collar so she wouldn't venture any further. He'd popped in last night and Erin had explained about Dorothy finding Marnie, and how she'd come to be in the practice, hoping he wouldn't object to another stray after the piebald pony that morning. He'd said immediately that she'd done the right thing in giving Marnie a chance and offered to keep an eye on her too.

'Good, thanks. Improving.'

'That's great, Erin. Glad to hear it, and Dorothy will be too.' Gil's eyes narrowed. 'Speaking of which, I've got to the bottom of what that pony's doing here. Somebody got in touch with Dorothy to say they'd seen it looking a state and that the owner obviously couldn't manage to look after it. She went straight round with the trailer, persuaded them to give Flo up and unbeknownst to me and Pippa, Harriet offered to give her a home and so here she is.'

'I wouldn't have minded seeing Dorothy persuading someone round to her way of thinking.' Oli grinned and Gil laughed.

'They didn't stand a chance.' His smile was a wry one. 'Dorothy thinks Flo would make a good driving pony and Harriet's determined to have a go when Flo's fit enough. She likes the name too. They say they didn't know Flo was in foal, but I'm not convinced, Dorothy's no mug. As if I needed another bloody pony, and now I've got three for the price of two.' He rolled his eyes. 'Ah well, it could be worse, Posy could be the one in foal. So are you two all set for Saturday? I reckon Elaine's thinking of fixing Secret Santa so she gets me. Apparently I'm a Grinch because I said I never wanted to hear "Last Christmas" being played ever again. Seems pretty reasonable to me.'

'Totally, I'm looking forward to it.' Erin was hoping to get Jess; she already had a gift in mind. Anyone would be fine really, except Oli.

It was time for the daily staff briefing, so she and Oli disposed of their gloves and masks, and made their way to the office with Gil and Lola.

-

By Thursday evening Marnie was making progress and Erin was in love. She'd known by the first morning that rehoming her was no longer a possibility; she simply couldn't bring herself to do it. Without a microchip or the unlikely prospect of someone coming forward to claim her, Marnie needed a home, and Erin had decided that hers was going to be it. Marnie was still wary whenever she and Oli approached but the catheter was out, she was eating and drinking on her own, and would tolerate brief touches. She'd already put on a little weight as the hunching in her tummy eased, and she had melted the hearts of everyone at the practice.

They gradually reduced her meds as her temperature returned to normal and even the way she sneezed was adorable. She was beginning to take an interest in her surroundings and although she wasn't well enough to have her vaccinations, Erin planned to do that just as soon as she could.

Tonight she was planning to bake for the mince pie tasting tomorrow. She hadn't done much baking since she'd moved into the cottage, preoccupied instead with settling in and her new job, and she'd missed it. For Erin her nan set the standard, her scones and mince pies were legendary. Joyce made good use of the produce Bill grew, and Erin always thought the house smelled like Christmas once the fruit for the cake Joyce baked had been left to steep in brandy for several days.

Earlier Oli had mentioned that he'd sort out dinner and she'd come home before him to find a chilli gently simmering in the slow cooker, loaded with peppers, beans and spices. She was so tired and grateful, she'd have hugged him if he'd been there. She put a couple of potatoes in the oven to bake as she'd be using it for the mince pies anyway, and headed to the shower, thankful he was checking on Marnie after early evening consultations. When he arrived he shrugged out of his coat and wasted no time in joining her in the kitchen, sniffing appreciatively.

'Smells amazing.' He found a teaspoon and stuck it in the jar of Joyce's homemade mincemeat Erin had got her mum to post. Her nan wouldn't entertain ready-made and used molasses sugar to give the mincemeat a thick, dark sweetness. 'Mmm, it is amazing. What!'

'Get off,' Erin told him, trying to be stern and failing when he laughed. She shoved his hand, about to dive in for a second time, away. 'There's not that much and you are not allowed to eat it.'

'What, ever?'

'Maybe I'll save you a bit as a thank you for sorting dinner. It too smells amazing.' There was nothing like coming home on a cold winter's night to a meal made. It was one of the joys of growing up with her grandparents; that there was often something delicious on the go. 'How was Marnie, did she eat again?'

'She did, every scrap. I think she's turned a corner, maybe you can bring her home at the weekend?'

'I'd love that.' Erin grinned at Oli, leaning against the stairs. 'I'll run down and check on her again in a couple of hours.'

'So can I help?' He pointed to the muffin tins on the worktop, already lined with butter. 'What would it take to persuade you to turn your entry into a joint one?'

'Are you kidding me?' she retorted. 'You think I want to share my mince pies with you? And don't you dare eat one because then you'll know which are mine when you try them at work. Don't look at me like that either, this is a serious business and I'm not going to be swayed.'

'So you think I could sway you?' Oli had lowered his voice and Erin's pulse jumped. She turned back to the pastry she'd been rolling out, more distracted by him than she'd like to be.

'Definitely not.' Hair was escaping from her ponytail, getting in her way. Hands covered in flour, she shook her head, trying impatiently to flick it from her face.

'May I?'

She nodded slowly as he took two steps to stand behind her. Throat suddenly dry, she swallowed, barely breathing as his fingers brushed her neck. He drew her curls together before re-fastening her ponytail.

'Thanks.' Her voice was a croak, and she was aware he hadn't moved away, other than to withdraw his hands.

'You're welcome.' He dropped the words into her ear, and her eyes slid closed as his breath skimmed her neck. 'It'll cost you a mince pie.'

'Oh well, if you'd said that I would've refused your help. No can do, they're strictly off limits until tomorrow.' This was turning into dangerous territory that felt very much like flirting. Erin was wishing he'd move and also trying to subdue a burning desire that he wouldn't. 'So, er, did you say you were going to shower before we eat?'

'I didn't, but it's probably a good idea.'

'Yeah. I need to get on with these anyway.' She waved a hand over the pastry and jar of mincemeat as Oli stepped away. 'Take your time.'

An hour later she had a dozen golden mince pies cooling on the worktop and he was doing his best to persuade her to let him try one. She refused again and when it was time to nip back to the practice and check on Marnie, she took the mince pies with her so he couldn't cheat. They laughed about it when she returned after settling Marnie, and she was grateful he'd cleared up while she'd been gone. She thanked him, ready to head up to bed for an early night.

In the morning Erin was happy to have the mince pie tasting coming up to distract her from the call she was making first. It was three days since she'd visited the dairy herd to test the cows for tuberculosis, and returning to assess the results was always an anxious time for everyone. On Tuesday she'd clipped two patches of hair from the neck of each cow and measured the skin thickness before injecting both sites with different tuberculins.

Marnie was making steady progress and would sometimes purr when they stroked her, which thrilled Erin. She was hopeful that without a feral mum to guide her, Marnie would lose some of her wilder instincts and learn how to settle into a home. Harriet was studying for pre-Christmas exams in between taking care of the ponies. Flo had officially been welcomed into the family and now had her own pink waterproof rug which she wore in the paddock each morning, with a different one for the stable at night.

Gil had scanned her and thought she would give birth in May, and everyone was excited about seeing her with a foal at foot in the spring, when she would be well recovered and enjoying the early grass. Neither Harriet nor Dorothy had any clue about the stallion who'd sired the foal. Harriet was hoping for a pony she could keep for riding when it was old enough, ideally one taller than Flo's thirteen hands as she was already five nine. Gil was still occasionally muttering about how they'd managed to become a two, nearly three-horse family, but he often popped into the stables to check on Flo, and he didn't stand a chance against Harriet, Dorothy and Pippa anyway.

When Erin arrived at the farm to complete the tuberculosis test, the cows were herded back through the crush so she could measure the skin thicknesses of each site she'd injected on Tuesday again. It was a fiddly, cold and noisy morning, and her arms were aching when she finished, thankful to advise the farmer that the second measurements were within normal limits and there were no 'reactors'. It was a huge relief that the herd had maintained their tuberculosis-free status, and the cows were released into their barn.

Back at the practice there was a festive air when the staff gathered in the office for the mince pie tasting before afternoon consultations got underway. Oli smirked when he caught her eye and she flashed him a glance, wondering if he had cheated after all and helped himself earlier, even though Elaine supposedly had all the entries under lock and key.

The seven different mince pies, each cut into manageable quarters for tasting purposes, went down a storm and everyone cast votes for their favourite in a sealed box Elaine had brought in specially. The results would be announced at the staff party tomorrow and the winner revealed. Nearly all of Erin's mince pies vanished, and she didn't think it was fair to vote for her own, so she chose another homemade batch instead, with perfect sweet short crust pastry and a frangipane topping. Dorothy arrived towards the end, and she whacked a bowl onto the table in the kitchen already scattered with pastry crumbs.

'Couldn't be bothered with mince pies, too finicky,' she declared, giving Oli a disdainful look. He'd been round to treat one of her Soay sheep this week and by all accounts, his anyway, it had gone quite well – he hadn't been banished from her farm at least. She tore off a tinfoil wrapping to reveal a rich, dark fruit cake in a metal tin.

'Is that a dog bowl?' Oli whispered to Erin incredulously, and she tried hard to stifle her laugh. 'It might even be the very one I saw her dogs slurping from the other day.'

'Could be, but who cares? It's obviously been well cooked, and Dorothy's cakes are apparently rare and revered,' she muttered back. Elaine was thanking Dorothy and trying to persuade Jess to nip to the village shop for some cheese to go with it. 'I'd eat it.'

'You might be on your own, not sure I will.'

'Are you going to tell Dorothy you're too scared to eat her cake, then?' Erin watched as Dorothy gave the tin a hefty whack with her palm and the cake flew out to land upside down on the table.

'No, and don't you tell her, either. I've got the perfect excuse not to.' Oli drew his phone from a pocket of his moleskin trousers, and checked it. 'I'll fetch the cheese, Elaine,' he said loudly. 'I've got a parcel to pick up from the shop anyway.'

'Thanks Oli, do you mind?' Elaine sent him a grateful smile. 'Jess has got patients due for a health check any minute.'

Erin saved Oli a slice of fruit cake for later, determined to get him to try it. It tasted amazing with a hunk of local Wensleydale cheese, and she nipped off to check on Marnie before her first afternoon consultation.

On Saturday Oli was on call and he spent it mostly at the practice. Erin was there in the morning too, taking care of Marnie and helping Harriet with the ponies, happy to see Flo brightening with excellent care, food and shelter. Dorothy had been round to clip her, removing the matted and dirty coat and replacing it with a heavyweight rug to keep Flo snug. The blacksmith had also called and trimmed her hooves to a manageable length that no longer caused her pain. Posy wasn't too thrilled with her neighbour and would thump her stable door, demanding to be fed first.

Yesterday Erin had reminded Jason about the party, and he'd said he would meet her there as he had a full day of clients and might arrive at the last minute. She didn't mind too much; she understood what working all hours looked like and wasn't in any position to object seeing as she'd once had to leave a date early when she'd been on call. She could check on Marnie while she was at the party and hopefully on Monday she'd be bringing her home, at least overnight. Until Marnie settled in the cottage, she might have to take her into work during the day and pop her in a kennel, as Gabi and Gil often did with their dogs.

Once Erin was ready she went downstairs and found Oli waiting, standing in front of the fireplace. He tugged his sweater straight to give her the full effect.

'Don't say a word. I've got a long-sleeved T-shirt on underneath in case it gives me a rash.'

'Can I not even say it's totally you?'

Even with the years of separation since university, every detail of his face was still fixed in her memory. The tiny scar below his left brow he'd got falling off his bike and the faint dusting of freckles, brows a shade darker than his hair. The black sweater suited his colouring perfectly, with a grimacing green sprout sporting a set of antlers above rows of white snowflakes alternating with miniature Christmas trees and prancing reindeer.

'Never in my life did I imagine I'd catch you wearing something like that. Are you actually going to keep it on all night?' Erin slipped her coat on. She'd gathered her curls at the nape of her neck into a loose ponytail and she hadn't missed his own stare as he took in her altered appearance. The comfortable work clothes and cosy lounging clothes she usually wore had vanished, and she felt more feminine in her favourite winter skirt, a dark green floral asymmetric one worn with long leather boots, despite her own ugly sweater.

'Isn't that the point? So are you saying I don't look good in it?' Oli raised a brow, and Erin felt the kick in her pulse at his lazy tone.

'You look passable. Like you're going to an office Christmas party.'

'Passable? Wow.' He clutched his heart. His gaze swept down her scarlet jumper to the glittery silver and black Christmas pudding adorned with a gold ribbon across her chest, and her stomach fell away. A tingle darted across her skin, and she was remembering standing before him at the May Ball in her bra above her black pencil skirt, the desire in his eyes. 'Whereas you look…'

'Don't say it,' she warned, finding a scarf to wrap around her neck. 'Either because it's rude or not appropriate for colleagues.'

'Erin, you and I are way more than colleagues,' he said softly, reaching past her to open the front door. 'You know we are.'

He closed it behind them, and they set off to walk to Home Farm. A huge star attached to the top of the church tower was glittering, brightening the sky and the still, cold evening. A merry group spilled from a holiday house opposite the green, heading for the pub. The door opened and Erin heard the cheery seasonal music drawing them in, a reminder of Christmas around the corner.

'So is Jason…'

'How did…'

'Sorry. You first.'

'I was going to ask how the collie is doing, the vomiting one. I saw it came back for a follow up.' She was doing her best to ignore the quiver of anxiety at the thought of Jason being with her tonight. It had been very kind of Gil and Pippa to include partners, but she and Jason were so new, and she hoped he wouldn't bang on about work and his clients all night.

'Yeah, it was fine, and none of the other dogs on the farm have been ill, so it was likely something she ate, as you thought. They've got a three-year-old bitch who's due to whelp in two weeks, so they'd separated her in case she picked anything up.'

'I know the one you mean, I scanned her last month. That's good news.'

168

They strolled past the green and across the bridge towards the church and the school next door, festive decorations outside homes cheerful and welcoming. At the entrance to the practice they swung left halfway up the driveway to the farmhouse instead. It shone from every mullioned window, jolly Christmas lights draped around the huge, studded wooden front door. Oli knocked while Erin was scanning the car park for signs of a dark van.

'I might wait here for Jason.' She folded her arms against the chill. A vehicle was approaching, though she knew from the size it wasn't his.

'Are you sure?' Oli gave her a doubtful look. 'Because it's literally freezing, and we both know you could be a while.'

'Oli, you've met him once!' Frustration with both men spilled into her reply. 'Could you just stop with the judgements, please?'

The door was pulled back and Pippa was there, welcoming them above the music and trying to prevent the dogs swarming all over them. Erin and Oli dropped down to greet Lola and springer spaniel Maud, well used to seeing them in the practice with Gil and Harriet or around the yard. Oli had treats in his pockets and he offered some to both dogs, who gobbled them up.

'Friends for life,' Pippa said fondly, managing to persuade the girls back inside. 'Come in and have a drink to warm you up. I take it you've walked? Gil's mulling cider and he's unearthed his gran's old jam pan so we've got bucket loads.'

'After you,' Oli said smoothly to Erin, and she shot him a filthy look as she followed Pippa, unwilling to miss her own staff party because the man she was dating hadn't seen fit to arrive on time.

Chapter Fourteen

Erin had been in the house before, but she usually entered through the back door via the garden. Woodwork in the hall was dull and every door was white with metal handles, not the more original and natural style she'd been expecting. Wallpaper decorated with over-sized green flowers appeared very 1970s and stairs turned halfway to the first floor, a huge Christmas tree shimmering on the landing in front of an arched window.

She glimpsed a sitting room on the left, another door into the dining room opposite. At the far end of the hall she spied Jess in the kitchen, sparkling and gorgeous in scarlet palazzo pants and a black jumper emblazoned with a silver Christmas tree, heels adding to her natural height. She caught Erin's eye and waved as Gil emerged from the dining room, bottle in hand.

'Erin, Oli, welcome. So happy you're both here.'

'Thank you.' Erin gave her boss a grin. 'Love the sweater.'

'Cheers.' Gil held up his bottle in mock salute. His sweater was black, with rows of tiny Christmas puddings and festive lights framing an image of Homer Simpson clutching a drink and declaring it was the most wonderful time of the year for a beer. 'Harriet looked like that too when she saw it, and wondered if it had been made with me in mind. Pippa chose it, and it seemed right to acknowledge a universal truth, as the saying goes.'

'It was either that or the Grinch, and in the end I went for the beer.' Pippa was smiling up at him, and he slid an arm around her waist to draw her close.

'You know me so well.' He dropped a kiss on the top of her head and tilted his bottle. 'This is non-alcoholic though, in case I get called out.'

Erin and Oli shrugged out of their layers and Pippa draped their coats from a suit of armour beside the staircase. She caught Erin's eye and laughed. 'It didn't make the cut when we cleared the house, Gil's strangely attached to it. We haven't done much else in here yet, apart from take up the carpets. Thankfully, we've had planning permission granted for the extension now, but we won't be starting before spring. Gil's got news to share about that. Let's get you both a drink, as usual everyone's crammed in the kitchen and Alfie's managed to squeeze his decks in there as well. He was thrilled when Gil asked him to do the music.'

'Where's Jason? On his way?' Gil was looking at Erin and she cringed, aware of Oli watching on. She hated having to make excuses for her date already.

'He's running late, he's with a client. He sends his apologies, I know he's looking forward to seeing everyone.' He hadn't sounded sorry at all, but she really didn't want Gil thinking badly of him as well. It was enough to know that Oli didn't approve. 'It's very good of you to include partners. Not that we're partners or anything,' she went on hastily. 'We're just dating.'

Inviting Jason and exposing herself to the excuses required to explain away his lateness was her own fault. She loved not having to balance her hours or commitment to her career against a partner's demands, but for once she hadn't wanted a space at her side. If she was honest she'd also wanted to make Oli aware she had moved on, in every sense. But tonight was already an uncomfortable reminder that he, who represented so much of her past, had been the only person she'd ever imagined in her future.

'So no Raf, then?' She'd heard that Pippa's brother might be here tonight and squirmed. She'd been hoping to change the subject away from Jason, but her clumsy question made her sound more like a desperate superfan. Raf had a reputation as a charmer and she'd seen him drumming online with Jonny's band and thought he was brilliant, as well as gorgeous. She'd never met a rock star before and wouldn't mind the chance if one came her way. It wasn't a bit of a crush on Raf, though. Definitely not.

'Yes, he's actually made it for once.'

'Oh wow!' Erin swiftly decided she'd better be careful what she wished for. She tugged at her sweater and tucked a loose curl behind her ear; she wouldn't normally have chosen to display a Christmas pudding across her chest to meet a bone fide rock star.

Oli was chatting with Gil, and Pippa pointed to the kitchen so Erin could go first. 'Just for the weekend, before he and my friend Cassie take her children to Lapland, then he's heading to Australia for Christmas. My dad's bought a place out there and he's planning a big family gathering.'

'That sounds lovely,' Erin said wistfully. Much as she adored the Dales and couldn't imagine living anywhere but Yorkshire, the thought of some proper sunshine in winter was very appealing.

In the kitchen she spotted Raf behind the decks with Alfie and Harriet. He looked up and caught her eye, offering a lazy grin that made her cheeks flame with colour. In the flesh he was even taller, his short nut-brown hair streaked with blond, and he was the only person not wearing a sweater. Erin doubted there existed one ugly enough to detract from his looks and a charisma that seemed to carry right across the room to her pink face. Harriet was sharing a set of headphones with Alfie, her dark hair a sharp contrast to his white-blond mop, and laughing at something on his phone.

Gil and Pippa had recently knocked through into the pantry to give them more space until the new kitchen and family room were built across the back of the house. Through a mullioned window onto the terrace Erin glimpsed a hot tub, covered for now. Maud and Lola were ignoring their beds to mingle amongst guests they knew well, accepting cuddles and hoping for more treats.

'Drink, you two? Mulled cider, wine, beer, or something soft?' Gil was alongside her and Oli.

'The cider would be perfect, thanks.' They accepted glasses from Gil a few moments later, and were soon caught up in the introductions. Jess was here with Noah, and Erin's discomfort returned when she had to refute Gabi's wife Michelle's assumption that Jason was also a vet and had been called to an emergency to explain his absence.

Steph's husband was a builder, and he and Gil were soon deep in conversation as Steph chatted with Elaine, who had come on her own. Erin would be loving every minute if she wasn't feeling quite so publicly stood up. Even the festive music and Gil's expression when Alfie played 'Last Christmas' weren't managing to distract her completely. Oli had been drawn into conversation with Jess and Noah, and Erin's dismay was rising at Jason's lack of courtesy. She pulled her phone from her handbag to check it, not even certain he'd let her know if he wasn't going to turn up at all.

'So you must be the brilliant new vet I've heard so much about.'

Erin's head whipped round, and she found herself staring up into wicked brown eyes, which seemed to be smiling at her as much as Raf himself was. Her mouth had gone dry, and she didn't need a mirror to know she was blushing like a teenager again.

'I'm Raf, Pippa's brother.'

'I know who you are.' She gulped a mouthful of cider to distract herself from that gaze. 'Doesn't everyone?'

'I guess, but it doesn't hurt not to assume.' Raf had to hunch to drop the words in her ear over the din. 'You're Erin, right?'

'Oh!' In what world did a rock star drummer know who she was? She really hoped her face wasn't giving away that in some of the videos she'd seen of Raf he'd been drumming topless, messy hair wild, his body glistening with sweat. She didn't often listen to rock music, but she was as appreciative of his talents as much as the next person.

'All good, I promise.' He leaned against the wall; Erin hadn't imagined he'd want to linger. 'Gil thinks you're brilliant.'

'That's very nice of him,' she said loyally. 'It works both ways. I'm so grateful to be here.'

'And the boyfriend?' Raf's gaze flickered across the kitchen to Oli. 'What does he do?'

'Oh, Oli's not my boyfriend,' she rushed out, following Raf's gaze and wanting to be clear. 'He's our locum, he's just working with us until Christmas.'

'Right.' Raf let the syllables on that word linger and his eyes narrowed. 'But you arrived together, and there's obviously something.'

'Something?' What could he possibly know about her and Oli? There was nothing to know, she'd been very careful at work to make sure of it. 'He's staying with me, that's all. We were friends at university. On the same course. Just friends. My boyfriend's not here yet, he's running late. He's on his way. Although we're just dating, he's not really my boyfriend. Jason. That's his name.' She snapped her mouth shut, aware she was massively over-sharing in front of the most gorgeous man she'd ever met.

'I hear ya. Just friends. And for the record, Erin, if I were Jason I'd have more sense than to stand you up.' Raf winked, straightening up as Pippa approached. 'Hey, sis.'

'I hope Raf's behaving himself,' Pippa said to Erin, who nodded hastily, her cheeks still burning. As if he'd ever misbehave with her – and she wouldn't want him to anyway. Well, not much, and a girl could dream.

'The food's ready, we've piled everything in the dining room away from the dogs so you can help yourselves. The caterers have been wonderful, I couldn't face cooking for us all in that prehistoric oven.'

'Thanks, Pippa.' Erin wasn't expecting Raf to walk beside her into the dining room and everyone soon followed, tucking into gammon roasted with cider, apples and celery, perfectly crisp roast potatoes and red cabbage braised with blackberries. Dessert was an indulgent and utterly delicious chocolate orange trifle, thick Baileys custard layered over orange and dark chocolate and smothered in a generous cream topping. Most people drifted back to the kitchen to eat, and when they were done, Gil called for quiet once Alfie had turned down the music.

'Thanks everyone. I'm not going to drone on like the office bore but I have got a couple of official duties to perform and something to share with you. So firstly, we'll announce the winner of the mince pie tasting competition.'

Elaine handed Gil an envelope. 'It's like the Oscars, only more secretive. Thanks, Elaine.' He tore open the envelope and grinned. 'Okay, so the winner is… Entry number five.'

Everybody was looking at everyone else and Erin beamed as she stepped forward. Joyce's recipes never let her down. 'That's me. It's my nan's recipe, with her homemade mincemeat.'

'Well, it worked. You and your nan came out on top, it seems everyone loves a traditional mince pie. Congratulations.'

'Thank you. And thanks for voting for them, my nan will be chuffed.'

'Elaine did ask me to sort out a prize and I forgot, so see me on Monday and I'll arrange something.' Gil put the envelope down. 'Anytime you feel like making them again, we won't say no.'

'I'd love to.' It would be a good excuse to bake again before Christmas. Joyce had promised Erin a small cake of her own, seeing as she wouldn't be around to share theirs.

'So now, Secret Santa.' He rattled a bowl with folded up pieces of paper inside. 'If everyone can take one, and obviously please don't share who you've picked. The budget is ten pounds max, and we'll exchange gifts on the twenty-third.'

The staff helped themselves and Erin unwrapped hers. She slipped it in her bag, happy with her choice.

'Great, that's sorted.' Gil held out a hand to Pippa; she made her way to his side and he slid an arm around her. 'And I want to say thank you, to each and every one of you. It's been a challenging year for sure, but we've already come a long way since taking on the practice in the summer. We're a great team and I couldn't be happier to be working alongside you all. And even though he's not here I must thank Jonny too, because without his generosity in remembering my dad and giving me a chance to keep the farm and grow the practice, none of us would be here.'

'Hear, hear,' Elaine called, and there was a lull as everyone raised their glasses to Pippa's dad.

'But.' Gil was looking at Pippa, and she reached up to kiss his cheek. 'None of this would have happened if I hadn't met Pippa, and much as I want to keep the practice going, I couldn't do it without this incredible woman at my side. I still can't believe she's taken me on and maybe one day I'll deserve the faith and trust she's put in me.' He offered a toast to Pippa, and she laughed as the glasses were raised again, and he kissed her.

'So that brings me to our news.' He ran a triumphant gaze over the staff. 'We heard yesterday that we've been granted planning permission to redevelop the barns and extend the practice. To say I'm delighted is an understatement, and I'm very much looking forward to building a future here with you all. It's going to bring a lot of new challenges, but I hope you'll meet them with me, and we'll work together to keep the practice here in Hartfell. So here's to us, Home Farm Vets, and the future.'

'Yay,' Jess yelled, and everyone laughed as Gil raised his glass again.

'Home Farm Vets,' they chorused, raising their own glasses.

Erin's three-month review was due, and she really hoped it would be a formality. The practice was adapting as it grew and she wanted to be at the heart of it, to fix her future to Hartfell. Her eyes sought Oli, talking with Elaine, and she was sharply reminded that they might never work together again once he'd gone. He was already becoming a part of this place, had slotted so well into the team. And yet he was leaving in less than two weeks, moving on to somewhere new, never standing still. She was scared of admitting, even to herself, that she was already wondering how her life would look when he was no longer in it. She checked her phone, a wave of despair following to see no more from Jason.

'Dancing. You promised.'

Erin started as Jess grabbed her hand, jolted from her uncomfortable thoughts. 'Jess, there's barely room to swing a cat!'

'Don't care. This is the only staff party I'm going to get this year and we're dancing.'

Erin abandoned her glass, happy to be distracted from her humiliation by a Cher Christmas party track and soon she and Jess weren't alone. Raf was on the decks with Harriet, and he grinned when he caught Erin's eye. Three glasses of mulled cider and several tracks later, she was dancing like no one was watching and it felt so good to release some of the tension she'd been unconsciously carrying all evening.

She leaned towards Jess to shout over the music. 'I'm going to check on Marnie.'

Outside the night was bitter as she crossed the court-yard and she shivered, wishing she'd thought to put her coat on. Apart from the embarrassment of Jason standing her up, she was having a wonderful time. It was his lack of courtesy she minded the most, but then what could she seriously expect, given that everything so far between them had been pretty casual.

The practice was eerily dark, and she switched on a light in reception after letting herself in. Marnie, still in her isolation kennel, seemed happy to see her and Erin was busy chatting to her as she topped up the water bowl and offered her some food.

'Are you okay?'

Erin shrieked, and the packet of food she'd been holding splattered on the floor. She spun around to find Oli leaning against the open door, and dragged in a breath.

'Sorry, I didn't mean to make you jump.'

'What are you doing here?'

'I just came to see if you and Marnie are okay.'

'I'm fine.' She grabbed a paper towel to wipe up the mess. 'Thanks for asking. Marnie's doing well, I definitely think she can come home on Monday.'

'That's great.' Oli joined her and he reached into the kennel to stroke the kitten, smiling at her quiet purr. 'So your boyfriend never made it?'

'Thanks for pointing out the obvious. And he's not my boyfriend. You just don't like him because he's a joiner.' She was busy wiping and part of her knew it wasn't fair to take out her frustration on Oli.

'Come on, Erin, you know me better than that. I don't dislike him because he's a joiner but because he's jerk who treats you with zero respect. If you really want to share your life with someone who'll celebrate and support you, then don't settle for a guy like him. One whose back will be turned the moment you really need him.'

'You don't know that!'

'Yeah, I do, and underneath you do too, because you're the smartest person I've ever met. Let me guess how it went when you met him. He tossed his drink over you, you shrugged it off and said it didn't matter. But because you weren't really interested, Jason wasn't having that. No, he told you he had to make it up to you and wore you down until you said yes. Because maybe you're getting tired of being alone and thought dating him was better than not seeing anyone.

'He doesn't give a shit about university and why should he, because he never went. But he should care that you did, because it matters to you, and it was six of the most important years of your life. That you're one of the few who made it into Cambridge and graduated with a First, one of the very best in our year. Is Jason going to say to anyone who'll listen, hey, look at this woman and everything she's achieved and how far she's come. She's amazing and I get to stand beside her and remind her every day how awesome she is.'

Oli thrust an arm in the air as his tone became sharper. 'Is he going to be there when you crawl into bed exhausted at midnight after you've delivered a dead calf or run out on him because a dog's been hit by a car and you're the vet on call? No, because in his world he's top dog, and you suit him perfectly because you allow him to think it. You don't make any demands and you're not some hot twenty-two-year-old he daren't let out of his sight for fear another guy will jump in front of him.'

'I can't believe you said that! How dare you?' It was way too close to the truth, but Erin was different now from the girl who'd fallen in love with Oli at Catz. Never again would she allow herself to fall for someone so completely that she almost lost sight of herself and the life she'd worked for. Hot tears were stinging her eyes, and she swiped a hand at her face.

'Because it's true. And don't think for one second that I don't think you're amazing or beautiful, because I do.' Oli went to take her hand and she almost jumped aside; she couldn't let him touch her now and blur her thoughts still more. 'I always have. Right from the day we met.'

'Don't say that! You can't say those words to me, not now.'

'But they're true, and I can't change that.' His voice cracked, and he pressed a hand to his temple. 'I knew it the moment I saw you again.'

'It's too late, Oli. You don't get to tell me who I should date or how to live my life,' she whispered brokenly.

'I just don't want to see you hurt or humiliated by someone who doesn't deserve you.'

'And you didn't humiliate me? When you were on holiday in France with Bella crawling all over you?'

'I've apologised for that, and I swear nothing happened. I made a mistake in letting her get close and I'll always be sorry for how that made you feel and breaking your trust in me.' This time Oli took her hand, and she was staring at their joined fingers, the reality of him once again within reach. 'I can't help that I still care, Erin. And if you can tell me honestly you don't feel the same, then I'll walk away and you don't have to hear from me again.'

He let go of her hand and turned, his footsteps fading as she leaned against the wall, swallowing back the tears. Both for the truths he'd shared about Jason and the fear that Oli understood how she felt about him too. But what could she do about that, when her life was here and Hart-fell was a stopping-off point for him, another interlude before he moved on? She turned to Marnie, thankful for the kitten content in her bed; she had more love in her life now, and maybe this was all she needed.

Back at the party and keen to avoid Oli, she slid into the dining room and helped herself to one of Violet's mince pies, baked for this evening. It was perfect and she was dusting crumbs from her sweater when Raf found her.

'Hey. So I take it the boyfriend slash non-boyfriend hasn't shown up.'

'No.' Erin hurriedly checked for more crumbs; being covered in bits of pastry wasn't a good look for chatting with a rock star, but then neither was the giant Christmas pudding. At least it didn't light up, and she already felt cheered by his company. 'Maybe he's had a better offer.'

'With you here? Doubt it, the guy sounds like a jerk. Manners cost nothing.'

That made Erin laugh despite her frustration: how many more people tonight were going to refer to Jason that way? She bet Jess would oblige, and she appreciated the compliment from Raf.

'You want to have a little fun?' He strolled across and halted front of her. 'Lend me your phone.'

'What! Why?' She unlocked it and held it out anyway, and he took it. He really was hot, and if she weren't upset with Jason and confused over Oli, then she might… She hastily shook that thought away – Raf was her boss's brother-in-law, good as. 'What are you doing!'

'Sending him a message.' Raf tugged her close and slid an arm around her shoulders. He turned the camera into selfie mode and began recording, his smile that famously wicked one she'd only ever seen online before tonight.

'Hey, Jase, it's Raf Jones. Sorry you had to miss Erin's party, but I thought you'd like to know I'm taking good care of her.' He turned the phone to the noise in the kitchen, the guests spilling into the sitting room, and back to them again. 'Hope you're having a great night too. And don't worry, I'll make sure she gets home safely.' He winked into the camera before turning it off, and Erin was lost for words.

'Oh, you're good,' she managed eventually. 'He hates being called Jase.'

'Then my work here is done,' Raf announced, dropping a kiss on the top of her head. 'Let's see what he makes of that.'

'We're just dating, it's not really anything, so it doesn't matter. I should probably never have invited him tonight.'

'Because your heart is otherwise involved?' He grinned and held up a hand. 'It's okay, you don't have to say anything. I know what it's like. So I guess Oli will see you home?'

'I suppose so, seeing as he's staying there.' That thought shouldn't be warming her as much as it was.

'Merry Christmas, Erin. You ever fancy a gig sometime, let me know.' At the door Raf turned and his grin was a mischievous one. 'Pippa'll give you my number.'

Chapter Fifteen

Oli was on call the next day and Erin heard him leave around seven. She was finding it impossible to escape his words at the party and the admission that he still cared about her. He'd promised to check on Marnie and Erin wasn't cooking the usual lunch as Heather was catching up with an online training course. Edmund was also absent, visiting a friend in London, so she had a rare day to herself. Even though she was looking forward to celebrating Christmas in her own home, she was finding it strange to be preparing without her family, sharing in the festivities together.

She was on the floor, sorting through the decorations her mum had brought, trying to untangle a fragile paper garland they'd made years ago. She'd already decided it wasn't a good idea to have decorations everywhere with a new kitten, so she was going to restrict herself to a few little touches here and there.

A knock came at the front door and she glanced up, wondering if Oli had forgotten his keys in his haste earlier. The last thing she expected to see when she opened it was a young woman waiting, a green beanie covering some of her gorgeous fox-red hair above a black puffer jacket and skinny jeans tucked into leather boots. She looked vaguely familiar, but Erin couldn't place her.

'Hi, I'm really sorry to bother you.' Her smile reached lovely hazel eyes too, framed by long lashes, and Erin was reminded of the girls who used to hang around Oli at Catz. This one had that same natural confidence and elegance, the sleek and glossy hair, perfectly applied make-up on her heart-shaped face. 'I hope I've got the right address, I'm looking for Oli. I'm Imogen, his sister.'

'Oh! Right.' Now Erin understood why she looked so familiar and felt a little self-conscious in her work clothes. Her hoodie was still sporting dog hair from a consultation with a St Bernard on Friday, and she was saving her shower until she'd finished with the decorations. 'He's out on a call, I'm not sure how long he'll be. Is he expecting you?'

'No, I thought I'd surprise him. I've got some news to share, but I'll find somewhere to wait until he's back.' She turned a shoulder to a dark SUV in the lane.

'Would you like to come in?' Erin stepped back, holding the door wide. 'There's a pub just up the road but it's not open until twelve and there isn't a cafe for miles.'

'That's very kind, thank you.' Imogen's curious gaze went to the sitting room and the jumble of decorations spilling from the box, the cheerful fire burning in the stove. 'Are you sure you don't mind? You're not too busy?'

'I was just sorting through some old decorations, it's fine.'

Erin closed the door, and she was doing it again, viewing the cottage through Imogen's eyes: the shabby chintz sofa and chair, and tired dining table and chairs parked in front of the window.

'Your home is beautiful, so cosy.'

'Thank you. I love it but there's still a lot I'd like to do.' Erin pointed to the sofa, swiping away stray dog hairs. No matter how much she brushed her clothes and cleaned, a few always made it home with her.

'It's so romantic and cute, it reminds me of the cottage in *The Holiday*. I love that movie.' Imogen slipped off her jacket and the beanie, draping them on the arm of the sofa.

'Me too. I watch it every year.' They shared an understanding smile before Erin edged towards the kitchen. 'Can I get you some tea, or a coffee?' Putting the kettle on was a given in any situation and her nan always said there wasn't much a proper brew couldn't fix. 'I don't really drink it, but Oli has a machine.'

'So I see. He takes it pretty much everywhere; my brother can't get by without coffee. And I'd love one, thanks. It's been a long drive. I stayed with friends in Manchester last night, so I haven't had to do it all in one go.'

'Where have you come from?' Erin switched the machine on and picked up the espresso cup she'd given Oli with its cute Christmas animals. It lived permanently on the draining board with her favourite mug; they never made it back into the cupboard because they were used so often.

'Marlborough, my partner and I have just bought a house there.' Imogen had got up to hover on the edge of the kitchen. 'I have to be back for work tomorrow, so I can't stay too long. I'm sorry, I don't know your name. Oli hasn't told me much about where he's staying, other than the address.'

'Oh sorry, it's Erin. I work at the same practice with Oli and he's lodging with me whilst he's here.' She was filling the kettle and her head snapped round when she heard Imogen's gasp.

'I'm sorry, did you say Erin?' Imogen's eyes were still wide. 'You weren't *the* Erin with Oli at Catz, by any chance?'

'Oli and I were in the same year, yes.' Erin switched the kettle on and reached for her mug.

'Bloody hell.' Imogen huffed out a laugh. 'No wonder he was so cagey about this job.'

'He won't be here for long, he's leaving on the twenty-third. He mentioned about you hosting a family Christmas.'

'I don't think that's why he's kept it quiet.' Imogen drew her long hair across one shoulder. 'That first year at Catz, whenever he came home he talked about almost no one else but you. He never actually said so, but it was obvious he was crazy about you. Mum always said she'd loved to have met you because anyone who could make Oli light up like that must have been very special.'

The mug in Erin's hand slid into the sink, splattering water up the tiles. She wasn't expecting to feel such profound sorrow at so simple a remark and that she'd never met the mum he loved. And guilt too, because she'd blocked him from her life and hadn't been there to support him when his mum had passed away so suddenly.

She'd made herself believe that his feelings mattered less because they came from different worlds, with very different backgrounds. But Oli had been right when he'd said that underneath they wanted the same things; love, home, security, support, and she'd denied him those because her courage didn't extend to offering her heart. She'd judged him by her mum's experience of marriage and her own expectations, and she'd let him down. Erin was gripping the sink, Imogen's words coming to her in a blur as she hurried to stand alongside her.

'Erin, are you all right? I'm sorry, I didn't mean to shock you.'

'I'm fine, thank you,' she muttered. Once again her past was colliding with the present and threatening to unbalance her carefully planned future. 'I'm sorry I never met your mum. I wish I had.'

'You didn't know, about how Oli felt…' Imogen's voice drifted away.

'Not for certain, not until recently. It was kind of always there, but then…' She wasn't sure how much Imogen knew about the summer after the May Ball.

'So you're the reason he took this job, other than the usual one, of course.'

'I don't think so. Oli didn't know I was here or that we'd be working at the same practice.' Erin took a deep breath, drying the mug and sliding a capsule into the coffee machine as Imogen stepped back. 'There was a change of plan, and I only found out he was coming a couple of days before he arrived.' Only the truth would do now, and she hoped Imogen would understand it was opportunity that had brought him to her door, not a deliberate choice. 'What did you mean, Imogen, when you said other than the usual reason?'

'Being a locum suits Oli because he can make the travelling all about his career, that he has to go where the work takes him. But actually I think he travels for a very different reason. Thanks.' Imogen accepted her coffee, smiling at the image on the cup. 'Ever since Mum died I've always had the impression he's scared of staying in one place too long, because he doesn't really know what home looks like for him, so his job gives him the perfect excuse to keep moving. He has a tiny flat, but that's just a space where he leaves his stuff, it's not a home.' Her gaze ran over the small kitchen, the boots he'd left beside the back door, the coffee machine on the worktop, a navy scarf slung over the newel post. 'Not like this one.'

Oli's life was beginning to make sense now, and Erin saw it clearly, the details finally falling into place. The front door flew open and both women started as he burst through it, a Christmas tree in a net clutched awkwardly in his arms.

'Shit, it's freezing out there, I seriously need a brew to warm me up. I thought I might never feel my feet again after that barn, but the calf was alive, so it was worth it. Brought you this, thought it might go in a pot as we can't have one inside with Marnie here.' He dumped the Christmas tree against the wall and tugged his hat off. 'Call it my contribution to Christmas, although I'm quite glad we're not actually living in a holiday movie set after all, thanks to Marnie… Imogen? What the hell are you doing here?'

'Hello, bro,' she said wryly, flashing Erin a glance before she crossed to Oli, holding out her arms. 'It's been a while. Gonna give your big sister a hug?'

'Of course.' Oli unzipped his coat and Erin watched them embrace. She finished making her tea and slid another capsule into the coffee machine.

'Like the beard.' Imogen pulled back to look at him, her hands still on his arms. 'It suits you.'

'Cheers. So what brings you all the way up here? Is everything all right with you and Alex?' Oli settled on the sofa and Imogen perched beside him. He thanked Erin distractedly when she brought another coffee through.

'More than all right, actually,' Imogen smiled and held out her left hand. Erin saw the stunning diamond and platinum engagement ring sparkling on her third finger.

'That's why I'm here. Alex proposed last week and obviously I said yes. He's sorry he can't be here too, but he had a golfing weekend in Portugal arranged and I really wanted to tell you myself before you saw it somewhere.'

'That's brilliant news, congratulations!' Oli shuffled forward until she was in his arms again and he hugged her tightly. 'I'm so thrilled for you both, it's wonderful.' He slid back and his grin eased into a wistful smile. 'Mum would be so excited.'

'Yeah, she would. She'd have been online already, looking at dresses and making appointments for me to try them. She always did love a good wedding.' Imogen glanced down at her ring and sniffed, finding a tissue in her handbag.

'Congratulations, Imogen.' Erin wasn't quite sure what else to say to someone she'd only just met.

'Thanks, Erin, that's very kind. We're elated. I sort of knew it was coming one day but I had no idea Alex had already planned it. It was wonderful, and his mum is so supportive.' Imogen looked at Oli. 'So that's partly why I'm here. Alex's family are hosting a Christmas party on Saturday, and they've very generously offered to turn it into an engagement one for us. Obviously, we'd like everyone we love to be there and that includes you, so...'

She paused, her tone suddenly pleading. 'And yes, before you say it, of course Dad and Christina will be there. He'll be giving me away at the wedding, Oli, and he's part of this. I want him to share it, especially as we can't include Mum.'

'I'll leave you alone to talk.' Erin leaped up; she really didn't want to be in the way of brother and sister and what sounded like a deeply personal conversation.

'No, Erin, please don't go.' Imogen turned a beseeching glance on her. 'I think you should hear this.'

'But it doesn't concern me.'

'Actually, I think it does. More than you probably realise.'

'If Oli doesn't mind…' This time Erin would stay if he wanted her to, and he nodded faintly. She retook her seat, twisting her fingers together as Imogen continued.

'I know it's very close to Christmas and you're busy here, but please come, we really want you to share it with us too.'

'Imogen…'

'No, Oli, no more excuses! I know things between you and Dad have been difficult since Mum died, and you blame him for having an affair and splitting up our family. But he's sorry, he's always been sorry about how things ended between them, and I don't want mine and Alex's wedding turning into a battlefield between you both. He'll be with us at Christmas too and this is our chance for a fresh start, as a proper family, if you want it to be.' Imogen's voice fell. 'Mum would be devastated to see you always on your own, never standing still long enough to let someone love you.'

Oli dropped his head into his hands and Erin knew the time for pretence was over. She crossed the room and knelt before him. Maybe it wasn't her place, maybe it should be his sister, but she wrapped her arms around him and pulled him against her. The last time she'd been in his arms they'd been sharing a goodbye kiss before he went on holiday to France. This was different, and she wanted him to know she was here, that he could lean on her if he chose, and she felt him begin to relax as he clung on.

'I'm really sorry if I've upset you.' Imogen stood and put the empty espresso cup on the floor. She placed a hand on his shoulder, squeezing it gently. 'The invitation is for two so of course we'd love to see you there as well, Erin. Thank you for looking after Oli and welcoming me into your home. I had thought we could have lunch before I go, Oli, but maybe it's best if I leave you two to talk. I hope we'll see you both on Saturday.'

The front door closed behind her, and Erin eased away from Oli. He raised his head to stare at her with bruised and troubled eyes weighted with sadness. 'Sorry. I thought I was over all that stuff with my dad, then one word from Imogen and…' He huffed out a laugh without humour as he dragged both hands over his face.

'Please don't be sorry, I hope it's helped.' She stood up, intending to gather their empty cups, but he caught her hand and tugged her onto the sofa beside him. The cottage was tiny and yet they'd found a way to make it work, had eased into a rhythm, living together even though she was only too aware it wasn't in all the ways she wanted.

'You know what it was like, because your dad left you too.'

'Yes.' Erin's fingers were stroking his. 'It was different for me though, because he never came back. There was a time when I would've wanted that, but then it was too late. He made himself irrelevant to us and our lives. Oli, I'm sorry I assumed life was pretty perfect for you and I was the one who'd had it tough. And I didn't really, apart from my mum's health and the worry. My family is everything, and we're always there for each other.'

'I think my dad would be there for me too, if I let him. But part of me is scared of forgiving him for what he did because then maybe it's not supposed to matter anymore, that it didn't hurt that much after all.'

'Maybe there comes a point when you have to find a way to forgive, because in the end it's also about how you live your own life. How much of that hurt you can let go of and how much you still carry with you.'

'How are you so wise?' Oli touched his forehead to hers. He was so close, and she'd only need to lean forward an inch or two to find his lips with her own.

'I think I was born that way.' They smiled and she eased back, trying to loosen the moment without shattering it completely. 'Thank you for the Christmas tree. I think it's a perfect size for a pot.'

'You're welcome. Do I get to help you decorate it?'

'What, string a few lights around that,' she quipped, and he grinned. 'It'll take us about five minutes.'

'I don't care,' he said softly. 'I'd still like to decorate it with you. I'll even make us hot chocolate.'

'Decorate the tree even though you won't be here for Christmas?'

'Yes, even though I won't be here for Christmas.' He paused, his words a breath against her cheek, landing like kisses on her skin, his mouth still tantalisingly close to hers. 'We really messed up at Catz, didn't we? So many missed opportunities.'

'Yes. We were so young,' she whispered back. His words from last night were in her mind again, etched on her heart too. That he still cared, and she knew it was the same for her. 'I was scared of admitting I'd fallen in love with you. Scared of trusting you.'

'I was frightened too,' he admitted. 'Worried that if my dad didn't love me enough to stay then why would anyone else?'

'Oli.' Erin's breath caught and she placed a hand either side of his face, the beard gentle and rough all at once against her palms. 'Never think that, because it's not true. Not for you. Your dad loves you. Mine didn't, and I won't let that define my life forever.' She was thinking of Imogen and Alex's party and Oli being there alone, not having a partner to stand alongside him and hold his hand when he needed it.

'I can't promise, not until I've cleared it with Gil, and then there's Marnie to consider,' she said quietly. 'But would you like me to drive you down to Marlborough on Saturday?'

Chapter Sixteen

Monday was hugely exciting because Marnie came home, and Erin wasn't sure how she'd ever thought Bramble Cottage had been complete without her. She'd nipped into town early and bought everything she needed, including the cosiest bed she could find, a soft nest of cream fur that she hoped Marnie would find comforting. It still chilled her to think of the kitten huddled beside a ditch, starving and sick with no one to care for her until Dorothy came along. Erin had no idea how she'd settle, having spent those first weeks of her life living with a feral mum. Marnie would be coming into the practice for now, until she gradually got used to Erin leaving her at home alone.

Oli arrived home soon after Erin and they were both distracted by Marnie, taking turns to sit beside her bed on the sofa. She was wary and unsettled after the change in routine, and still weak, but Erin was heartened that she ate a small feed and went to her litter tray afterwards. However much she wanted Marnie to understand the cottage was home now, and she'd be loved and cared for, it was a huge change in her circumstances. Busy serving chicken arrabbiata from the slow cooker, she was also watching Oli with Marnie and trying not to like the sight too much. The kitten was soon tired, and she curled in her bed as they ate on their knees.

'So I spoke with Gil,' Erin said casually. 'And he said it's fine for me to take the weekend off.'

'You're sure?' Oli shifted to look at her. 'Because I know how you feel about personal relationships at work, and when this gets out – and it will – everyone's going to wonder about you and me.'

'You don't want me to come?' She tried to quash a flare of panic before it took hold. Had he changed his mind, didn't want her there?

'What? No, of course I do. I want you to be there with me, as long as you want the same thing.'

'I want to be there, Oli, to support you,' she told him softly. 'We'll deal with work when we have to, and anyway, there's nothing to tell. We're just friends and I'm your plus-one for a party.'

He found her hand but stopped short of threading his fingers between hers. Gradually the barriers between them were being diminished and Erin was aware she'd broken another one down when she'd offered to accompany him to his sister's engagement celebration. Revealing their plan to Jess was trickier, as Erin also had to ask her friend if she'd mind taking care of Marnie for the weekend. Jess agreed at once and alongside a knowing wink, told Erin she hoped they had a brilliant time.

Last night Jason had sent her an apology after Raf's video message, but Erin knew it didn't matter anymore. In her reply she'd suggested they call it a day as they both had different priorities and there seemed little point in continuing. He'd responded a few hours later, informing her there were no hard feelings and to give him a call if she changed her mind.

She'd read the message twice, wondering how she had ever thought he might be someone with whom she could envisage any kind of future. There was no shared life to divide, no real sense of an ending. They'd made no plans for the holidays together, no cosy nights in front of the fire and a festive movie, or wintery walks around Christmas markets. She also felt a little untethered around Oli without Jason's presence in the background, as though she needed him there to help keep her feelings about Oli in check.

Already this was Oli's last week, with just another ten days until Christmas. As the weekend approached, she and Oli kept an eye on Marnie at work, depending on which of them was in the practice or out on calls. At home they took turns to feed and play with her; she was becoming used to being handled, and once she'd sat on Erin's lap and purred contentedly. He was endlessly kind and patient, emptying the litter tray if he was first down in the mornings and feeding her. He seemed to find as much pleasure in Marnie's company as Erin did, and on Thursday evening she'd gulped back tears when she'd come downstairs and found him sprawled on the sofa asleep with Marnie curled on his chest.

It hadn't taken long to decorate the little Christmas tree in its pot outside the front door, but they'd done it together, and it was a cheerful reminder of the season every time she came home. She'd reluctantly cancelled the festive movie night with Jess as having a houseful of guests might be too much for Marnie right now.

On Saturday, she was surprised at how difficult it was to leave Marnie with Jess, who was staying overnight in the cottage so as not to disrupt the kitten's routine too much. As a third-year nurse well on her way to being fully qualified, Erin had absolutely no qualms about Jess, but it was still hard, to close the door and get into the pickup.

Jess had hugged them both, told them not to rush back tomorrow.

For Erin, making the offer to accompany Oli to the party had been an instinctive one when he'd been feeling vulnerable and unsettled, and she hadn't needed to think twice. But sitting beside him as they set out for Imogen and Alex's house on a grey and sludgy day, it felt very different and also familiar. They'd come a long way since they'd shared a long journey that first Michaelmas term at Catz. They'd graduated university and were members of the Royal College of Veterinary Surgeons, had survived the pressure of exams and those early years in practice when theory had threatened to vanish when presented with the sudden realities of the swift and tough decisions they had to make.

She cast a sidelong glance at Oli as she drove, and her stomach dropped with a longing she'd been trying for days to deny. Since Imogen's visit and Erin's break up with Jason, there had been a subtle shift in their relationship, as though they were both afraid to ignite a flame that might never burn out. She was beginning to dread him leaving in just three days, when she would wake each morning in the cottage without him, and once again their lives would lead them along different paths.

They grabbed a quick lunch from the services and set off again, and once they'd left the motorway it was still another forty-five minutes to the house. Imogen and Alex lived a few miles south of the town in a new-build they'd moved into three months ago. Erin glanced at the sat nav and her nerves fluttered again. She knew Oli had messaged his sister to let her know Erin was coming, but she had no idea what his family would make of her being at his side for such a personal and special event.

'So has Imogen said anything about the house, what it's like?' She glanced at Oli again; that familiar profile, the hair swept back from his face and the scattering of freckles over his skin. She liked the growing beard and thought it suited him, and when she'd teased him about it the other day, they'd both fallen silent when he'd laughingly informed her it wasn't coming off until he was living somewhere warmer.

'Not much. Just that they love it and it's small. Probably still cost a fortune down here.'

'How did she and Alex meet? I know Imogen's an architect, you mentioned that.'

'He's a builder, they met on a project about three years ago after she moved back from London.'

The roads became quieter as they headed into the countryside, and although it was beautiful, for Erin it couldn't match the wildness of the Dales they'd left earlier. Here all was gentle meadows and neat red brick houses, not the stone barns and moorland farms she was used to. Following the directions, she turned into a wide driveway, a huge sweep of flawless green lawn and a small lake set before a curved row of more contemporary and perfectly elegant, red brick houses.

'Nice,' Oli remarked, and she laughed.

'That's quite the understatement; they're stunning.' She didn't imagine she'd find any charity shop chintz sofas in the impressive show house near the entrance. She took a deep breath, forcing away more comparisons with her own home. 'Which one is theirs?'

'Nothing quite so grand, Imogen said it's a terrace in the courtyard around the back. Alex has left his car at his parents' place so we can use his parking space.'

'Are you okay, about seeing your dad later?' Erin's hand found his, resting lightly on his thigh, and his fingers tightened around hers, holding them in place. The contact had been natural, born out of a desire to impart support, but still she felt the thrill of his touch dancing across her skin.

'Think so,' he said quietly. 'I'm delighted for Imogen and Alex of course, and I am glad we came. I suppose a party is a good place to see Dad and Christina, given that everyone will be busy chatting to someone else.'

Erin drove past the first row of houses and turned right into a beautiful courtyard, made up of three blocks of immaculate terraces, low evergreen planting and matching red brick paving interspersed with gravel parking places. Alex and Imogen's house was at one end of the furthest block and Erin parked in the allocated spot. She covered a yawn as they got out – she'd done a couple of hours' consulting this morning before they'd left to save Gil a job – and she and Oli both stretched. Checking her phone, she beamed at a message from Jess, holding it out so Oli could see.

'Don't think Marnie's missing us.'

'No, she looks happy.' They shared a smile at the image of Marnie asleep on her bed in the cottage before the fire. Noah was joining Jess later and they were planning a takeaway; a rare night off from renovating the house they'd just bought. Oli was at the boot removing their bags when the front door opened, and Imogen rushed outside.

'Guys, I'm so happy you're here! You made great time, come in and have a drink to celebrate. There's a taxi picking us up later so no one has to drive.'

Imogen hurried down the path and flung her arms around Oli, who grinned as he hugged her back, a bag slung over each shoulder. She turned to Erin and hugged her too, murmuring a 'thank you for coming.'

'Alex sends his apologies, by the way. He had to go into work, and he's been delayed on site.' Imogen pointed so Oli and Erin, who had a garment bag with Oli's suit and her dress draped over one arm, could go first. 'His company are renovating a hotel and there's a crisis with a crane. He shouldn't be too long.'

'It's beautiful, Immi,' Oli remarked as they stepped into a narrow hall, and he caught his sister's eye. 'What?'

'Nothing.' She bumped into him on purpose, nudging his arm with hers. 'You haven't called me Immi for ages, that's all.'

'Yeah, well,' he retorted, giving her a brotherly shove. 'Mum always said…'

'What?' There was a questioning note in her voice, urging him to continue.

'Nothing.' He glanced down. 'Do we have to take our shoes off?'

'With these carpets? You betcha!'

Erin slipped her boots off and Oli did the same, leaving their bags in the hall for now and being careful not to rest them against the white walls. A compact, sleek white and grey kitchen was on their left, the window looking onto the courtyard. For a moment she almost envied its orderliness and clean lines, and then she was reminded of her cottage's comforts and cosiness, the stories of people who'd lived in it long before she had. She was just a chapter in its history, a guardian readying it for the next person who would come along after her.

'Sitting room and dining area.' Imogen threw open a door at the end and they were in another white room with a pale grey carpet matching the one in the hall. The furniture, apart from a cream sofa and an armchair, was dark and contemporary, a huge flatscreen TV sat on a low cabinet, and French doors led to a narrow garden planted with evergreens, gravel in place of a lawn and bordered by metal railings. Everything was glossy and gorgeous, and Erin was checking her jeans for signs of mud just in case; sometimes it seemed to get everywhere, especially at this time of year. A tiny Christmas tree sparkled in a corner, the only nod to the season.

'It's gorgeous, Imogen. Congratulations,' Erin said. She'd never lived anywhere so tidy and couldn't imagine curling up on this perfect sofa without worrying she'd mark it in some way. She'd felt at home in the cottage from the first day, and mud falling from boots or dog hair from patients was easy to clean from stone-flagged floors, even if they were freezing beneath her feet. This house was a contemporary home for contemporary lives, and she didn't picture Oli living in such pristine surroundings either.

'Yeah, it's stunning, Immi, congrats.' He lowered himself onto the sofa and Erin chose the armchair. She could attempt to maintain a physical distance from him at least, even if the emotional one was retreating with every day they spent together.

'Thanks, guys, so happy you like it.' Imogen turned back to the door. 'Glass of bubbly to get you started before the party? The taxi's picking us up at six thirty, so we've got plenty of time.'

'Why not?' Oli looked at Erin. 'We don't often get to relax and spoil ourselves, do we?'

'You need to up your game, bro, if you think that's spoiling someone,' Imogen retorted. 'No wonder you're still single. Sorry, forget I said that.'

'It's fine,' Erin assured her. 'Oli and I are just friends.'

'Yeah, about that.' Imogen threw out a grin. 'Before I open the bottle, let me show you to your room.'

Room? Erin subdued a moment of alarm. She hadn't known exactly what to expect but the house was tiny, much smaller than she'd imagined. Surely, though, there were more than two bedrooms? They followed Imogen upstairs and she opened one of only three doors on the landing.

'You two are sharing,' she said bluntly. Erin caught Oli's eye. He appeared as startled as she did, and his gaze slid to his sister as Imogen carried on. 'The bathroom's between your room and ours.'

'Imogen…'

'What?' She jammed her hands on her hips and glared at him. 'Don't even think it, that sofa is velvet, and you are not spending the night on it. You two just need to get on with it or get over it, you decide which. Come down when you're ready but don't leave it too long.'

She backed away and running footsteps on the stairs disappeared. Erin took a hesitant couple of steps into their room. It was just as beautiful as the rest of the house: white walls offset by pale grey furniture, a narrow mirror above each of the bedside tables, and wardrobe space that was a rail with hangers. A wraparound suede headboard made the bed look very inviting.

'It's not much bigger than your spare room.' Oli grinned and she laughed nervously.

'No. But I bet the bed's a lot comfier.' And a double, at least.

'It'll be fine, I'll sleep on the floor,' he said decisively.

'Don't be ridiculous.' Her laugh this time was more of a protest. 'There wouldn't be enough room for that if you slept bent double. I'll do it, I'm smaller than you.'

'If you think I'm letting you sleep on the floor whilst I take the bed then you're crazy.' Oli fixed her with a look and she made herself hold it, trying not to turn away from the determination in his gaze.

'So we have to share then.' Erin attempted to land her thoughts on staying professional but even that didn't work as well as it usually did. She was thinking instead about what it would be like to fall asleep beside him, to wake up together in the morning and see him smiling across at her. And about how she was going to make herself maintain the distance they needed to keep as colleagues.

'I guess.' He was at the window overlooking the court-yard, and he turned. 'It's only for one night and we won't be back from the party until late. We'll both be ready to crash by then, we'll probably fall asleep the minute our heads hit the pillows.'

'Absolutely.' She edged towards the door. 'So shall we get that drink then?'

Oli nodded and they returned to the sitting room. Alex came home while Imogen was opening the wine, and she made the introductions. He and Oli shared a hug, his dark hair and olive skin a contrast to Oli's auburn colouring, and he hugged Erin too, telling them how happy he and Imogen were that they'd come all this way to celebrate with them.

One bottle of bubbly turned into two and when it was time to change for the party, Oli went up first so Erin could have a little more time and the room to herself. She was in the bathroom freshening up when she heard him go down and she closed the door to their room once inside, nerves fluttering in her stomach as she unpacked. She sat on the bed to do her make-up, trying to recall the instructions about blusher Jess had imparted earlier in the week. Erin didn't often wear make-up; there seemed little point when she was battered by the elements outdoors most days. She was happy with the results and the slightly different face staring back at her in the mirror when she'd finished, hair fastened into a knot at the nape of her neck. At least she'd found the time to have her nails done.

The taxi was due in half an hour and Imogen wanted them to be ready fifteen minutes before so they could take a few selfies. Erin had found her dress online during the week and had sent a link to Jess for her opinion before she clicked 'buy' in case her friend thought it wouldn't suit her. But Jess had loved it as much as Erin did, and bluntly informed her to buy it or else.

She'd never worn anything so elegant or dramatic in her life and the navy silk felt amazing when she stepped into the dress. The skirt fell to her ankles and the split to her left thigh was evident every time she moved, the silk sighing against her bare skin. A cowl neckline was just high enough and spaghetti straps on her back crossed to fasten in corset style, which she'd found very tricky to tie just above her waist. She quashed a flare of panic that perhaps her outfit was too dressy. But she knew Oli was wearing black tie as it was a formal event, and hoped very much the dress would do.

Black ankle-strap heels were unfamiliar as she descended the stairs, and the second Oli's astounded gaze landed on her Erin knew she'd got it exactly right. She couldn't help but think of Catz and the May Ball, and the missed opportunity to be his date that night. To be on his arm and wear a dress like this, to have him look at her in exactly the way he was doing now. She didn't need him to utter a word to let her know what he thought, every single syllable was written in his eyes.

'Erin, your dress! I adore it.' Imogen's colouring was perfectly complimented by a strapless green grown with a fitted bodice and flared skirt. 'Oli, doesn't Erin look stunning?'

'You do. You look perfect.' His quiet murmur was for Erin alone and for once she wasn't going to subdue the butterflies dancing in her stomach or the faint flush on her skin. She felt amazing and his hand on her back, as Imogen assembled them for the selfies, felt like a promise for the evening ahead. She wasn't going to think of having to share a bed with him and pretend it was fine, before tomorrow arrived and they returned to their normal lives. This evening she was his date, and she wanted to hold on to every single second of the next few hours together.

Chapter Seventeen

The taxi journey took twenty minutes, and the car was soon sweeping up a long driveway, pulling up outside an historic house built of ancient golden stone. Erin was aware of Oli's tension in the set of his face when they followed Imogen and Alex out of the vehicle, hanging back so the newly engaged couple could enter first, some guests and a photographer waiting to greet them.

Oli caught her eye in the light of a large pair of illuminated Christmas trees outside the entrance. 'I'm glad you're here,' he told her softly. 'I wouldn't have wanted to do this with anyone else.'

'You numpty,' she told him sternly, emphasising her Yorkshire accent on purpose. He laughed, as she'd meant him to. He hadn't even touched her and still those few words felt like a caress. She shivered, her only smart winter coat and the silk dress unequal to the chill winter night, and it felt perfectly natural when he took her hand.

Once inside the hotel another Christmas tree was cheerful, shimmering in shades of gold and silver in a low-beamed reception area. Erin slipped off her coat, aware of Oli watching, as she left it in the cloakroom. They accepted glasses of honey-coloured champagne and followed more guests into a marquee at the rear of the building. The air was scented with spices, huge church candles on the tables surrounded by evergreen wreaths.

She was clinging to his hand as though they really were a couple, and she wasn't just an old friend here to support him. Imogen and Alex had already been swallowed up by guests eager to congratulate them and admire the exquisite diamond ring glittering on her hand.

Hundreds of white fairy lights shone from the ceiling, reflected in the scarlet baubles at every place setting. Staff were mingling, offering canapés and more champagne. Erin hadn't quite finished the first glass yet and she drank it quickly, the fizz hitting her bloodstream as she and Oli accepted another. A string quartet on a low stage was playing classical Christmas carols, a wooden floor ready for the DJ and dancing to follow. But first there was the formal dinner, and they saw from the seating plan they were sharing a table with some of Imogen and Alex's friends.

Erin's gaze was darting over the guests, and it came to rest on an older man sitting at a table; she knew he must be Oli's dad. It wasn't just the similarities in height or the breadth of shoulder – there was something watchful in his gaze that reminded her of Oli. Oli's fingers tightened around hers and she squeezed back, letting him know she would be alongside him if he wanted her there.

'It's much easier to see your eyes when you're wearing heels,' he murmured. 'They look more golden in this light.'

'Don't get used to it, these shoes are strictly a one-off,' she warned, smiling up at him. 'I'll be back in my boots on Monday.'

'Shame. I like you in heels.' He didn't attempt to disguise the desire in his eyes and her skin was heating yet more with every look he gave her.

'That's not a very professional thing to say to a colleague,' she remonstrated. Clinging on to the pretence was getting more impossible by the moment.

'If that's what you want me to think of you, then maybe you should have worn a different dress.' Oli's murmured words skimmed her ear as his eyes swept down her again. Erin blushed furiously, something she'd never quite grown out of. She was so used to her winter work layers, and she felt virtually naked in the navy silk, which was caressing her body every bit as much as his gaze was.

But then movement caught his eye, and Oli forced his attention to the man watching from his table across the room. He sighed. 'Shall we get it over with?'

'Are you sure you want me to come with you? I can wait at our table or the bar if you'd rather do this on your own.'

'I want you to be there,' he said simply. 'If that's okay?'

'Totally.'

Oli's hand was on her back as they approached the table opposite theirs. The man stood up and the blonde woman in an elegant black dress beside him remained seated. Although he glanced at Erin with a brief smile, his attention was all on Oli.

'Oli, it's so good to see you.' He cleared his throat and offered a hand across the table. His grey hair was cropped short, and his dark blue eyes were quite different to Oli's more cerulean shade, colouring Erin guessed Oli had inherited from his mum. Erin felt a glimmer of sorrow at the thought of him and Imogen celebrating the first family engagement and planning a wedding without her.

'Dad. Christina.' Oli shook his father's hand and smiled at the woman next to him, who smiled back, tension evident in the gesture. 'How are you both?'

'We're well, thank you. How about you, I heard you had a blast in Costa Rica.'

'Yeah, I'm great, thanks.' Oli's smile skimmed over Erin, and she squeezed his hand. 'It was brilliant, the animal sanctuary does amazing work, and I got to treat some of the two-toed sloths, which was pretty incredible.'

'That sounds perfect, you always were fascinated with exotics.' His father turned that sharp gaze on Erin, softening it with a smile, and she offered her own in return, hoping this encounter would go smoothly for both men. 'Would you please introduce me to your friend?'

'Dad, this is Erin Hardy, who is an old friend and a brilliant colleague. We met at Catz.' Her breath caught as Oli's hand went to her back again, his fingers grazing the straps holding her dress together. 'Erin, my father, Michael Sterling, and his wife Christina.'

'Mike, please. That all sounds so formal.' He shook Erin's hand with both of his and she saw him attempting to make sense of her presence at his son's side. How much did he know of her and Oli's history, their fractured past and uncertain future? 'How do you do?'

'Very well, thank you. It's lovely to meet you both. Hello, Christina.' Erin's Yorkshire accent was always more evident when she was nervous and she tried not to measure it against Mike's more modulated tone as she shook hands with Christina as well, who'd stood to greet her. 'What a gorgeous party, you must be delighted for Imogen and Alex.'

'We are, yes.' Mike looked to his daughter and her fiancé across the room, still greeting guests. 'It's wonderful to be planning a wedding in the family, but of course it's not the same for Imogen without…' He hesitated and glanced at Oli. 'Without her mum to help her.'

Erin was conscious of Oli's tension at her side, the press of his body against hers. The conversation felt so stiff and unnatural, a million miles away from her own family all chattering at the same time.

'Erin, shall we find our seats?' Oli smiled at her. 'It looks as though they're getting ready to serve the meal.'

'Oli?' Mike came around the table and his hand settled on his son's arm. 'I know we can't talk here, but I was hoping we might catch up before you head back north. Christina and I are staying in the hotel, and we wondered if you'd like to join us for brunch tomorrow. Both of you, of course.'

Oli shrugged as he looked at Erin, as though he didn't mind either way, and she nodded. They'd come a long way to celebrate with Imogen and Alex, and she very much hoped there might be more for him and Mike this weekend. That they wouldn't go their separate ways after one formal handshake and so very few words.

'We don't have to rush home,' she told him quietly. 'I think that sounds nice.'

'Great,' Mike said quickly, pressing home his advantage. 'Shall we say ten thirty then, so we're not keeping you too long if you need to be on your way.'

He seemed relieved as he backed away and Christina smiled as he rejoined her. Erin guessed she must be a good ten years younger than Mike, and wondered if this was the woman for whom he'd left his marriage. If so, no wonder Oli felt awkward around them, even if it had been years ago. Sometimes those things never quite went away.

'Right, well, we'll see you then.' Oli nodded at them both and Erin slipped her arm through his as they left the table.

'Are you okay?' Even in heels she had to reach up to place the words in his ear above the music and laughing chatter. 'And I don't have to join you tomorrow if that's simpler.'

'I'm fine, thank you for asking, and Imogen's right. It is time he and I talked. I can't avoid him forever, especially with a wedding coming up. And please do come with me, if you're sure you can stand it? I'd really like you to be there to hold my hand.'

'Then I will be,' she told him softly, and he smiled when she squeezed his fingers.

'But what would Jason think?' Oli's brows drew together as he halted. 'Doesn't he mind, that you're here with me?'

'It doesn't matter if he minds or not, because Jason and I are no longer dating. I can't even say we broke up because we didn't have anything to break.'

'I'd tell you I'm sorry if I really meant it, but the only thing I'm concerned about is whether you're okay?'

'Do I not look okay?' She realised immediately it was the wrong question as it gave him another excuse to run his eyes over her, and that scorching gaze ignited every nerve ending yet more.

'You look so much more than okay,' he murmured, bending to speak against her ear, brushing her skin with his breath, teasing and tantalising. 'You look incredible and entirely too distracting.'

'Oli!' That single word of remonstration did nothing for her composure after such a stare, and she tried to drag her mind back to the reason she was here. 'So tomorrow at brunch, I'll be there as your friend. Just to be clear.'

'Friends,' Oli echoed, giving her a wicked smile. 'That's a step up from colleagues and I'll take it. For now.'

'Don't push it, Sterling, or you might be spending your last few days cleaning out kennels.'

They took their seats and introduced themselves to everyone else on their table, a few Oli had met before. Imogen and Alex's friends and family welcomed them, and Erin found it lovely to laugh with Oli beside her, as though they really were a couple, and she eventually gave up trying to refute that they weren't. Dinner was outstanding: prime rib of beef and roasted stuffed cauliflower served with hasselback roast potatoes, caramelised shallots, and sprouts with baby carrots. Dessert was mini hot toddy pavlovas, meringues flavoured with whisky, pears and spices. Afterwards Imogen and Alex were first on the dance floor, and Oli pushed back his chair and stood up.

'Shall we?' He offered a hand to Erin, a smile on his lips. 'I've waited a long time to dance with you wearing a dress like that.'

It was impossible to say no; she too had longed for this moment. Champagne had been flowing, but it wasn't that heightening every sense, it was his eyes and the way he'd been looking at her all evening. Her hand was in his as they walked onto the dance floor, Erin dizzyingly aware of every touch.

Oli's right hand went to her back and hers was on his left shoulder, resting on his black tailored jacket as the opening notes of Nat King Cole's 'Christmas Song' filled the room. Everyone but Oli was a blur, his fingers splayed across the laces on her back. Their feet were following one rhythm as their bodies danced to an entirely different one; with every beat of the music they drew closer until his chest beneath the open jacket was against her breasts. His fingers slid beneath the corset fastening of her dress and her breath caught. She was trembling in his arms and even her legs felt unsteady as they danced on. His hand slid slowly up her back until it reached the knot of curls at the nape of her neck.

'I love your hair like this.' His new beard was rough against her cheek as he murmured the words. He gently tugged a curl free and wrapped it around one finger. 'Let me take it down for you when we're alone.'

'Oli, we can't!' Erin tried to summon some sense, and her laugh was more of a shocked gasp. 'We're really not meant to be doing this.'

'Actually, I think you're wrong.' He pulled back to stare at her, and she was lost all over again at his eyes glittering with desire. 'I think we're meant to be doing exactly this.'

There was no reply she could offer and already the song was ending. Slowly they separated. The DJ switched to classic Christmas party songs but Erin didn't want to leave the floor, to think about the end of the party on its way. They carried on dancing, and she was remembering what it was like to let go and have fun, to leave behind their responsibilities for this one magical evening together. All too soon midnight arrived, and everyone was saying goodbye, promising to see each other again at the wedding.

Oli found his dad and Christina to say goodnight to, and Mike confirmed how much he was looking forward to seeing them again in the morning. Imogen and Alex were following on in a separate taxi later, not yet ready to end their celebration. Erin and Oli got into their taxi, and all she could think of was how she was going to manage to share a bed with him after tonight and emerge from the weekend with her professionalism intact.

Back at the house, Oli let them in with the key Imogen had given him, his question deceptively casual. 'Brew before we go up, to offset all that champagne?'

'Actually, I think I'll just go straight to bed.' Erin hadn't drunk that much and didn't think she could spend a minute alone with him until she was wrapped in the duvet and trying to pretend he wasn't actually there. She tugged her eyes free from his and he nodded.

'Okay. Give me a shout when you're done in the bathroom.'

'I won't be long.' It was a terribly flat reply after the evening they'd just shared, and she trailed upstairs. But it was also the lifeline she needed to pull her back from the brink, to prevent them falling straight into bed together. Despite the disappointment, she was glad he'd made the decision to wait downstairs because she wasn't certain she could've done.

She was sitting on the bed when he came upstairs after her call, snug winter pyjamas laid out behind her, and trying to focus on the latest Marnie update from Jess. Erin's heart was racing when Oli appeared, and she put her phone down. The black dinner jacket was draped from one shoulder, the bow tie loose. He'd undone the top two buttons of his white shirt, and her breath caught.

'Sorry. I thought you'd already be in bed,' he muttered, halting at the sight of Erin still in her dress, the heels discarded nearby. 'Do you think Imogen did this on purpose?'

'Totally.' She stood up, her fingers trembling. 'I can't undo my dress. Could you help me please?'

'You want me to unfasten your dress?'

'What else am I meant to do? I don't want to ruin it,' she replied helplessly. 'I wouldn't ask otherwise.'

'Okay.' His voice was very low. 'Turn around.'

She did, slowly, and his fingers were cool on her warm skin. She held in a gasp as she felt them slide underneath the crossed straps, working slowly to unfasten the knot she'd managed to tie in her haste to be in bed before him. His breath was skimming her neck, and she knew from its unevenness that he was finding it as difficult as she was to maintain that everything must stop here.

The moment he'd undone the knot she felt the dress loosen as the straps slackened and she clutched the bodice tightly, not daring to let it fall away. He inched a finger beneath the strap on her left shoulder and she couldn't move; even her breath had halted at this exquisite, questioning touch. He slid the strap from her shoulder to her elbow and she closed her eyes, fighting the impulse to lean her head back.

He repeated the gesture on her right shoulder, this time allowing one finger to follow the path of the strap down her arm. But her arms holding up the dress were the only barrier between her and scalding embarrassment when she had to face him in front of their colleagues on Monday. Her pulse was pounding, and she was trying to summon all the reasons why continuing what they'd begun was such a bad idea.

'It's undone now.' His low words were a whisper against her face as he bent his head, both hands resting lightly on the top of her arms.

'Thanks.' Whatever she did next would determine the rest of this evening, as well as his last few days in Hartfell, and she longed to continue. She took a deep breath and snatched her pyjamas from the bed, fleeing to the bathroom to change. When she returned Oli was in bed and he offered a smile.

'Night. Sleep well.' He turned over, hunching onto his side as she hung up her dress.

'Thanks. You too.' Erin got in beside him, wrapped in her winter pyjamas. She lay still, utterly aware of Oli. She knew the moment he'd fallen asleep when his breathing changed, one arm tucked beneath the pillow. She lay awake for an hour, staring at her phone and alternating between relief and profound regret. She eventually dropped off and woke again a couple of hours later, turning over and rearranging the pillow as she tried to settle.

'What's the matter?' he muttered sleepily.

'I'm too hot,' she replied irritably. 'Sorry, I didn't mean to wake you.' She punched the pillow and turned over again. She definitely couldn't sleep facing him and she inched across to the very edge of the bed.

'I'm not surprised. Those pyjamas could probably take you on a polar expedition.'

'I didn't know we'd be staying in a boiling new-build and not some draughty old manor house,' she shot back, trying to keep her voice down lest they wake Imogen and Alex in the next room. She'd heard them return about half an hour after Oli had fallen asleep. 'I was expecting freezing temperatures and high ceilings, not underfloor heating.'

'Imogen can't stand the cold, she always has the heating turned up to tropical.' Oli sat up. 'Can't you change into something else?'

'Like what? I only packed enough stuff for one night and I need my clothes for tomorrow.'

'You can have my T-shirt. I'm too warm anyway.'

'Oli, no!' She flipped over in time to see him yank it over his head and he dropped it on the duvet between them. 'Sharing a bed with you is bad enough, how you do expect me to sleep if you're…'

'I'm not naked,' he muttered. 'I'm wearing shorts.'

'No, but you're…' She'd rarely seen him like this, so close, and not since the incident back in the cottage with the peelings when he'd been heading to the shower. Years of rugby and surfing had kept him fit and he'd retained those muscles, his arms, shoulders and chest perfectly defined. 'Almost.'

'Do you want the T-shirt or not?' He picked it up, dangling it through the darkness.

'Okay,' she replied steadily. 'But only because I don't think I'll be able to sleep otherwise. Please can you turn away?'

Erin sat up and she felt the mattress sink as Oli turned over. She undid her pyjamas with clumsy fingers, remembering his own, deft and sure, on her dress earlier. Her pulse was beating to that dangerous rhythm again as she wriggled out of her top and snatched up his T-shirt, tugging it hurriedly over her head.

It was still warm and smelled of him, that same vanilla and bourbon scent that lingered whenever he was near. She lay back, as tense and taut as before. It was tricky to get the bottom half of her pyjamas off lying down under the duvet, but she managed it, and they hit the floor too. She breathed out a calming sigh now the heavy cotton was no longer covering her body. In truth it wasn't just the house making her overheat, but trying to feign indifference to Oli beside her. Erin closed her eyes, willing sleep to come.

Chapter Eighteen

Erin woke again later, sunrise still a while off yet. She lay back and stared at the ceiling, wanting strangely to cry. They had managed it; she and Oli had spent the night in the same bed, and the knowledge should have been a triumph. She was trying to recall why being sensible had been such a good idea and instead all she could think of was his fingers on her back, undoing the spaghetti straps of her dress and how she'd longed for him to continue.

Oli's bare chest was revealed by the duvet he'd pushed away, and she was loath to disturb him again. Trying to banish the indecision racing around in her head, she slid out of bed and crept to the bathroom. She freshened up and stared at her reflection in the mirror. The make-up had gone, her hair was returned to its usual long, loose curls and she looked like ordinary Erin again, not the woman who'd worn a beautiful silk dress and danced in the arms of the only man she'd ever loved.

Her family and her career were everything to her, but Oli was moving on soon. What if they missed this final chance to be together? At least she understood after the conversation with Imogen last weekend that creating a home wasn't for him, and their priorities were different. They were leaving for Hartfell in a few hours, and she knew, absolutely understood, that there her resolve would be stronger. She returned along the landing, her pulse banging with nerves and something much more dangerous. It was desire, and she was so tired of pretending.

She opened the bedroom door and halted abruptly. Oli was sitting up, illuminated by faint golden lamplight. He looked sleepily dishevelled and utterly gorgeous, and Erin swallowed as he ran a hand through his hair.

'Sorry,' she croaked. 'I didn't mean to wake you again.'

'Don't be.' He smiled slowly as he eased the hand behind his head. 'Much as I love you wearing my clothes, I'd like my T-shirt back now please. I'm cold.'

'No you're not.' This was the moment, and her decision was made. A tremor darted over her skin as she closed the door, her low tone matching his. 'You're just saying that because you want me to take it off. At least that's what I think you meant.'

His eyes darkened as they went to the T-shirt skimming her thighs, and his lazy smile widened. 'That's exactly what I meant.'

She was remembering the last time she'd worn something of his; when he'd tossed a drink over her at the May Ball, and she'd made him swap shirts. That rush of confidence and joy after their first kiss, the powerful high of realising he'd wanted her as much as she did him. She wasn't that same young woman now, caught between their past and an uncertain future. She was stronger, capable and decisive. And she wanted him.

'If you want it you'll have to come and get it.' The husky note in her voice was new and she raised the hem of his T-shirt an inch, that same confidence surging again as he watched.

In a second he'd flipped the duvet aside and got out of the bed. As he slowly walked towards her, she was drinking him in too, those shoulders and the arms that had held her before. The bare chest she couldn't stop thinking about, night after night in bed with Oli sleeping just the other side of the wall.

He halted six inches away and her senses were full of vanilla again, her heart full of him. A tear slipped free at the longing and passion she read in his eyes, and he caught it with a finger, gently brushing it away. It was as though she was seeing him for the first time, without the barriers of before and the differences in their backgrounds she'd always thought had mattered.

'If this isn't what you want, Oli, then say so now.'

'Erin, I've waited years for you.' He tilted his head to murmur the words into her ear, letting his lips brush her skin, and she was already lost. 'Don't ever doubt that I want you. I always have, and that won't change.'

'So that's a yes, then,' she whispered. She couldn't close her eyes; she wanted to drink in the desire in his. Oli's lips were making their way to her mouth, leaving soft kisses along her neck and then her jaw.

'A most unequivocal, absolutely, definitely yes,' he murmured. 'What about you? And please, I beg you, don't mention work.'

'Totally yes, how could you doubt it now?' She stood on tiptoe, loving the muttered groan he uttered when she kissed the corner of his mouth. 'And I'm not really thinking about work.'

'Not really thinking about it?' There was mock outrage now, too, and he tugged on a curl. 'I'm obviously not doing enough to distract you.'

'You are, honestly,' she said breathlessly. 'But we can't take this into the practice, not ever. We can't let anyone suspect. Promise me?'

'If I promise not to sneak you away into the kennels so we can be alone, will you promise to stop talking about work?'

'Promise.'

'So do I. And I've finally realised there's only one way to stop you talking.'

'Oh?' She arched an eyebrow, and her hands inched up his arms to his shoulders, allowing her fingers to explore him at last. 'Are you going to tell me?'

'Nope. I'm going to show you.'

Then his mouth was on hers, parting her lips as he kissed her. Erin was frantic to make up for lost time and rediscover him again, already drowning in the passion she'd only ever felt with him. The only man she'd ever loved. Her hands were tangled in his hair as he pushed her back against the door and slid a firm thigh between her legs. His beard grazed her skin, and he groaned again when she curled into him, her curves soft against the hard planes of his body.

He pulled back to run his hands through her curls, tousling them some more. 'You looked beautiful with your hair up, but I love it like this as well.' His arms fell and he took hold of the hem of his T-shirt. 'And this looks much better on you, but I still want it back.'

'Take it then,' she whispered. She raised her arms above her head, and he tugged it off, tossing it to join her discarded pyjamas on the floor. Heat was curling in every part of her, and her stomach dropped as she watched his eyes on her body. Last time they'd done this she'd been wearing a white lace bra and now there was nothing to hide her from his gaze. His hands were on her waist, and he muttered something she didn't hear as they inched higher, until his thumbs and then his hands were on her breasts.

'You're stunning,' he ground out, sliding one hand to the small of her back to pull her into him. 'Completely beautiful. I love you in nothing but lace.'

'So are you.' She truly felt it, saw the truth of his words and his desire for her laid bare in his eyes. Her breasts were pressed against his chest, dark hair grazing her nipples and heightening every sensation already burning. 'I've dreamed about this so many times. I want the reality of you, I want to feel you against me.'

His reply was to take her hands so she could slide his shorts down and he hurriedly kicked them away. His eyes darkened yet more as she ran her hands from his chest to his shoulders, and she pulled his head down to kiss him again, his mouth expert and demanding on hers.

His thumbs were inside her lace thong, and he quickly slid it down until it was at her feet, and she stepped out of it. Then there was nothing but their nakedness and she was glorying in it, and him. Oli turned her swiftly, one arm hooked around her waist to hold her against him as he kissed her all the way back to the bed and scooped her up to drop her onto it.

–

'Oli, wake up.' Erin leaned over him, her breasts and long hair brushing his chest. His hand went to her back, holding her close.

'I'm asleep, but I won't be for much longer with you like that.'

'It's eight fifteen! We can't stay here all morning, we're meeting your dad and Christina in a couple of hours. And

I can hear Imogen and Alex downstairs. What are they going to think if we're not up as well?'

'They'll think we don't want to get up because we've been making perfect and incredible love all morning.' He opened one eye, and she laughed at the expression on his face. 'Which is the truth, so what does it matter?'

'Because it does!'

'Does it?' He opened the other eye, and that same languid smile Erin wore was parting his lips. 'And I don't want brunch, I want you.'

'We can't, it's too late and they'll hear us!'

Something caught in her memory, the half promise she'd made to herself a few hours ago; that this one night would be enough, and she knew now that it wouldn't, not ever. She wanted this morning, tonight, tomorrow; she wanted it all with him. But Monday was a reality they'd have to face, and she tried to hide it somewhere it couldn't intrude on these moments. She loved the smug look of satisfaction he wore, the lazy desire in his gaze, the hand exploring her bare back and holding her captive as his fingers tucked her hair behind one ear.

'And you don't think they might have heard us before?'

'I hope not,' Erin said vehemently, a flare of embarrassment brightening her skin into a blush. 'It was very early, and we were quiet.'

'Fairly quiet.' Oli grinned as he pushed himself into a sitting position, taking her with him. 'See look, I am very awake.'

'That was never in doubt,' she murmured, unable to resist another kiss, easing herself onto his lap.

'If you're serious about getting up then that's really not helping,' he said sternly, both hands on her waist.

'Maybe another five minutes,' she said softly, smiling at his muttered groan as she trailed her lips from his jaw to his ear, nibbling at his neck on the way. 'Is that enough?'

'Nowhere near,' he whispered back, settling her on his thighs and shoving the duvet away. 'Not ever.'

Afterwards they showered together, Oli overruling Erin's protest; she relented when she realised Imogen and Alex had gone out. Downstairs Oli made espresso for himself and tea exactly how she liked it, and they sat together at the small breakfast bar, heads bent over her phone and smiling at the latest Marnie update. Imogen and Alex returned soon after with shopping, and Erin was too late to ease away from Oli's hand on her thigh. Imogen took one look and rolled her eyes knowingly.

'So that's clear, then. Good to see that you two have made the best of sharing one bed.'

'We haven't, I mean, we didn't…' Erin tried to refute it as she stood up hurriedly, and couldn't when Oli, still sitting on the bar stool, pulled her back between his thighs.

'Oh, we did, Erin,' he said wickedly, running a hand over the blush staining her cheek. 'We very much did, and you're rubbish at pretending. That's another thing I love about you, that you can't hide whatever you're feeling.'

Love? Had he really just said that word, out loud, in front of his sister and her fiancé? Erin's blush deepened and she longed to say it back, to let him know what was in her heart. But perhaps it was just a throwaway comment, one of those things said in the moment, and he didn't mean it that way at all. She shook her head to chase the thought away and slid her arms around his neck instead.

Alex made more drinks, and they settled in the sitting room, going over the party last night. Imogen got up to hug Oli and tell him how much it meant that he'd been

225

there to celebrate with them, and her eyes were glittering with tears. She sat back down with a sniff and her laugh was a quick one.

'Dad's messaged me to say how much he's looking forward to seeing you both.' She paused. 'He really wants an opportunity to talk and put things right between you so we can move on, together.'

Erin squeezed his hand. They were pressed together on the sofa, and they'd barely let go of each other all morning. They'd gone so many years without touching, and now they'd started they couldn't seem to stop. It was so easy to be together like this, with Imogen and Alex too, and she was wishing they had another day, that they could stay in this other world until tomorrow; a world where work and a separate future for her and Oli wasn't at the forefront of her mind. She was going to have to produce some performance at work to remain indifferent to him after this weekend and all they had finally shared.

'I've been running a long time, Immi, maybe it is finally time to stop. Maybe he and Mum just weren't meant to be together.' Oli sighed. 'But whatever age you are, it's still hard to accept that home isn't what you thought it was.'

'I know, I get it.' Imogen leaned over and she touched his hand. 'But I'd hate to see what happened stop you from having your own home and maybe a family one day.' She glanced at Erin and her smile was a faint, knowing one. 'You've got to trust yourself, trust that you're worth loving too. That because Dad left doesn't mean you'd do the same, or that he doesn't love you. I know he does.'

It was time to leave, and at the door Imogen hugged them both fiercely, reminding Oli that she'd see him again soon, for Christmas. 'I know Oli won't thank me for saying this, but I'm going to.' Imogen flashed her brother a glance after Alex had hugged them too, and held up her hand. 'Don't say a word, Oli, I want Erin to hear this. He's always loved you, Erin, ever since that first year at Catz. He never said so, but he didn't have to, it was perfectly obvious, and I know my brother. A home is all he's ever wanted, no matter how much he tries to pretend otherwise. So if you're both thinking there's a reason you can't be together, you'd better find a way past it, because what you two have doesn't come around very often.'

'Immi, it's not that simple.' Oli sighed and Erin was shocked to realise he hadn't tried to refute Imogen's startling declaration.

'You think? Because just sometimes, it really is that simple. Drive safe, see you soon. Hope brunch goes well.'

The silence was a tricky one once they were in the pickup and Erin drove out of the courtyard. She didn't know where to begin an ordinary conversation after that, one which would lead them away from thoughts of the future. Oli was the first to speak and he made a suggestion, his hand finding its way to hers.

'After brunch, do you fancy seeing the Christmas market in town? I haven't been for years, and it would be nice to have the time together. And maybe you don't have enough decorations at home yet?'

'I'd love that.' She'd take any excuse to be alone with him, and Jess was staying until they returned. 'And there's always room for more decorations.'

When they arrived at the hotel it seemed very different in daylight, busy with weekend guests checking out. Erin recognised a few from the party, and she and Oli greeted them without pausing to chat. In the restaurant a table had been reserved for them, where Mike and Christina were waiting. They both stood as Erin and Oli reached them, and handshakes were offered all round. Erin was aware of Oli's tension in the hand holding hers on the table, his fingers taut.

'Thank you for coming, we're so glad you're both here.' Mike glanced at Christina, and she followed up with her own smile. Erin knew from Imogen that Christina was a corporate lawyer with a large London firm, and she'd met Mike through work. 'Have a look at the menu, the choice is excellent.'

'Thank you.' Erin accepted the one Mike was offering, then the waiter was there, taking a drinks order and promising to return shortly. She wondered if this was a mistake after all; if Oli and Mike should have met in private and discussed their differences alone instead of in the full glare of a busy restaurant. Perhaps she and Christina were meant to be buffers between father and son and their longstanding differences.

Erin and Oli went for the full English and Mike decided to join them as Christina settled on an omelette. Their drinks arrived soon after and Erin waited for her pot of tea to brew as Oli knocked back an espresso. Christina was drinking green tea, and Mike had also finished an espresso.

'I know there's a lot to say, Oli,' he began quietly, fixing a stare on his son. Erin thought she saw a glimpse of hope amongst the steel, and it wasn't difficult to picture him as a tough city banker all about the deal. He was lean and sharp, but there was a softness in his look now on Oli too. 'And I want to start by saying how sorry I am for leaving this conversation so long and not trying to explain the truth earlier.'

'We know the truth, Dad,' Oli replied bitterly. 'You and Mum sat us down one day and said it was over, that you'd met someone else. We didn't even meet Christina until two years after you left, and then you went and got married right after Mum died. Why do you think we didn't come to the wedding and celebrate with you? Whatever happened between you and Mum, Immi and I didn't deserve that. Why didn't you postpone it?'

Erin slid a hand onto Oli's thigh, hoping somehow it might help ease the tension set in his jaw, the lips she'd kissed right before they'd got out of the car pressed together in a firm line.

Mike glanced at Christina, his hand going to the back of his neck to rub it, and she took his other one. 'Oli, I'll always be sorry about what happened between me and your mum and how it ended. I know it was a terrible shock for you and Immi. And for not being there for you after your mum died. I know that's unforgiveable and why it hurt you both so much.' He picked up his cup and put it down again when he realised it was empty.

'Christina and I had found out she was pregnant after IVF, and we were all set to tell you. But your mum suddenly passed away and we were all reeling from the shock. Then whilst we were planning the funeral, we lost the baby as well.' Mike blinked, pressing his eyes closed for a second, and Christina squeezed his hand, before he refocused.

'It just didn't seem like the right moment to add to what you were already going through. We hadn't intended to get married then, it was something we'd talked about doing once the baby had been born. After the funeral we decided to go away on the spur of the moment as Christina was feeling better physically, and the wedding gave us something else to think about. Something to remind us that we did have a future together, and it helped, a bit, with the grief. I know I hurt you both, being so distant, and I'm so sorry.'

Mike's voice cracked. 'You probably don't want to hear it, but I've always loved you and Immi, and nothing will ever change that. I was in shock about your mum passing away so suddenly, and between that and the baby, I kind of lost it for a bit.'

'It was more than a bit, Mike,' Christina said gently, and she looked at Oli, her lovely blue eyes glittering with tears. 'Your dad had a breakdown and had to take six months away from work. I wanted him to tell you, but he was adamant that we shouldn't. He felt he'd let you down enough already.'

'Shit, Dad.' Oli's voice was shaky, his breath rapid, and the thigh beneath Erin's hand was trembling. 'I wish you had told us.'

'I wasn't sure you'd want to hear it as you still blamed me for the divorce, and I thought you had enough to deal with, after your mum. We weren't seeing much of each other anyway, you'd just graduated and found your first job. I didn't think it was fair to drag you into our worries. The doctor said it was likely caused by a reaction to all the emotional stress. It felt as though a lid had been blown off and I couldn't keep on top of everything.'

'I'm so sorry about the baby.' Oli looked at Christina and her smile was an understanding one as she nodded. He turned his sympathy to his dad, who gripped his hand across the table before letting go.

'Oli, what I'm going to tell you next is in no way meant to reflect badly on your mum, and I've agonised for a long time, years really, about whether I should even mention it,' Mike began hesitantly. 'But in the spirit of telling the truth and helping you understand why we separated, I thought you should know.'

He took a gulp of water, placing the glass carefully down on the table. 'It was your mum who'd met someone else and wanted to start a new life with them. I'm sorry we lied and let you think otherwise, but at the time she was distraught, and we didn't know what else to do. I was travelling and I believed then, and I still do, that it was best for you, Immi and your mum to be together, and the easiest way to achieve that was for me to leave. There was no going back on her decision, and we made sure of it by telling you I'd met someone else. Christina and I actually met about eighteen months later, at a conference.'

Mike coughed and reached for the glass again, and Christina passed him a tissue. He wiped his eyes and Erin was sharply aware of Oli, silent and frozen at her side, the tension thrumming through him and evident in his thigh set like steel beneath her hand.

'Don't ever doubt your mum loved you and Imogen best of all,' Mike said quietly. 'She adored you both and was so proud of you.'

'But, Dad, there wasn't anyone else,' Oli whispered hoarsely. Erin gripped his hand as he leaned forward. 'We never met another man and she never once mentioned someone else.'

'That's because it wasn't another man,' Mike offered slowly. 'It was Gillian.'

'Gillian! But she was a client who became Mum's friend, and they travelled together, she stayed with us sometimes...' Oli's voice fell away, and his head was in his hands. 'She never said. Why didn't she tell us? At least we would've known the truth, and it wouldn't have changed how we felt about both of you.'

'She always said she was waiting for the right time, and I think she was afraid you'd think badly of her for being the one to break up our family.' The sigh Mike eased out was a long one. 'Please try and understand your mum never saw this coming, and it hit her, both of us, as an absolute bolt out of the blue. She hadn't planned it, and she was tormented for months about what to do, and about letting me take the blame. I knew she still loved me, but I felt it was right to give her that chance of happiness with someone she loved more. Someone I know she thought of as the love of her life.'

Mike leaned forward and he clutched Oli's arm. 'They were happy together, Oli, in their way. Time just went on and maybe they wanted to keep what they had to themselves.'

'Gillian was with Mum when she died. She must've been bereft, and we didn't even notice,' Oli said hollowly. 'It wouldn't have mattered, nothing would have changed how we felt about Mum. And Gillian helped us organise the funeral, and she read a poem. How did she get through it? I wished I'd known, because then Gillian would be our family too.'

'She still can be. She is family.' Mike picked up the glass again and swallowed more water. 'I'm sure she'd love to see you, or hear from you. We email from time to time.'

'Right. Email. Bloody hell, Dad. This is turning out to be some brunch.' Oli eased back in his chair as though all the air had been knocked out of him as their food arrived. 'I'm sorry for…' His voice cracked as he stared at his dad and Mike's hand found his across the table. 'For everything, really. For us missing out too, and thinking badly of you when it wasn't your fault.'

Erin was still clutching his thigh, trying to convey every bit of strength and support she could after such revelations. And love, it was pointless trying to pretend otherwise. It was simply how her heart was made, to love Oli Sterling.

Chapter Nineteen

The Christmas market in Marlborough was enchanting, and Erin and Oli wandered around it mostly in silence, holding hands. He was still reeling from the revelation about his family at brunch, and the time with his dad and Christina had passed far too quickly. They'd parted with hugs this time, and Mike had said he hoped they'd see Oli at Imogen and Alex's for Christmas. It was going to take more than one conversation to heal a rift which had been simmering for years, but Erin was hopeful that Oli was on his way now he understood the truth.

Festive stalls stretched the length of a charming high street on either side, and Santa in his grotto was greeting excited young children, with a pair of reindeer outside drawing lots of admirers. A rock choir was performing later, and buskers dressed as elves were wandering through the crowd, making merry with music and stopping for selfies. Erin and Oli joined a queue for mulled wine, with Erin choosing the non-alcoholic option as she was driving home.

After last night it seemed perfectly natural to wrap their arms around one another as they strolled amongst the stalls. Their lovemaking had been perfect, and had lived for so long in her imagination. She wanted to keep him close, especially after seeing his dad and Christina earlier. To let him know that she cared and hated to see him hurt.

She was looking forward to going home for Marnie, but it was difficult to think of tomorrow, of his leaving in two days, and balancing their professional relationship against the swerve their personal one had finally taken.

Oli bought her a midnight blue beanie because he said the colour reminded him of her dress from last night. She was smiling as he slid it over her hair and dropped a kiss on her lips, their faces chilled from the cold. She couldn't resist more decorations for the cottage, even if she had to put them away until Marnie was older, and picked up some felted mince pie baubles, which Oli thought were a fitting choice after her triumph in the mince pie tasting. A delicate, fused glass robin and a silver snowflake embellished with tiny red stones found their way into her bag as well, and she gave him a pair of red socks made from soft alpaca wool to keep his feet warm in wellies out on calls. They finished with hot sausage rolls filled with black pudding and cranberries before they set off on the long journey back to Hartfell.

Without a stop they made home in good time. Jess was very happy to hear they'd had a lovely weekend. Erin tried to hide the new light in her eyes, but it was impossible in front of her intuitive friend, especially when she was making a brew and Oli forgot about Jess in the sitting room and came through to kiss her. Marnie was in a mischievous mood and getting the hang of living in a home, and they played with her after they'd thanked Jess and she'd left.

But Monday was approaching, bringing with it the last working days before Christmas, and a return to normality after these precious few hours alone. She was aware that Oli had left his bag in his own room, and she loved him all the more for not assuming that everything here had changed as well, and he could share her room without questioning it first.

After a light supper she glanced at her phone on the coffee table. She wasn't on call, but she was always alert to notifications, especially from her mum, and she'd never miss an emergency if she could attend. She unlocked the phone when she saw a message from Gil; it was unusual for him to contact her out of hours unless it was important. At least she could still drive tonight if she needed to.

She scanned the message; he was apologising for contacting her but wondered if she could come in early on Monday for a meeting? It was nothing of concern but there was something he needed to discuss with her. Erin replied at once to agree and arranged to head in at seven before the rest of the staff arrived and the working day began in earnest. Already her mind was going to what lay ahead tomorrow, and she was startled from her thoughts when Oli spoke.

'Sorry, I missed that.' She smiled at him to make up for her distraction.

'I wondered if you were ready for bed?' He found her hand and she was staring at it on her lap, the simple connection that meant so much more. 'I'm not going to presume, I want you to know it's fine if you'd rather I stay in my room. Well, mostly fine.' He leaned in as though he was going to kiss her and thought better of it. 'Not that I wouldn't rather be naked with you in yours.'

'Are you sure you're not just saying that because you're tired of sleeping in a single?' she teased, knowing her reply was enough to make her decision clear. 'Are you trying to make me feel sorry for you?'

'Is it working?' He gave her such a sad look that she laughed, and she was the one who reached over to kiss him.

'Naked sounds good,' she murmured. 'Although this house is not heated like Imogen and Alex's. We'll probably freeze to death.'

'We definitely won't, I'll make sure of it.' Oli got up and held out a hand. 'You lock up, I'll settle Marnie.'

In the morning Erin found it very difficult to get out of bed, but then she didn't usually share hers with Oli. They'd fallen asleep after making love and he stirred when her alarm went off, slinging an arm across her. She allowed herself the luxury of curling into him for a few more minutes, loath to leave him yet. But the meeting with Gil was starting soon and she couldn't linger. She got ready and was parking at the practice just before seven, wrapped up against the chill. Snow was forecast in the coming days and the landscape was glittering white with frost, and another sharp sunny day beckoned.

Gil had already nipped down to the village shop, which opened early to accommodate hungry farmers and those in search of a hot breakfast before work. Erin's stomach rumbled noisily as she caught the smell of bacon sandwiched between fresh rolls. The coffee machine was already on, and she made herself a quick mug of tea as Gil cleared space for them to eat at a desk in the office. He pushed a bottle towards her as they sat down, and Lola settled down beside him, hopeful of a treat.

'Brown sauce, right?'

'Yes thanks.' She'd brought their drinks and slid his coffee across, and he thanked her. She wasn't worried about this meeting, but she'd be glad all the same to discover what it was about. Her three-month review was coming up, but surely he'd have said if it was just that, and given her time to prepare?

'Thanks for coming in early, Erin, I really appreciate it. I hope I didn't worry you but as I said, it's nothing to be concerned about. Just some potential changes to the rota over the holidays.'

'You're welcome.' Well, that sounded fine, and she savoured another bite of her breakfast, wondering if she'd have time to run down to the shop and fetch one for Oli, too. They usually just grabbed cereal or yoghurt before work, and she'd like to treat him if she could.

'The thing is, you know my boys are in Australia for Christmas.' Erin nodded and Gil carried on. 'Luca's just got there, he's staying at the vineyard with Joel until he heads back to university next month. And with Jonny buying his own place and the rest of the family joining him, Pippa and I would love to be there too, and we thought we'd go if we could get away. Harriet and Alfie have finished their exams, so he'd be along for the ride as well. Everything's running smoothly here, and it would only be a flying visit, ten days or so. Elaine would be happy to house sit and look after the dogs and the ponies.'

He leaned forward and Erin's pulse spiked as adrenaline shot through her. Did he mean what she thought he did?

'Obviously I don't want to put undue pressure on you, but if I go, and it's not decided until we've had this conversation, then you'd be the senior vet in charge whilst I'm away.' He paused to let this sink in, and nerves were fluttering through Erin's stomach. 'I also want you to understand that you have my complete confidence, and I hold you and your commitment to the practice in the highest regard. Sometimes these conversations get lost in the day to day, but they shouldn't because I need to be clear.

'Next year is a really big one for us with the redevelopments. I'm looking to the future, and I see you very much as a partner who can work alongside me and help me take those tough decisions when we need to. I trust you and your judgement absolutely. In fact, I feel very lucky to have found you. Gabi's an excellent practice manager, and I know all the staff will support you totally. So what do you think?'

Erin wasn't sure she could think. She'd abandoned her bacon roll and her mind was spinning with this news coming at her out of the blue. She hoped one day she'd make partner and lead a team; she wanted a long-term career in a practice where she could treat companion animals alongside farm and equine ones, but so soon?

Was Gil actually serious? He was a brilliant colleague, and they always had a laugh, but he was totally committed to the practice, and he expected the same high standard of care from everyone else. But was she ready for this, to take on the responsibility that came with leadership until the new year? The adrenaline was still flooding her body, and she made herself sit still, forcing down the fight or flight sensation, so familiar from those first months after qualifying.

The thought of the practice without Gil, even for just two weeks, was making her nervous too. Although she'd been qualified for seven years, this was her first winter here and she was still getting used to the clients and the location. But she also very much appreciated his experience and his willingness to share it in support of her own career growth. She was elated that he trusted and valued her, and wanted her to step up. But there was fear too, that she'd fail because she wasn't ready for such a role.

'Wow, thank you. I really appreciate your confidence and trust in me.' She landed on the first question in her mind. 'When are you thinking of going?'

'Tomorrow, actually, so we'd be there for Christmas Eve. We'd be flying back on the second.' Gil picked up his coffee and finished it. 'I'm sorry, Erin, I know that doesn't give you much warning. If you're not comfortable with it, then Craig Blackwood, who was one of my partners at the practice in town, would be prepared to step in, I'm certain. He wouldn't be here day to day, but he'd act as senior vet if that's what you'd prefer. And we will be closed for the bank holidays, apart from out-of-hours.'

And tomorrow was Oli's last working day here. Already his three weeks were almost over, and Erin couldn't believe how quickly that had come around. She was in no way ready for that, and she refocused sharply as Gil continued.

'Irrespective of my trip, Gabi and I have arranged to continue with the agency cover for out of hours until mid-January at least. Obviously you and Oli are covering some of it, and I think it would be good to have two vets on call once we get into lambing season.' Gil ran a hand over his jaw, eyes flickering over his phone as it lit up, and he swiped the notification away. 'I'd like to ask Oli to stay on until I get back, and maybe through lambing season as well if he's interested. Like you he's a team player, great with clients and even Dorothy's offered the occasional compliment. And if he agrees, it will mean that he'd still need somewhere to stay. I realise this is a lot to ask you over Christmas, but would you be happy to continue hosting him?'

'I'm fine with all of those things,' she replied steadily, trying to subdue a rush of joy. The adrenaline was receding now, and she was thinking more clearly. She didn't have to consider whether Oli should stay, they needed him. But he had made plans for Christmas, and much as she longed for him to spend the holidays with her, she didn't want to be in the way of his family arrangements.

'That's brilliant, Erin, thank you. I can't tell you how much I appreciate it, and Pippa will too, she's so excited about having both our families together.' Gil leaned back and eased out a long breath. 'So when I get back, you and I need to sit down and have a proper three-month review, but as far as I'm concerned that's a formality. I couldn't be happier, and I have no concerns. But if you do, then we can talk about them before I leave.'

'No, I'm fine. I love it here, it's exactly what I was looking for.' Warmth was stealing through her at Gil's words. This was where she wanted to be, making a life on which she could depend. 'I promise to do my best not to let you or the practice down.'

'That's great, I'm delighted. And I know you will, I don't doubt you.' Gil reached across the desk, and they shook hands firmly, and Erin laughed. Her life had taken an unexpected turn in the last two days and this one felt brighter still, filled with excitement and promise. And pressure, there would be plenty of that.

'Craig is a good friend, and he will absolutely help you out should you need him. And don't forget I'm only a call or a Skype away, you can contact me anytime, day or night.'

'I hope I won't have to, but thank you.' Erin was trying to remain professional, but it was hard in the face of anticipation of more time with Oli. This was another step in her career plan. She tried to ignore the little voice reminding her that she didn't have everything she wanted in Hartfell. Because eventually Oli would leave, and she'd stay to grow her career and remain close to her family.

'So let's pass on the news to the staff when they come in, and you and I need to go through the diary.' Gil had saved Lola some of his bacon buttie and she wolfed it down, staring up at him with hopeful eyes. 'Sorry, Lola, that's your lot.'

An hour later he broke the news and to Erin it still sounded incredible, almost unreal, that she was now effectively senior vet. She'd been preparing herself for this ever since she'd arrived at university with little in her pocket but a strong work ethic and a lifelong desire to care for animals, but it was still astounding to realise it was now in her grasp.

'Erin, that's fantastic. I'm so pleased for you, and you'll be brilliant.' Oli was the first to step forward and she thrust out a hand in case he was thinking of hugging her. She would definitely have appreciated one right now, though, the certainty of his arms tight around her and letting her know she was up to the challenge. The rest of the staff offered their own congratulations and support in turn, and Jess did hug her.

'Oli, Erin and I would like a word before you head out please.' Gil pointed to a chair as everyone else trooped out, and another blast of adrenaline shot through Erin when he looked at her. 'Would you like to take the lead on this?'

'Of course.' She drew in a breath; it was one thing to spend half the weekend making love with Oli; it was quite another to face him across a desk and keep those intimate and meaningful moments they'd shared together private. 'We'd like to ask you to stay on until Gil gets back, possibly into lambing season as well. Of course you may have other plans, and it would impact your own with family for Christmas, so I'm sure you need some time to think about it. I'd be happy for you to stay at the cottage.'

She stopped talking lest her expression was doing it for her. It was so difficult to look at him and pretend they hadn't shared a lingering kiss before she'd left home earlier.

'I don't need time to think about it; I'm more than happy to accept. I haven't made any plans for January yet and I'd love to stay on.'

'But what about your family?' she rushed out. Her heart was aching that she and Gil had presented him with a difficult choice, and for a fleeting moment she wished things were different, that work hadn't suddenly stepped between them in a way she hadn't seen coming. 'Won't they mind not seeing you for Christmas?'

'I'm sure we can catch up in the new year.' His eyes caught hers and she read the glimpse of pleasure amongst the professionalism, the realisation that Gil's sudden new plans would give them more time together over the holidays, too. 'And you need me here.'

That much was true, and it would be almost impossible to find a new locum in time, especially one who fitted so well into their small team. He shared in the fun, he made them laugh and Erin had seen time and again that he was an outstanding vet who had boundless compassion for his patients. And he was so good with Marnie, and she knew he was as attached to her as she was.

Gil shook Oli's hand delightedly, and after Erin had thanked him too she made her escape. She had a full list this morning and needed to get on. It was evening before she saw Oli again and she was at home when he arrived, sitting on the floor playing with Marnie. The kitten liked to leap onto the sofa and stalk along the back with an important air before sliding down the other arm.

Oli had left chicken, chorizo and peppers in the slow cooker this morning and Erin added rice to finish it off. It smelled wonderful and she was hungry after an early start and a busy day, with clients making last-minute appointments before the practice closed for the holidays. She would be on call on Christmas Day, with Oli taking Boxing Day. This wasn't anything new, but at least her mum would be here to share the day with them, and Erin had booked the luxury of a taxi for Heather to make sure of it.

They ate with plates on their knees after she'd fed Marnie, who'd fallen asleep in her bed, tired after racing around. Tomorrow was Christmas Eve and Erin was hoping the snow on the way wouldn't impact their work too much.

'How are you feeling, after seeing your dad yesterday?' She put her empty plate aside and he did the same. Other than on the drive home, when he'd been quiet and reflective, they hadn't had any more opportunity to talk about this.

'I'm okay, thanks.' He leaned back, letting his head rest against the sofa. 'It's hard though, after years of believing it was Dad's fault their marriage ended to suddenly find out that it wasn't him at all. And if I'm honest, I'm sad for all of us because I think the truth would have hurt less. And Mum, all those years with Gillian. Imogen messaged me and said she suspected but it wasn't obvious. I think I was too busy being angry at Dad after Mum died to see it, so what does that say about me?'

'It says you were hurt and trying to protect yourself,' Erin said gently. 'Please don't beat yourself up about your mum. She never found a way to tell you and maybe she thought that was for the best. From what your dad said she was happy, and he's happy too, with Christina.'

'Yeah. I'm glad he has that, because I've blamed him for so long.'

'I'm sorry that work has got in the way of your Christmas with them.' Erin found his hand to hold it; she simply couldn't not. 'Imogen's going to be disappointed.'

'They're used to it,' he said lightly. 'We haven't done Christmas together in a long time. Hopefully we can do it next year.'

'But what about you?'

'I'm fine, we'll be busy and you need me here,' he said firmly. 'Like I said, I don't do much to celebrate.'

'Well, at least you can thank Marnie for not having to live in a holiday movie set,' Erin told him, and he laughed. 'And of course you're welcome to share in everything Mum and I do.'

'Like what?' he said suspiciously.

'Christmas lunch and something on telly, then probably a board game and a movie.' It would be strange to spend the day without her grandparents, but that was their choice, and she couldn't push them. Her nan would be cooking lunch at home come hell or high water, run off her feet and loving every minute. Joyce always said she'd never step aside while she had breath in her body and two legs to keep her upright.

'That doesn't sound too bad. I think I can cope.' He squeezed her hand. 'Erin, I really am thrilled about your role at the practice whilst Gil's away. I know you'll be excellent, and I'll support you totally.'

'Thank you, that's lovely and I so appreciate it.' She took a deep breath; there was something she needed to say, and she was dreading it. 'But I have been thinking, about you and me. If you agree, I think we should put our relationship on hold until Gil gets back. And that you should stay in your own room for now. We're so new, and I really can't afford any distractions whilst he's away.'

'You're not serious?' Oli shifted a shoulder to stare at her. 'Because I don't have any problem with you being my senior at the practice if that's what's concerning you. I understand that we have to be careful, but we're both adults here, and more than capable of doing our jobs, even if we do feel a lot more than professional respect towards one another.' He paused. 'The last couple of nights with you have been incredible, and of course I want that again. I want us to fall asleep together after making love, to wake up in the morning with you beside me. And I want the hand holding, the laughter and the coming home together.'

'But you won't be here, not forever,' she burst out, unwilling to let such thoughts settle in her mind. She wanted all that too, but she didn't see how they could have it, not when his own plans were so uncertain. 'You're leaving, Oli, and we both knew that settling down isn't what you want. My life is here, my family, my career, my home, Marnie. My everything, and I can't just take off when I feel like it. Are you seriously saying that you'd settle here, in this house, so we can be together?'

'And what if I am?'

Erin's shoulders crumpled and she couldn't allow herself to believe it, not really. Not when her mind was full of the coming days at the practice, and the thought of being senior vet was still making her stomach swoop. 'That's not something we should talk about now. Please,

Oli, let me do my job, and if you still feel the same way in January we can discuss it then.'

Chapter Twenty

The following morning Gil, Pippa, Harriet and Alfie had already left for Australia and Erin found it strange to be taking the morning staff meeting without him. She'd done it before when Gil had been unavailable, but this time it was different, and she struggled to meet Oli's eyes. He'd moved back into the spare bedroom last night and she'd missed him horribly. It felt like a very backward step in their relationship, and she was confused by the conflicted emotions filling her mind.

Elaine was house sitting to look after Lola and Maud, plus the ponies, and both dogs knew something was amiss without their family around. Posy hadn't thawed towards Flo yet and before he'd left, Gil had erected another strand of electric fencing in the paddock so they could graze separately but within sight. Flo was slowly putting on weight and Harriet had been practising leading her around the yard and getting her used to being handled. Dorothy had mentioned that she used to drive a skewbald cob around the dale and Harriet had already asked her to teach Flo in the summer.

It was a full-on morning of farm calls and Erin felt chilled from the inside out as she drove, as flat and heavy as the grey skies laden with snow, after the decision she'd made to ask Oli to sleep in the spare room again. She was glad to return to the practice for a late lunch, trying to summon a more festive feeling.

In the evening she wrapped her gifts and left them in her bedroom, not wanting Marnie to assume they were toys and rip all the paper off. Oli had gone out and the cottage, even with Marnie and a festive classic on the television, felt diminished without him. She settled Marnie and went up to bed before he arrived back, aware that the return to their first difficult days here was her own fault.

On Christmas Eve she left Marnie at home as she wouldn't be out all day. The morning was still a working one of routine consultations before they closed for all but emergencies. Everyone was in a merry, festive mood and she loved how they'd pulled together in Gil's absence, including Oli. She'd heard him return last night and had turned over alone in her bed, missing him beside her more than she'd ever imagined.

By the time Erin returned from her two farm calls, snow was falling steadily, and she messaged her mum, checking in that the taxi was still okay to bring her over tomorrow. It was costing a fortune, but she really didn't care; it was worth every penny. At the practice Christmas carols were playing in the office and Elaine had brought in homemade vanilla cupcakes decorated with snowmen. Lola and Maud had their own treats and were curled in their usual spot behind Elaine's desk. Erin took a picture of them and sent it to Harriet, who'd apparently been tearful when she'd had to say goodbye to the animals.

Jess, sporting an antler headband decorated with flowers and scarlet berries, organised everyone into the kitchen once they'd closed, and the staff sat down with brews and Gabi's delicious traditional Polish poppy seed cake, which disappeared in moments. Gabi also handed out paper cups of mulled non-alcoholic punch as Elaine passed around their Secret Santa gifts. Gil had already received a Grinch travel mug before he'd left and it had pride of place on a desk, ready for his return. Their out-of-hours locum was covering the evening and Erin was aware she'd probably be called out at some point tomorrow; it came with the territory. But as long as her mum got here safely then all would be well.

She suddenly realised that everyone was looking at her, and stood up hastily. She hadn't planned anything to say but now seemed the right moment to express her gratitude. 'So before we open our gifts, I'd like to thank Elaine for arranging Secret Santa.' Everyone else murmured their thanks, and she was aware of Oli at the back of the group, his eyes on her.

'I know Gil's already thanked you for your work since he took over the practice and wished you all the best for Christmas. I'd also like to say thank you for your welcome and helping me find my place here. You all know how much I love it, and it means the world to be working alongside you.' She held up her paper cup. 'Merry Christmas, I hope you have a wonderful one.'

That hurt too, as she imagined what kind of Christmas Oli was going to have without his family. Erin sat down and they opened their gifts. Elaine was delighted with a cream tote bag covered in black paw prints; Steph loved her scrubs bag decorated with cats and dogs; and Gabi was thrilled with a water bottle emblazoned with 'fifty shades of vet medicine' in scarlet. Erin thought that Jess, who loved to be glamorous even when she was cosying up at home, might guess that she'd chosen the pair of fluffy white slippers decorated with diamante hearts. Jess gave her a knowing look and declared them perfect.

Oli unwrapped his gift and he laughed at a green travel mug with 'good luck finding better colleagues than us' written around it. To Erin it was a stark reminder that he'd be leaving soon after Gil returned, and she listened with half an ear to the teasing as he promised it was absolutely true. She unwrapped her own gift to discover an A5 notebook, but it was the image of a woman wearing scrubs and the words written beneath that made her gulp. Holding a stethoscope in one hand, a cat on the woman's right with a dog on her left, the inscription read 'never forget the difference you make'.

It could have come from any one of her colleagues, most likely Jess, but when she caught Oli's eyes on hers, she was in no doubt. At Catz they'd talked about their future careers, and she'd told him then she wanted to make a difference to the lives of animals and help those who cared for them. She saw the memory in his gaze, and she felt it again; the realisation that he knew her so well. It was impossible to imagine anyone else could ever touch her life in the same way. She blinked back the emotion before it became apparent, and he turned away to laugh at something Steph was saying.

The staff parted in the snow outside the practice, and Erin was thankful to pick up a message from a local farmer who'd be coming later to clear the driveway. They needed access to the surgery at all hours and Gil had asked him to keep an eye on the weather and help if he could. She replied to thank the farmer gratefully, aware that his own work didn't end with the holidays. She'd definitely be ready for the week off she had planned in early January, before lambing season kicked off in earnest.

She'd ordered a veg box from Violet and Daphne at the shop and she called for it on the way home. The two sisters were looking forward to having Dorothy over for lunch, something they'd been doing for years, and they were busy with customers calling for last-minute shopping. Erin also picked up some more mince pies before wishing them a happy Christmas and lugging the box out to her pickup through gathering snow. She'd bought plenty so she could send an extra lunch back with her mum, and her family could enjoy it at home on Boxing Day.

She already had the turkey in the fridge and Heather had brought over one of Joyce's Christmas puddings on a previous visit. She'd also be fetching a trifle as well and Erin couldn't wait; no one made trifle like her nan. She let herself into the cottage, shaking the snow from her hat as she carried the box through to the kitchen. Oli was already changed after a shower, and he settled on the floor with Marnie to play with her. Erin plugged her phone in to charge so she was prepared if she had to go out, and after her own shower she was in the kitchen to make a start on tomorrow's lunch preparations.

'Can I help?' Oli appeared at the door. 'Marnie's crashed now, I've tired her out.'

'You could do the sprouts, if you don't mind?' Erin pointed to the stalks still sitting in the box on the floor; there simply wasn't room on the worktop. She had a playlist of brass band carols going and found it soothing and sad all at once; reminding her of family and the traditions they loved.

'So what do I need to do?' He lifted a stalk from the box. 'I had no idea that sprouts grew like this, I thought they came in plastic bags from the supermarket.'

'Ha ha.' She pointed to a spare chopping board as she carried on peeling potatoes; there could never be enough roasties. 'Just take the bottom bit off and tidy them up.'

'So I suppose you're going to tell me they're essential with Christmas lunch.' Oli started snapping sprouts from the stalk and she smiled.

'It's not even a discussion. Although my nan and grandad can't agree on how to serve them. Nan likes them plain and Grandad prefers them with a bit of crispy bacon, so she makes both.'

'Which are you going to serve?'

'Both,' Erin said promptly. Until this moment she hadn't even considered how awkward lunch might be. Her mum knew her so well and was bound to sense the new tension between her and Oli. 'Got to stick with tradition.'

'You'll really miss your grandparents tomorrow,' he said quietly. Bits of sprouts were spilling on the worktop as he peeled.

Erin nodded. She was breathing him in again, thinking of falling asleep with him beside her. It was worse now, to step back to what they'd been before last weekend. Before she'd had the reality of making love with him to remind her how wonderful it really was.

'That's why I need to keep some of our traditions and create my own. It helps keep them close.' Hopefully next Christmas she wouldn't be on call, and she could go over and spend the day with her family. Her nan and grandad weren't getting any younger and she didn't want to think of how many more Christmases they might have together.

'So what new traditions have you come up with?'

'I'm going to walk around the village later, have a look at the lights, and watch *The Holiday* before bed. That's going to be my new Christmas Eve. Usually I'd help Nan with the lunch while she makes the trifle. Then she'd get out the best glasses we only use at Christmas, and we'd drink snowballs and watch *The Royle Family* Christmas special. The one with Caroline Aherne, not the actual royal family.'

'Right. It sounds great.' Oli seemed wistful.

'So what about you?' she said quietly. 'How do you usually spend Christmas Eve?' She wondered if he'd reply or tell her that it was no longer any of her concern.

'On call sometimes.' They shared an understanding smile at that. 'When we were little Dad would track Santa with us, and we'd hang up our stockings and put out food for the reindeers. But after Honey died and he left we were too old anyway, so Mum would arrange a movie marathon, and we'd have a takeaway. It was nice, but it was never quite the same. I don't have any traditions now. Imogen and Alex are hosting some friends tonight, and Dad and Christina will be with them tomorrow.'

'I'm so sorry you're not with them.' Erin laid a hand on his arm. 'I hope you don't miss your family too much.'

'It's fine, Erin, I'm happy to be here and help you.' His eyes were telling her more; that he was hurt about the change she'd brought about in their relationship in order to have the space she needed to run the practice without Gil. 'I'll take a few days off when I leave and see them then.'

Oli slid the peelings into the recycling bin by the back door. Marnie had come to investigate and Erin bent to pick her up gently, a rush of love following as the kitten began to purr. They tried not to crowd her so she didn't feel threatened or afraid, and it was wonderful to be taking these tiny steps as she gained confidence. She wasn't far off a normal weight now and yesterday Erin had vaccinated and microchipped her, making Marnie's new home official.

'Would you like to come with me tonight?' Erin asked impulsively. She wanted to be with him, for Oli not to feel alone without his family. 'Obviously you don't have to, but…'

'I'd like that.' He reached out a finger to Marnie, stroking her head, his care for the kitten another thing Erin loved about him. He was so gentle and patient, and it wasn't difficult to imagine the kitten would miss him too when he left.

They needed wellies with snow still falling steadily. The village was quiet, everything draped in a thick white blanket, Christmas lights and decorations shimmering through the dark. They called on Edmund to make sure he was okay, and he assured them he was fine; he would also be joining Violet, Daphne and Dorothy for lunch tomorrow.

'So any thoughts about work in the new year?' Erin had been worrying about this and it was a coming reality she had to get used to. Spending the holidays in Hartfell was an interlude for Oli, and one he would leave behind once his contract at the practice ended.

'Nothing yet. A couple of recruiters have got in touch, but one job was in the Highlands, and I'd prefer to be further south for a while.'

'To be nearer your family?' She hoped that was true.

'Yeah.' Oli's eyes caught hers in the lights glittering outside the pub. It was busy despite the weather, packed with people enjoying these last few hours of Christmas Eve. He kicked some snow with his foot, scattering it over Erin.

'Watch it,' she warned, brushing it from her jeans. 'Or else.'

'Or else what?' He'd paused and she recognised the dangerous glint in his face, sending her pulse spiking.

'Or else you'll regret it.' She dropped down and gathered some snow into her hands, launching it at him. It landed on his shoulder and his splutter was an astonished one.

'So that's how you want to play it? Now who'll be the one regretting it?'

'Not me. I was goal shooter in netball at school and I've got a brilliant aim.' She'd already scooped up another fistful of snow.

'Is that right? And I was a fast bowler in my school's first eleven, so let's see who's best, shall we?'

Erin lobbed it and darted out of his way. Too late to completely avoid him though, and his first caught the back of her head, falling down her collar. She squealed in outrage, and they fought mercilessly, pelting one another until they were both soaked and laughing helplessly.

'Let's go into the pub and have a snowball, a drink this time. To keep with tradition, cos we haven't got any at home.' Oli took her hand and tugged her to the entrance. 'You'll still be fine to drive tomorrow if you need to.'

Had he really just said home? She felt it too, the rhythm and routines they'd developed naturally, caring for Marnie too. How it felt more of a home with him and Marnie in it. There were so many ways she was going to miss him.

She let him lead her into the pub, packed with party-goers celebrating the season. Kenny was delighted to see them and sent over a glass of punch to get them started. After that they had snowball cocktails; rich, creamy advocaat topped up with lime and lemonade and finished with a cherry on top. Oli pulled a face at the sweetness when he tried it, and Erin laughed. Then they were ready to return home, their clothes still damp after the snowball fight.

They went to change after greeting Marnie, and Erin was first back downstairs, sliding the homemade fish pie she'd bought from the shop into the oven. She checked her phone; she wasn't on call, but she wanted to be available if anyone needed to get hold of her. It was already Christmas morning in Australia, and happiness quickly followed at the thought of Gil, Pippa and Harriet celebrating with their families and enjoying the sunshine. She still wouldn't trade the chill of her traditional Dales Christmas, though.

Oli appeared on the stairs, and she was thinking of kissing him just two nights ago, the scratch of his beard against her face, the memory of his mouth once again on hers. She flushed, hoping he couldn't read her mind as well as she suspected. They watched *The Holiday* while they ate and even though she adored it, it was strange to share something so hopeful and romantic with him beside her. Afterwards they agreed on *Gavin and Stacey*'s first Christmas special, and she was almost asleep when it was over, Marnie on her lap.

'I need my bed.' She stood up, snuggling Marnie close. 'Thank you for everything you've done.' The veg for lunch was ready and the turkey in the oven, gradually reaching room temperature before she switched it on in the morning. This felt too stilted a goodnight after all they'd shared; but it was her choice and she had to see it through.

'You too, Erin,' he said softly. He stood up and stroked Marnie in her arms, the kitten purring softly. 'See you tomorrow.'

She was jolted awake a few hours later by her phone and she picked it up, squinting at the screen as she swiped to answer. Within seconds she was in work mode, and she got up and dressed quickly. At the window she pulled back the curtains, thankful to see that no more snow had fallen overnight. Downstairs she fed Marnie quickly and switched the kettle on for her flask; she might be gone for hours. Another message arrived as she poured hot water into the flask, unrelated to the veterinary emergency, and she read it twice, blinking back a rush of tears. This was a disaster, and her mind was racing between the message and the emergency she was about to attend.

'Morning.' Oli appeared on the stairs, one arm on the ceiling above him. 'What's the call? I heard your phone.'

'It's a ewe, she's lambed overnight and prolapsed.' Erin grabbed one of the cereal bars she kept for mornings like this. 'They think she must've got caught by the tup before the rest of the flock. She wasn't meant to be in lamb and they didn't scan her. Sorry for waking you.' She swiped at a tear before it slid down her cheek.

'Right. Hope it's okay, drive safe.'

'Thanks. The farmer's cleared her track, she reckons my pickup will get through.'

'Good. Merry Christmas, by the way.'

'What?' She blinked at him; it didn't feel very merry right now. 'Oh yeah. Merry Christmas.' She huffed out a laugh that very nearly became a sob.

'What's the matter? Is it the ewe?'

He joined her in the kitchen, smiling a hello at Marnie as she wound a path between his legs. Erin was on her way to the front door, trying to focus on what might lie ahead on the farm eight miles away. She yanked her coat from the hook and pulled on her hat. Thankfully, the farm was lower down the dale and not at the top of what would be a very tricky climb over precarious roads in this weather. At least someone, probably a farmer, had been out with a snowplough around the village last night so she wouldn't have to dig her vehicle out of a drift.

'My mum isn't coming, that's all. The taxi's cancelled because of the weather.' Erin's throat felt scratched, and the tears were blurring her vision. 'It was always a possibility she wouldn't make it with me living here. But as long as she and Nan and Grandad are okay, then that's all that matters. You and me can still have the lunch, I suppose.' She paused. 'Please would you switch the turkey on, it's all ready. Give it forty minutes and then turn it down again.'

'Absolutely. Is there anything else I can do?'

'Look after Marnie, please. I'll be back as soon as I can.' She opened the door, already braced for the cold. She was needed today, and Christmas would just have to wait.

The sun was low in a moody sky, and she breathed in cold, crisp air, helping to clear her mind. The silence and stillness always seemed different on Christmas Day, as though the world had paused to acknowledge its significance. The windscreen of her pickup was frozen, and she thanked Oli when he came out to help, his feet stuffed into wellies. She'd already put the heated seat on, and she leaped in the moment it was clear and took off as fast as she dared, thinking about the sheep who'd just given birth. It was essential she reached it as quickly as possible.

It took longer than usual to reach the farm, and she was very glad of her all-wheel drive vehicle as it climbed a steep but short and rocky track to the farm. The ewe was in a pen with her new lamb nearby, and Erin very quickly got to work once she'd examined her. She cleaned and disinfected the prolapse before reinserting it and completed the process with a suture to keep everything in place.

On the way back she picked up a call about a calf with suspected pneumonia and she diverted, heading further away from home. The signs when she examined it were reasonably positive, and she left additional medication for the farmer to inject over the coming days. It might be Christmas Day but that didn't stop animals needing to be cared for, and she'd been given a very welcome bacon roll at the second farm which went a long way to warming her up after an early start.

A third call came in when she was close to the practice, and she headed there to meet a dog which had swallowed some chocolate. The frantic owners hadn't wasted any time in turning up, so Erin got to work, giving it the appropriate medication, and mentally preparing herself for the mess. She adored her job but there were occasions when it seemed like a continuous process of clean-ups from either end. The medication worked and she gave the very sorry-looking spaniel charcoal treatment as well to help absorb any remaining traces of chemicals or toxins.

Satisfied after a while that it wasn't dehydrated and was comfortable enough to go home, she called the owners to let them know and told them to get in touch again if they had any further concerns. She'd left the cottage six hours ago and she just wanted to go home. Never mind Christmas lunch, especially without her mum – a turkey sandwich would do now, and at least thanks to Oli it would be ready.

She parked outside, thinking of lighting the fire and curling up beside it with Marnie and a movie to cheer her from missing her family. She let herself in and stopped

dead on the mat behind the door, her empty flask crashing
to the floor as she burst into tears.

Chapter Twenty-One

'Ooh, our Erin, I thought you were never comin' back,' her nan shouted from the kitchen, a ladle in her hand. Her grandad was in the armchair whisking cream in a bowl balanced precariously on his lap and her mum was setting the table. Oli was stirring something on the hob, and she swiped at her face when she caught his eye. His smile quickly became a laugh as Joyce peered inside the pan and told him to 'stir a bit quicker, lad, if you're thinkin' of 'avin' gravy with your dinner this side of t'new year.'

'Oh, it's so brilliant to see you, I can't believe it! How did you get here?' But she knew, and she barely trusted herself to look at Oli again as she brushed the tears away. Her mum came over to hug her, murmuring, 'As if you didn't know, Erin, love.' She went to her grandad and bent down to kiss his dry cheek, and he grinned up at her. 'You look like that's always been your chair, Grandad. It suits you.'

'Aye, it does.' He winked. 'Better watch out or I might be swappin' with you. Go an' see your nan, she's been itchin' for you to get back before her Yorkshires spoil.'

Her nan paused making the lunch long enough to let Erin bend down and hug her, and then she was chased from her own kitchen as Joyce informed her that she already had another pair of hands to help, and she should get her feet up while she could after the morning she'd just had.

'But Nan, you're on your feet, doing all this.' Erin waved a hand to the organised chaos scattered over the worksurfaces. 'You're supposed to be taking it easy, and I thought you weren't coming.' Her voice stuttered as she caught Oli's eye again.

'Aye, well we weren't, not until this lad turned up an' said he was fetchin' your mum back 'ere. No point in us sittin' on our own when I could be makin' meself useful with you out at work all hours. Now get out from under me feet, I've a dinner to make.' She shot Oli a look. 'Lewis Hamilton can stay. Nearly 'ad us on two wheels on the way over. I thought I wasn't goin' to live long enough to get me Yorkshires in t'oven.'

'Lewis Hamilton?' Erin's laugh was a spluttered one and Oli pulled a wry face.

'I'm not sure your nan's used to being driven,' he said, laughing. 'I wasn't going that quickly, honestly. There were a couple of tricky moments in the snow, that's all. How did you get on?'

'All fine for now.' Erin's shoulders loosened as her tension eased, and she checked her phone anyway, just to make sure. 'Probably won't be the last call of the day though.'

The little house was bursting, and she was over the moon that Christmas had finally arrived. The telly was on as her grandad kept an eye on repeats and her mum was setting out glasses and waving at someone through the window, Marnie perched on the back of the sofa and watching all this action warily. Erin desperately wanted a word with Oli, but she didn't imagine her nan would approve if he left the gravy alone at this crucial stage. She went over anyway, almost drooling at the thought of a proper Christmas dinner after her early start.

'Thank you.' The words were a whisper, and she hoped her eyes were telling him more. 'It means the world, especially when you can't be with your family. I hope you feel welcome in mine.'

'I do,' he told her softly as Joyce muttered at the sink. 'Although your nan said she'd knock my block off if there was any more messing about between you and me. I'm starting to realise you don't mess with Joyce.'

'You really don't.' Erin adored her nan's loyalty. 'But actually I think that's high praise. If she didn't like you, she'd have knocked it off already.'

She was trying to picture her life before Oli had landed back in it; her single-mindedness in focusing on work and her family, her small group of friends and the new ones she was making in Hartfell. She loved the community here and was so grateful to be a part of it, something she hoped to build on for the future. She'd never imagined sharing her life with someone else, not fully. Not like her grandparents, whose lives were melded together with a bond that seemed stronger than steel. They might bicker all day long and grumble constantly, but their partnership had endured almost sixty years, and the rhythm of their lives flowed as one.

Oli understood her career and its demands, the long and often unsociable hours. She knew he recognised her desire for independence too, to create a life that gave her security and satisfaction. In the years since they'd graduated, she'd never once come close to loving anyone else. And for all that she longed to remain professional at work, was it really so impossible to think they might be together and keep that part of their lives separate from their colleagues? Was she trying to push him away because she was afraid he wouldn't stay? But if she didn't give him a reason, then why would he stay?

The lunch was amazing, and Erin and Oli ate on their knees because there wasn't room for five around the table. No one made Yorkshire puddings like her nan, and they were perfect: golden, fluffy and crisp. Oli had wondered aloud why they were eating them when roast beef wasn't being served, but he'd been faced down by four outraged stares and very firmly informed that Yorkshire puddings went with everything. Joyce even promised to make her speciality for him one day, a large Yorkshire filled with steak, chips, peas and gravy, and Oli said he'd hold her to it.

Heather topped off the trifle with the cream Bill had whipped, and they paused for the king's speech before desserts were served. Joyce and Bill always had Christmas pudding followed by trifle, while Erin and her mum preferred it the other way around. Joyce had brought a pot of thick, creamy custard she'd made, and warmed it before pouring it generously over the Christmas pudding and ignoring Oli's protests that he was on call tomorrow, and he'd definitely need to be able to bend.

'Give over, you numpty, a big fella like you needs a proper dinner.' She dolloped on a bit more custard and Erin wasn't sure she'd ever felt so content in her life. She was full from her lunch and prayed she wouldn't get called out in the next couple of hours; she doubted she'd be able to bend. Maybe a second dessert hadn't been such a clever idea after all.

She'd already sent her nan and grandad's presents ahead as she hadn't expected to see them today, and they'd opened them at home this morning. She and Heather always made each other a stocking filled with small gifts they knew the other would love, and she was speechless all over again when her mum produced one for Oli too and set it on his lap.

'I know you couldn't be at home with your family, Oli, seeing as you're supporting Erin with Gil away. I didn't want you to miss out, it's only a few little bits but I hope you like them.'

Erin caught the bright shine of tears in his eyes as he was looking at her mum. 'Heather, gosh, this is so kind of you, and I really didn't expect anything. We haven't done stockings since I was a kid. I'm so sorry, I didn't get you a gift.'

'Oh you did, love, you did.' Heather leaned across to squeeze Erin's knee. 'You got us here to spend Christmas with this one, and that's all the present I needed. You'll never know how much it means.'

Erin had to gulp back the emotion clutching at her throat, both at her mum's words and her thoughtfulness towards Oli. She also felt a shiver of shame; she'd been so busy protesting they must maintain their profession-alism and pushing him away that she hadn't thought to do anything quite so caring or reminiscent of home for him. His support towards her was almost invisible but she knew it was there, nonetheless. It was the flask he made for her in the morning if he was down first; the acceptance of her decisions these past few days at work and his efforts to make sure they were implemented. The recipes he was following and the shopping he collected; all of it made a difference to her. She was the one failing here; she was the one trying to convince herself that independence didn't need to include love.

She and Oli were on the floor, and they unwrapped their stockings as Heather and her grandparents watched on. In hers she found the usual gifts she cherished, like the orange lip balm she used every day in winter, a pair of bamboo socks and an indulgent hand cream she'd save for weekends. There was chocolate and sweets too, plus a gift card for books, a gorgeous pair of Fair Isle knitted gloves, a candle from her favourite well-being range and a tangerine at the bottom.

Oli was unwrapping his gifts too, discovering a hat made from snug green wool, a trio of Old-Fashioned cocktails and a lip balm. He loved the mini travel set of shower gel and shampoo, and promised to use his own book token wisely. Alongside salted caramel chocolate buttons and a chocolate orange, he also discovered a chocolate first aid kit. He opened it immediately, declaring he was in need of some first aid after such a magnificent lunch, and passed it around. It took Joyce a moment to convince Bill, who'd been dozing, that he wasn't about to cut himself on a pair of real scissors. He said they were very nice but what was wrong with a tin of good old-fashioned Quality Street?

Erin made tea for everyone and coffee for Oli, and it was clear her grandparents were getting tired after all the activity. Oli insisted he would drive them home, and she accepted the offer; she was still on call and couldn't be too far away. The moment Erin had hugged her family and seen them safely into his car, she flopped onto the sofa with Marnie, who promptly fell asleep, shattered from the excitement of the day. The resemblance to that starving and sick kitten had all but vanished now, and the sight of her playing and darting around the cottage made Erin smile every single time.

Twenty minutes later her phone rang, and she left Marnie in her bed, hoping she'd stay there, and wrapped up against the freeze. A cat had cut itself quite badly on a shattered bauble, and as the nurse on call, Steph met her at the practice to assist. It was a nasty wound, and the cat had to be sedated so Erin could stitch the cut on its jaw back together. She was still home before Oli, and she cleared away the last of the lunch and gathered the discarded wrapping paper into the basket of logs. She had a quick shower and, by the time he returned, she was settled on the sofa in comfy lounging clothes, her work for the day finally done.

'Fancy a game of Uno?' She reached for the card game she'd left nearby. 'We always play it on Christmas night.'

'Love to.'

'Thank you for taking them home.' She found it difficult to meet his eyes, and the decision she'd made while he'd been gone was making her skin tingle with anticipation. 'And everything else you've done. It means the world.'

'My pleasure. It's been a wonderful day, despite the hours you've had to work.'

'I hope it's been okay for you, spending it without your family.'

'It's been a lot better than okay, I had the best time,' he said wistfully. 'It felt like Christmas for the first time in years. I video-called Imogen this morning and they were having a blast. She gets it, she knows why I'm here. Come on then, let's play. You'll have to remind me of the rules because I've haven't played it since that weekend at yours.'

'Seriously?' Erin laughed as she divided the cards between them. They played for an hour, other than a quick pause for hot chocolate, getting more competitive with every round.

'You win,' he said finally. Marnie had abandoned his lap and was stretched out along the back of the sofa. 'I'll be seeing little gingerbread men in my sleep after that.'

Oli reached into his pocket, and he took her hand, opening it to place a small gift wrapped in paper decorated with elves on her outstretched palm. 'I know we said no presents, but I saw this and thought of you.'

'Oli, you shouldn't have!' Erin unwrapped it slowly, not wanting to rush the anticipation and taking an extra moment to appreciate his thoughtfulness. Inside a box, sat a silver keyring with five charms attached to it. Warmth was flooding her body, and she had to blink before she could take in every detail. One charm was a tiny paw print, another depicted a family tree inside a heart, there was a letter E, a tiny silver kitten and a key. He'd encapsulated her world perfectly and she was staring in wonder at what felt very much like love in her hand.

'It's the most perfect gift I've ever had,' she whispered. 'I absolutely adore it, thank you.'

'You're welcome. I'm happy you're pleased.' He eased away, putting back the distance she'd insisted upon. She hated how they'd been moving around one another at home and at work as though they were strangers, trying to avoid every look, every accidental touch. She loathed how disconnected she felt from him now, almost from her own heart. It hurt more every day to think of him leaving Hartfell and beginning again somewhere else, when they would be once again out of reach.

'I got you something too.' It was also small, and she removed it from its hiding place behind a cushion. He opened the beautifully wrapped box and removed a silver chain and an ingot attached to it, turning the ingot over.

'It's a St Christopher,' she whispered. 'I wanted you to have something to keep you safe when you're travelling.'

'Erin… I love it, thank you.'

All those years without him, and she'd never feel for anyone what she felt for Oli. And he was here. Gently she reached across and cupped his face, the beard rough against her palm.

'I'm sorry I pushed you away,' she said quietly. 'Today's been amazing in between all the chaos, and it's made me realise it would be a mistake to miss out on what we feel. And my heart's telling me I don't really have a choice in the matter. But I understand if you don't, after everything I said about working together.'

'I want that too,' he said softly. 'And my heart's saying exactly the same thing. I think it would be a very good idea to work out how we feel about the future and take it from there. We have some time before we need to decide what's next. And I promise that nothing we share at home will alter my behaviour at work, or my respect for your leadership.'

Erin closed her eyes to prevent a tear escaping, her mouth dry. She knew where this was leading now, and it felt wonderful.

'Speaking of positions…' Oli's hands went to her waist, and she wriggled across to sit on his lap. She smoothed a hand across his face at the look of longing and love in his eyes, too. For now, the questions and concerns about the future were banished, and she wanted only him and this precious time together. She picked up his St Christopher and went to fasten it around his neck, but he stilled her.

'I don't need it yet,' he whispered. 'I'm not going anywhere.' He returned her gift to its box and one hand was on the zip of her hoodie as she lowered her head until her lips found his. His other hand went to her curls to hold her as they kissed, and already she was impatient with the barriers between them. She helped him tug her hoodie off and his hands were on the cream silk camisole she wore underneath.

'You're perfect,' he murmured, and she laughed softly.

'I'm really not, but I'm glad you think so.'

He raised his arms so she could lift his own sweater and the T-shirt beneath over his head, and he pulled her into him. Erin leaned down to kiss him again, her lips teasing a trail to his ear.

'Marnie's awake. She's watching.'

'So?' His hands were busy with the straps on her camisole.

'We can't let her watch, Oli! It's weird.'

'So what do you suggest?' His grin was a mischievous one as he kissed the shoulder he'd bared, his tongue tantalising on her skin.

'We'll have to go upstairs,' Erin muttered distractedly, and she went to pull back.

'Oh no you don't,' he said, standing up and taking her with him. 'Now I've got you in my arms I'm keeping you there.'

'Is that right,' she whispered as his hands hunched beneath her thighs and she wrapped her arms around his neck.

'Consider it a promise.' In the kitchen he turned to the stairs and the warning flew from her lips just in time.

'Oli, duck!'

Chapter Twenty-Two

Oli was on call on Boxing Day and he had to leave when he took a call from stricken owners about a cat they suspected had been run over. She made him a coffee while he dressed, and she'd already offered to join him at the practice if he wanted assistance. He suggested she stay home for now and he'd let her know when he understood more about the cat's condition. She followed him to the door and kissed him quickly, smiling as he sprinted to his car. The snow was beginning to thaw, and the lane was sludgy with slush.

He messaged later to say that X-rays had revealed a fracture in a hind leg and he'd be operating once the cat was stable. That meant he'd be gone for hours, so she tidied the cottage after she'd fed Marnie and changed her litter tray. She also checked in with her mum, and Heather replied to say they were all fine but tired after a wonderful day and it had been worth every minute of the journey. With Oli busy in surgery for some time, Erin kept an eye on calls as well, but she was thankful not to be needed.

When he returned late in the afternoon, they settled on the sofa with Marnie between them and *Elf* on the tele-vision. After a while he stopped laughing, leaning against her, and she saw that he was asleep. They were both tired after a manic few days and tomorrow the practice would open again as usual. Suddenly she couldn't wait for her week off in January, daydreaming about where she might spend it and if Oli would join her. She hadn't had a proper holiday for ages and the thought of her own short getaway was very appealing.

The practice was busy as ever when they returned in the morning. Everyone was either full of cheese or trifle, and they barely even knew what day of the week it actually was. There were no farm calls and Oli took the routine companion animal consultations, most of which had been booked in before Christmas. A couple of last-minute emergencies cropped up, so Erin saw those, dispensing antibiotics for a dog with a suspected bacterial infection and a cat which had had an allergic reaction to a change of food.

She also popped into the stables to check on the ponies and sent a couple of pictures to Harriet. Flo was steadily gaining weight as well as confidence and even Posy appeared to be thawing towards her, allowing Flo to graze nearby without pulling faces. May and bright spring weather, when the foal would be born, seemed a very long way from these cold and grey days.

At work Erin and Oli were very careful not to reveal the alteration in their relationship and he deferred to Erin's decisions every time. But she liked to discuss them with him first, and listen to his own advice and experience before making up her mind. Gil had also messaged to check in and she assured him they were fine, and the practice was running well.

The out-of-hours locums were on call in the evenings and although she felt braced for an emergency at any time, she also found it wonderfully relaxing to come home to Oli, sharing meals and playing with Marnie, watching old movies, and going up to bed together. His St Christopher

273

sat in its box on his side of the bed and occasionally it seemed like a metaphor for his leaving, the plans he would eventually make to take him away. But not yet. For now, they still had time together in Hartfell, and New Year's Eve in the pub with Jess and Noah to look forward to first.

–

'You look amazing.' Oli paused buttoning his shirt as Erin picked up her dress. Falling to mid-thigh, it was silver and long-sleeved, gathered at the waist with a thin belt. She'd bought it for a party with Carys ages ago and had only worn it the once, with the same choice of metallic ankle boots. Getting ready in here with Oli was a squeeze even with his clothes still hanging on the rail in his room.

'I'm not dressed yet.'

'Exactly.' He drew her towards him for a kiss and the silver dress fell onto the bed when she wound her arms around his neck. 'You look perfect just as you are.' His fingers were on the clasp of her bra, and she felt it come loose.

'Five minutes,' she told him sternly, belying the playfulness in her gaze. 'Or we'll be late.'

'Five minutes?' He added his own pretend outrage to that statement. 'It'll take me longer than that just to kiss you.'

In the end they were ten minutes late to the pub, and Erin hated that Oli freed his hand from hers as they entered. She sent him a grateful smile nonetheless, appreciating that he was trying to make this evening with their colleague as easy as possible for her. She checked her phone before sliding it into her bag as she hung up her coat, surprised to see that Jason had sent her a happy new year message. She replied with a brief one of her own wishing him all the best, wondering if he'd sent his by mistake.

This evening was ticket-only and the Pilkington Arms was packed with locals and guests sitting down to a five-course tasting menu and paired wines. Erin and Oli went for the non-alcoholic version as she was on call tomorrow, and she didn't want to wake with a hangover. All these altered nights out, when she couldn't quite party like everyone else, weren't something she'd factored into her career at the start. But she wouldn't swap it, not for the world, and having Oli beside her felt magical.

They were laughing at a funny story of Noah's from work, leaning together, shoulders touching, and Erin was sure Jess suspected she and Oli were now more than just friends and colleagues. But on this final night of the year, she was full of hope and happiness, certain that she and Oli would find a way around work if he decided to stay on once Gil came home and her role returned to normal.

A few minutes before midnight everyone hurried outside to watch silent fireworks lighting up the sky with showers of colour. A piper stood nearby to play 'Auld Lang Syne', and they joined hands to sing along, laughing through the cold. Erin didn't want to let go of Oli's hand when it was over and he was the first person she kissed once the year had turned, even if it was only on his cheek. Then they rushed home to make sure Marnie was okay before tumbling into bed.

They managed a lie-in in the morning and once he'd fed Marnie, he cooked breakfast, and they ate it in bed. The other day she'd discovered Marnie curled up on Oli's chest as he dozed on the sofa after an early start, and the sight had made her heart clench with joy. Just a few weeks ago she'd had neither of these loves in her life, and she realised just how rich they made it.

The practice was quiet over the next couple of days. Erin knew Gil and Pippa had returned when she bumped into Harriet and Alfie in the stables, straight off the flight and keen to see all the animals. Lola and Maud were ecstatic to have their family home, and the dogs were leaping around in excitement as Posy nuzzled up to Harriet in search of the treats she always carried. Erin thought Harriet looked lovely, her brunette hair shot through with lighter streaks from an Australian summer.

They'd had a fabulous time, she told Erin as they led the ponies along the drive to the paddock, but having so many of her family under one roof had been an enlightening experience. Apparently even Pippa was ready for their own space and a Yorkshire winter once the new year was over. Jonny was perfectly settled, and he and Vanessa were planning to stay for a few years at least.

Gil arrived at the practice on Monday morning soon after Erin, and once he'd greeted the staff and filled them in on his trip, and thanked them for all their hard work, he asked Erin if she'd join him once morning consultations were over. He also looked well, suntanned and fit, his blond hair even lighter.

She had a dental on Dorothy's lurcher arranged for the afternoon and Oli was castrating some ferrets – she'd teased him about who had the better job, and it wasn't him. Catching them first to anaesthetise them without being bitten would be the trickiest part, and she hoped he would get on okay when she sat down with Gil in the office later.

'We had a fantastic time, and it was so great to meet everyone properly.' He was cradling a coffee and had already made tea for Erin. 'Jonny was excellent company and my boys fitted right in. Pippa adored having everyone together and Jonny wouldn't let her do a thing. We managed to squeeze in a visit to Joel's vineyard too, and he's coming over in the summer.'

'It sounds amazing,' Erin replied wistfully. She was starting with a cold, and she knew her mum worried that she'd got run down over the holidays. It often happened when she was really busy so she couldn't deny she was relieved to have Gil back, even though a part of her was going to miss the pressure of being senior vet.

'I want to thank you for all you've done, Erin.' He leaned forward, one hand clasped around his coffee. 'Gabi and Elaine are full of praise for how brilliantly you've coped, and I really appreciated you not having to call me. It was so good to get away and have a proper holiday together.' He glanced out of the window towards the cobbled farmyard, the last of the snow still evident in slushy grey puddles. 'Coming back to this weather is going to take a bit of getting used to after an Aussie summer.'

'I can imagine.' Erin had never taken a holiday in winter, so she didn't know any different. 'Thank you for saying that, but I had a lot of support, and everyone's been wonderful. We pulled together, and I couldn't have done it without Oli too.'

'That's great to hear. So, going back to our discussion about the future before I left. I know we didn't have time for a thorough review but the clear thought in my mind is that I'd like to offer you a partnership, Erin. Of course you'll need some time to consider it.'

'Gil, I don't know what to say!' Her voice rose and her stomach was fluttering with excitement. 'That's incredible, thank you. It's everything I dreamed of for my career. Thank you for your confidence in me, I so appreciate it. If I'm honest, I hadn't imagined a partnership so soon.'

Her family would also be over the moon, and Erin was imagining her mum's pride, the sacrifices she'd made down the years, the thousands of hours of study and work it had taken to get here.

'You're very welcome.' Gil leaned back, and she knew from his smile he was pleased with her response. 'And much as I want you to progress your career, the selfish bit of me wants to hang on to you. I know you've got a week off coming up soon, so don't rush your decision. Have your holiday and we can talk when you get back and see how you feel then. I want you to be sure this is right for you, as much as I believe it is for the practice.'

'Thank you, I will give it serious thought and I'll let you know as soon as I've decided.'

'Perfect. So that brings me to Oli.' Gil slid his empty cup away and his gaze was so direct that Erin flushed guiltily. Did her boss know how things were between them? Had he heard about the kiss they'd shared on New Year's Eve outside the pub? Was he about to ask her to choose between Oli and her career? Could he even do that? She very much doubted it, but it was a concern all the same.

'I'd like to offer him a full-time job, with your agreement. He's settled in brilliantly and made himself very much part of the team, and I know everyone rates him highly. His preference for companion animal work complements you and me perfectly, Erin, and I'd like to keep him if we can. What do you think?'

'I think it would be wonderful if he stayed,' she replied steadily, trying to remove all trace of elation from her voice. But it was hard to disguise her pleasure; the final piece in her life was falling into place and this would be the perfect reason to anchor Oli in Hartfell. 'He's an outstanding vet and the clients love him.'

'So do you think he'll accept?'

'I hope so. I think he might, yes.'

Suddenly the day looked brighter. Perhaps she really could have it all: a meaningful career that made a difference to the animals under her care, one that sustained and fulfilled her. And love, beyond the love for Marnie, her family and friends. Oli's love, the one that made her hurry home of an evening to be with him, to settle in front of the fire and talk, watch a movie or read before they'd make love and fall asleep together. It was the kind of love she'd daydreamed of back at Catz when they'd first met, and she'd never imagined sharing with him then. And now it was within her grasp, she didn't want anything to stand in the way of holding on to it, least of all Oli not having a role here so he'd have to find one elsewhere.

'I'll talk to him as soon as he's finished with those ferrets. I'd like to get it settled as soon as possible so we can think ahead to lambing and what kind of cover we'll need.'

Erin floated into surgery with Dorothy's lurcher later, anaesthetising him and removing one infected tooth and cleaning the rest. It wasn't a difficult task, and he was soon recovering in the kennels on a cosy bed. A call came in just before four about a cow having difficulty calving and she set out into the night, her plans for an early dinner on hold. It was after eight when she returned home, tired but lit up too, at her news about the partnership and Oli's job offer, and she couldn't wait to talk with him.

Another message from Jason arrived before she got out of the pickup; a reminder this time about his cousin's wedding at the weekend, checking in that she was still okay to go with him. She pulled a face and shoved her phone into a pocket as she let herself into the cottage; she was pretty sure that meant he hadn't found anyone else, or he'd been let down. She'd reply later and let him know she wasn't going. She bent down when Marnie came over, thrilled that the kitten let Erin pick her up for a cuddle. Oli was in the kitchen, and she called across, the sight of him there now achingly familiar.

'Hey, you, something smells amazing.' She had to pass him to go upstairs and change. She slid her arms around his waist, holding him from behind and curling her tired body into him. He turned, kissing her and gently holding her face with both hands.

'Hello. You're cold.'

'So would you be if you'd just done a caesarean in a bloody freezing barn,' she retorted. 'The calf was alive, and the heifer was fine, so it was all good. Anyway I'm not cold now, not with you here.'

'That's great.' His smile was a distracted one and she wondered if something had gone wrong at the practice this afternoon. It was an effort at work to pretend they were just colleagues and friends, but they managed it.

'Has Gil spoken with you today? He said he was planning to.'

'He has.'

'And?'

'He's offered me a full-time job.' Oli's hands on her face tightened.

'Oli, I'm so pleased for you. Congratulations. I know you're going to be brilliant and so does Gil.' Erin reluctantly stepped back and his hands fell away. 'Have I got time for a shower before we eat? I'm sure I can smell the farm on me. And I've got some news to share.' She backed away to the stairs and Oli caught her hand, tugging her to a halt.

'Erin, I turned the job down,' he said quietly. 'If you'll just let me explain…'

For a frantic moment she wondered if she'd misheard him, or he was going to laugh and say he was teasing her, that of course he'd accepted the job. But the truth was written in his eyes and the world seemed to have fallen from beneath her. Blood rushed into her face and slipped away again, leaving her pale and trembling.

'Explain?' Her voice was a hollowed whisper. 'How can you possibly explain that you're leaving?'

'Because it's not what you think.' A muscle was twitching in Oli's cheek.

'You don't know what I think! Your contract is over, and you were always going to leave. I can't believe I've let myself imagine it could ever be different.'

'It's because…'

'Don't.' She yanked her hand free, shaking her head as though that might dislodge the hurt clouding her mind. Marnie would miss him too, and that was another level of sorrow. 'I'm going for a shower, and I think you should leave,' she whispered brokenly. 'There's no point in dragging this out.'

'Erin, don't do this, please. You have to let me explain.' His voice had fallen, but she couldn't allow herself to acknowledge the ache hovering in his eyes.

'I really don't, Oli. You've decided to leave Hartfell and that's all the explanation I need.' Her phone was in her hand, and she glanced at the screen as it brightened. Another message from Jason had popped up and she thrust it towards Oli. 'Jason's invited me to a wedding on Saturday and I've said yes.' She'd agreed weeks ago but she'd never have seen it through if Oli hadn't been planning to walk right out of her life.

'You're not serious? Why the hell would you do that?' His shoulders slumped and he shook his head in disbelief.

'Because I'm beginning to realise Jason's just what I need,' she told him. 'Someone who gives me the space to work and do my job without taking over every part of my life.'

'Someone who doesn't respect you, your career or your achievements, you mean.' Oli snatched up his phone and keys from the worktop, their meal abandoned. 'Someone who doesn't care about you, not in any way that matters.'

'It's better that way. Jason can't hurt me.'

'So what are you saying? That you and I are over?' Oli folded his arms, and she was on the edge of the cliff again, staring into another life. One she was going to have to live without him, and her heart was already crushed.

'We'd barely even begun. And we both knew it was always going to end.'

Chapter Twenty-Three

At work the next morning Erin sat through the staff briefing on automatic pilot, aware of the concerned glances coming her way. She'd hardly slept and was pale, barely equal to her job today. The row with Oli and her refusal to listen was lodged in her stomach like a dead weight, and even thoughts of the partnership with Gil were gone. She left Marnie in the kennels as she would be away from home all day. She had no idea what Oli had said to Gil to explain his absence since he'd packed and left the cottage last night.

She tried hard to behave as normal, but all the staff were a little flat without Oli. He'd made himself at home so quickly and even some clients were disappointed when she faced them over the consulting table and had to explain that he'd left, had moved on as planned. She set out for her calls, barely noticing the landscape that usually lifted her mood every time she laid eyes on it.

Experience and training carried her through those first few days, examining the animals who needed her care with her usual compassion and meticulous attention. She'd made herself reply to Jason, confirming she would go with him to the wedding, and she cringed every time she thought of what her mum or Jess would have to say about that. It was a stupid decision and she was already regretting it, with dread soon settling in too. He was a nice enough guy, but she knew he wasn't for her, nor she for him.

The weekend was also the beginning of her time off and Jess had offered to look after Marnie so Erin could have a holiday if she wanted to escape for a few days. Jess and Noah's house was coming along but she was happy to leave the mess and the dust behind for time at Erin's with Marnie. Erin had thanked her and said she'd think about it; there didn't seem to be anywhere she wanted to go.

It almost broke her heart all over again when Marnie looked at her sometimes, head tilted to one side, as though asking where Oli had gone and why wasn't he here to look after her too? There was a stillness in the house, one Erin might have imagined was peaceful before he arrived. But it wasn't peace she felt now, it was emptiness, and it matched the hurt at what she'd done in refusing to listen to him. The coffee machine was gone, and his boots no longer stood on the rack with hers; his coat wasn't hanging from the same hook. But for her shattered heart, he might not even have been here at all. His room was tidy, the bed neatly stripped, and the duvet folded back.

On Friday before work she packed for the wedding; she had a busy day and couldn't be sure she'd finish on time before her week off began tomorrow. The very last thing she felt like doing was attending the wedding of a happy couple madly in love and setting out on a bright new future together. And with Jason of all people, who wouldn't know how to be romantic if she'd written him a set of instructions.

She and Oli hadn't even had to try to find the romance in those days together, it had always been with them. It was the hot water he made sure to leave for Erin if he showered first, the morning cup of tea he made and the fire lit when she got home after him, Marnie settled and fed. The meals she cooked and he cleared up, the coffee she brought him in bed if she had to leave first. The laughter they shared and the understanding when an animal couldn't be saved, and they had to act on a decision often made swiftly and in distress. How they held one another afterwards, knowing they'd done all they could, and it wasn't meant to be. She hadn't realised quite how heavy her own load was until he'd helped her carry it.

She'd listened when he'd talked of his family, her arms wrapped around him, how it felt to watch his parents divorce for reasons he only now understood. How he wished his mum could share his life still, that she was here to enjoy the excitement of Imogen and Alex's wedding, and he could remind her he loved her. He was in contact with his dad most days and Erin knew just how much this meant to Oli, forging a different future as a family.

At the practice only Jess knew how she felt, after she'd walked round to Jess and Noah's house the other night, desperate to talk to someone who would understand. Jess was sympathetic and Noah had tactfully left them alone, as Erin wondered how she might put right her terrible mistake, or if she even could. She planned to accept Gil's offer of partnership and would let him know when she returned from holiday. It was a relief to pin her future to the practice and she'd always felt the life she was making in Hartfell was the right one, even if she was alone again.

After her calls on Friday morning she was in the kitchen at work, staring at a lunch she didn't feel like eating. With Oli gone, Gil had been taking companion animal consultations and he walked in to make a coffee. He asked how she was, and her reply was a flat, distracted one. He put the kettle on, closed the door and made her a brew.

'Erin, I know this is none of my business,' he began. 'But it's common knowledge that you and Oli were friends at Cambridge, and my guess is that it's clearly something more.'

She hung her head, both to hide her distress and the truth of those words, one hand clutching the mug of tea as though her life depended on it.

'Your personal lives are none of my concern and I had no qualms about the two of you continuing to work together if Oli had accepted the job. Can I take it he told you why he turned it down?'

'Not in so many words.' She swiped at her face, ashamed of her haste that day when Oli had tried to explain. 'I didn't give him the chance, my default where love is concerned is usually to expect the worst.' Erin blushed; had she really just said that word out loud and as good as admitted to her boss that she was in love with one of their colleagues? Ex-colleague, she reminded herself bitterly. Something else that was probably her fault.

'I know what that's like, believe me.' Gil was still leaning against the worktop, and she was glad he'd kept some distance because she wasn't sure she could cope with sympathy, she didn't feel she deserved it. 'But if me and Pippa can make it work given what we were up against, then I'm sure you and Oli can find a way too, if you want one. So here's the thing. Oli and I had a very frank conversation when I offered him the job and he turned it down for one reason only, Erin. Because of you.'

'Me?' Her head snapped up as she fixed red and puffy eyes on Gil. 'But why would he do that? It doesn't make any sense. I thought it was because he didn't want to give up travelling, to live in one place and make a home here with me.'

'It makes perfect sense when you know the truth,' Gil said quietly. 'I explained I'd invited you to become a partner and I was very much hoping you'd accept, and that we'd like him to stay on to manage the companion animal work. Oli did say he'd reflect after you and he had talked, but his initial response was to turn it down. This is the part you may wish I didn't know, but I do, so here goes.' Gil offered her a sympathetic smile and she was hanging on every word as though her entire future would depend on what he said next.

'Oli turned us down because he informed me that you and he were in a very meaningful and important relationship, and that you feel strongly about maintaining a professional distance at work. He felt, in order to give you space to succeed if you accept the partnership, that you'd be happier if he was working somewhere else but near enough for you to stay together. He didn't actually say the words out loud, Erin, but I know what being in love looks like,' Gil finished wryly.

Most uncharacteristically she burst into tears again and cried all over her boss, who handed her a tissue and tactfully disappeared after telling her to go home and begin her holiday early, they would manage. She drove home in a daze, horrified by her refusal to allow Oli to explain his reason for turning down the job, and utterly lit up by the realisation that he must love her. Or had. Given that she'd ejected him from her life a second time, perhaps he was already feeling very different.

She felt drained, as though every ounce of her energy had vanished since he'd left, and she crawled into bed after feeding Marnie. She had been planning to find a last-minute getaway in search of some sun, but since the conversation with Gil she couldn't get Oli and his generosity in turning down a fantastic job out of her mind. She was dreading the wedding sixty miles away with Jason tomorrow, just wishing it was over and wondering why she'd been stupid and stubborn enough to tell Oli she was still going when it was the very last thing she wanted.

Distracted by everything else this week, she'd let Jason take care of the arrangements, and she went cold when he let her know he'd booked them a room. Not at the lovely hotel where the wedding was taking place but in a lodge on a main road fifteen miles further on, and he'd asked her to share the cost of the taxi back.

In the morning she was ready early, her case packed and waiting in the sitting room. Jess and Noah were due later to look after Marnie, and Erin just wanted to be on her way. But first, she had something to do, and it was going to be in person. Jason arrived twenty minutes late and she watched his van pull up outside. As he got out he looked like a stranger, someone she'd never really known even though his features were familiar. She heard his cheery whistle as he thumped on the front door, the greeting he called to someone passing by. She took a deep breath as she opened it to him.

'Babe! You ready? The roads are looking pretty shit after the rain so we'd better get going. You look great, by the way. Have you done something different with your hair? I said we'd meet Kieran and his girlfriend in the bar for a quick one before the ceremony. You remember Kieran? Girl's new but same old story, hey?' He winked at her, then seemed to realise she wasn't moving. 'What's up?'

'Actually Jason, I'm really sorry, but I'm not going with you to the wedding.' She couldn't believe she'd ever thought this was a good idea. She'd wondered before if he called her 'babe' because he sometimes forgot her name and the generalisation covered all bases. 'I'm sorry to let you down on the last minute, but I know what that's like. Maybe you can find someone else. We both know I wasn't your first choice.'

'Yeah, but I'm here now and...'

'And I'm not going.' She found a smile, trying to soften the blow, probably more to his pride than anything else – she didn't imagine he'd appreciate showing up without a girl hanging on his arm. 'I've realised I'm not really the sort of person who can do casual relationships after all. I want something more; love, commitment, a family one day. I'm not sure you want that too.' She'd spoken the truth, but she imagined those words might send him leaping back into the van in search of his dating apps.

'Yeah, one day, maybe.' A frown creased his brow and the laugh he offered was a brief, puzzled one. 'But that's years off, and we both agreed to keep things simple.'

'And what if I've changed?' Erin hadn't planned this conversation, but she was feeling lighter already. 'I've made a terrible mistake, and I have to see if I can put it right. So let's just part as friends, and if I ever hear of someone after a personal trainer I'll send them your way.' Probably. Maybe. And they'd never be friends, but she could be friendly.

'You'd do that?' Already he'd brightened and a hand went to his back pocket. 'Take some cards, you never know.'

'I will.' She took a step back, impatient to set in motion the plan she'd formed just a few hours ago. 'Take care,

I hope you have a wonderful weekend. You'll probably meet someone amazing.'

'Bound to. See ya.' He turned away and she locked the door with relief, her knees still trembling. Right now she needed a quick brew before the taxi showed up.

–

The flight from Heathrow was uneventful and she slept through some of it, waking about an hour before they stopped in the Bahamas. The views were incredible: white sand, palm trees and glittering blue sea. After taking off again, they landed in the Cayman Islands less than two hours later and when Erin stepped off the plane she felt the incredible rush of a Caribbean sun envelop her in warm, welcoming air. It was the longest she'd ever flown, and she waited for her luggage nervously, still wondering if she was making another mistake.

It was a short journey to the hotel, and she was trying to absorb the sights as they drove along: bustling streets busy with people and lined with low, colourful build-ings. The light was extraordinary after the Dales winter she'd just left, and she understood some of how Gil and Pippa must have felt when they'd landed in an Australian summer. At the hotel she stared in wonder at lush green planting in the gardens, clutching the handle of her case and half wondering how she'd even got here. It had been such a rush, and she felt dazed by the flight and the difference in her surroundings.

Inside the lobby, the front desk sat between white and green walls, highlighting a glorious view of the beach. Artwork was bright and contemporary, and guests looked relaxed as they strolled by or lounged around a bright blue infinity pool falling away to the sea. Erin was welcomed warmly and had soon checked in. On the way to her room her breath stuttered at more tropical plants amongst tall, stately palms and soft pink walls, comfortable loungers placed between them. It was glorious and she couldn't wait for a swim before dinner to freshen up. She was tired after the journey, but her body felt hyped too, at the real reason she had come all this way.

Her room was stunning and simple; a huge queen size bed between white walls with a ceiling fan above it. She had her own sofa, and the luxury of an en suite bathroom nearly made her weep when she thought of her own back home in Hartfell. It was cool inside, and she threw open the doors to her balcony, blinking in wonder at the sight of the sea again, the blue water vivid beneath a Caribbean sun, and those skies. It was paradise, and for the next few days it was hers.

After a shower she changed and strolled through the gardens to the pool. She'd explore the beach tomorrow; today she just wanted to be in the water. She slipped off her shoes, the tiles hot beneath her feet, conscious of her pale skin in the heat as she tied her hair back. Suncream was essential and after she'd applied plenty she stepped into the pool. The water was exquisite and refreshing, and after a few minutes Erin abandoned swimming to float on her back. She flipped over, trying to calm her nerves as she thought of tomorrow and what she'd really come here to do.

Dinner later was plentiful and rich, blackened Cajun-spiced red snapper with rice and a glass of wine, after a cocktail to start. By the time she'd finished, her body was lamenting the five-hour time difference, crying out for rest, so she wandered back to her room and crashed into bed.

After a fitful sleep and a fabulous breakfast, she downloaded the map she needed and set off to explore, sunhat and glasses on. She got lost a couple of times, but Google put her right and twenty minutes later she arrived at the practice. It was so pretty, and she could see exactly why he'd chosen it. A white picket fence bordered a garden stuffed with plants, and green and white walls complemented the sign perfectly, a black paw print above white lettering confirming the name of the practice. She opened the gate with trembling fingers and took a deep breath before walking up the path.

It was cooler once she opened the door and entered the reception area. A desk stood to her right, the walls lined with chairs and only one person was waiting, a dog at their feet on a lead. She smiled; so many miles from home and yet it was all so achingly familiar. She approached the woman on the desk who beamed a greeting, and once Erin had explained why she was here she sat down to wait, clutching the sunhat on her lap with clammy hands. Even with the ceiling fan the air was warm, and she drank some water from the bottle in her bag, a tremble running through her body.

One of the two doors opposite her opened and she started, eyes flying to the woman in green scrubs who'd emerged and called her next patient. The woman with the dog got up and Erin felt a sharp pang of yearning for home and Marnie as they disappeared into the consulting room. Even exams had never made her pulse pound quite like this.

A few moments later the second door opened. Oli was there and her stomach clenched with longing. The beard he'd grown to keep him warm in the Dales had already gone and she saw the emergence of another suntan on his face, the scattering of new freckles as she slowly got to her feet.

'Who's next, please?' His eyes swept over the waiting room and when his gaze landed on hers, his mouth fell open in a gasp. His shoulders slumped as he swayed, letting go of the door, and it swung back to bounce against the wall, clattering through the stillness.

'I'm hoping that might be me.' Erin made herself take one shaky step after another. Coming here to find him had seemed like a sensible decision from the safety of her home in Hartfell, but facing him now she was terrified she'd got it wrong. What if he wouldn't listen to what she'd come all this way to tell him?

'Erin? What are you doing here?' His voice was a hollowed-out whisper as he ran a hand through his hair, and she just wanted to hold him, to tell him how sorry she was.

'Because there's something I really need to tell you, and it has to be in person,' she began shakily, grateful for the ceiling fan helping dissipate some of the heat racing through her. Thankfully, the receptionist was taking a call and not paying them any attention. 'I messaged Imogen to ask where you were, and she told me you were working here. I came to apologise for my mistakes and to ask you if we can find a way to fix what I've broken.'

'You don't need to…'

'Oli, I do,' she rushed out. She really hadn't wanted to cry but tears were already forming, and she tried to blink them back. 'I didn't go to the wedding with Jason. Please let me tell you this and then it's up to you, what you want to do about it. I'm so sorry about how I reacted when

293

you told me you weren't going to accept Gil's offer. He explained you turned it down because of me and I can't get my head around it. That you'd pass up a wonderful opportunity for me. I've spent years trying to convince myself we could never work, that we're from different worlds and we want different things.' She paused, swallowing down her sadness before continuing. 'But none of that is any use when it comes to loving you. I just do. I always have, pretty much since we first met and having you back in my life again made me realise that had never changed. I think it's how I'm made, to love you.'

It felt amazing, scary and wonderful to say it out loud, to see the glimmer of hope as a smile hovered on his lips. She knew then, and she didn't even need the words, they were in his eyes too.

'I'm not very brave when it comes to falling in love and nearly half my life I've been afraid of admitting what I've always known here.' She touched her heart. 'I love you, Oli Sterling, and I'm hoping you might give me a second chance. Or is it our third, I'm not really sure.'

'Erin, the only world I want is one with you in it, you numpty. I've loved you for what feels like my entire life, and I'm home when I'm with you.'

She laughed and then they were holding one another tightly, his hands firm and sure on her back. She wondered that she'd ever imagined or lived a life without him in it.

'I'm not a romantic,' she told him teasingly. 'The best you can expect is a hot meal when you come home and a warm bed. But I'm willing to do better.'

'You can leave the romance to me, I've barely even got started.' His whisper had her trembling all over again and she wrapped both arms around his neck, trying to tug him closer still. 'Wait until you see what I can do when I really put my mind to it.'

'I'll hold you to that.' But the mention of home was troubling her, and she pulled back to stare at him. 'Oli, what will you do? I can't leave Hartfell or my cottage, at least not yet.'

'Maybe the cottage can be our starter home,' he said softly, tucking a curl behind her ear. 'Maybe one day we'll want something bigger, something that has room for your mum if she needs us.'

It was the way he'd said 'us' and had included her mum that had the tears sliding down her face again. That he understood one day Heather might need more support and he was prepared to help offer it.

'It'll need to be big enough for both our families,' she muttered. 'Can you imagine all of us in our cottage at Christmas?'

'I can actually.' His hands went to her face, thumbs smoothing away the wetness. 'It'd be a squeeze, but as long as your nan's in charge of cooking the lunch, we'll be fine.'

'She'd love that.' Erin laughed and it caught on a sob as she stared into the face of the only man she'd ever loved. 'So would I, I can't think of a nicer way to spend Christmas.' She needed to share what was in her thoughts about work too, their future hinged on it. 'Oli, I know Gil would have you back in a heartbeat if you wanted that too.'

'So are you saying you think we could work together?'

'We've done it before, I'm sure we could do it again. And everyone already knows I'm madly in love with you,' she told him softly. 'Jess didn't need telling and when I cried all over Gil after he explained why you'd turned him down, he knew as well. I'm so sorry I got in your way of a job, and you stepped away so I could do mine.'

'It's totally fine,' he said softly. 'I want you to succeed, to stand alongside you and cheer you on. We'll make it work at the practice, Erin, I promise.'

'Only if I get to stand next to you and cheer you on. Marnie really misses you, she wants you to come home as much as I do.'

'I miss her too. If you'll have me?'

'Always.' The St Christopher she'd given him for Christmas was nestled against his chest and she picked it up. 'Maybe when you come home you won't need to wear this anymore.'

'Actually, I'd like to.' Oli kissed her fingers, her gift held between them. 'Because our lives will still be a journey, but one we'll travel together, and I already know the destination.'

Acknowledgements

Returning to Hartfell to write about Erin and Oli has been wonderful, and exploring the Dales on foot very much helped to inspire their story. I was fortunate to spend time with Alison O'Neill, shepherdess in the Yorkshire Dales, and her insight and enthusiasm into farming and the Dales was inspirational. Alison's story of life on a hill farm with her animals is an incredible one. To vets everywhere, who work long hours caring for their patients, often in difficult conditions; you're all amazing! Any mistakes in veterinary procedures are my own.

I'm very grateful to my agent Catherine Pellegrino and everyone at Canelo, especially my editor Emily Bedford, to have the opportunity to write more books set in the Yorkshire Dales. Thank you for your continued faith in my writing. Thank you, too, to Kate Shepherd and all those behind-the-scenes who make everything happen, and a huge thanks to the amazing illustrator who created such a perfect and beautiful cover for the book.

To Emma, Katie and everyone at EDPR, thank you for your support and tireless enthusiasm! Working together has been brilliant, and I appreciate all you've done for me. Thank you to Katie Sadler for marketing advice and always providing a solution just when I need it. To my wonderful writing buddies and cheerleaders, thank you for your friendship and encouragement, it makes such a difference and I'm very grateful for it.

Connecting with readers who love romance is one of the joys of writing, and a huge thank you to everyone who reads my books. I very much appreciate all that readers and bloggers do to support our fabulous genre and share the books they love.

Thank you to my amazing family for offering endless support, and especially to Stewart for always encouraging me to take opportunities when they come along. Teamwork really does make the dream work!

To Jen, all-round superwoman and one of the most talented, kind and generous people I know. Thank you for being a very early reader of my books, long before they were published, and for encouraging me to carry on. We share many happy memories of singing together, and I've never seen anyone conduct a brass band with more skill, enthusiasm or joy. Erin and her grandad would love to play in yours.